KU-368-466

Duty, Honour, Truth, Valour

The tenets of the **Knights of Champagne**
will be sorely tested in this
exciting Medieval mini-series by

Carol Townend

The pounding of hooves, the cold snap of air,
a knight's colours flying high across the
roaring crowd—nothing rivals a tourney.
The chance to prove his worth is
at the beating heart of any knight.

And tournaments bring other dangers too.
Scoundrels, thieves, murderers and worse are
all drawn towards a town bursting with deep
pockets, flowing wine and wanton women.

Only these knights stand in their way.
But what of the women who stand beside them?

Find out in
Carol Townend's

Knights of Champagne

Powerful swordsmen for passionate ladies

Author Note

Arthurian myths and legends have been popular for hundreds of years. Dashing knights worship beautiful ladies, fight for honour—and sometimes lose honour! Some of the earliest versions of these stories were written in the twelfth century by an influential poet called Chrétien de Troyes. Troyes was the walled city in the county of Champagne where Chrétien lived and worked. His patron, Countess Marie of Champagne, was a princess—daughter of King Louis of France and the legendary Eleanor of Aquitaine. Countess Marie's splendid artistic court in Troyes rivalled Queen Eleanor's in Poitiers.

The books in my Knights of Champagne mini-series are not an attempt to rework the Arthurian myths and legends. They are original romances set around the Troyes court and the town of Provins, which is also in Champagne. I wanted to tell the stories of some of the lords and ladies who might have inspired Chrétien—and I was keen to give the ladies a more active role, since Chrétien's ladies tend to be too passive for today's reader.

Apart from brief glimpses of Count Henry and Countess Marie, my characters are all fictional. I have used the layout of the medieval cities to create Troyes and Provins in these books, but the stories are first and foremost fictional.

MISTAKEN FOR A LADY

Carol Townend

First published in Great Britain 2016
By Mills & Boon, an imprint of HarperCollins*Publishers*
1 London Bridge Street, London, SE1 9GF

Large Print edition 2017

ISBN: 978-0-263-06751-4

Our policy is to use papers that are natural, renewable and recyclable products and made from wood grown in sustainable forests. The logging and manufacturing processes conform to the legal environmental regulations of the country of origin.

Printed and bound in Great Britain
by CPI Antony Rowe, Chippenham, Wiltshire

Carol Townend was born in England and went to a convent school in the wilds of Yorkshire. Captivated by the Medieval period, Carol read History at London University. She loves to travel, drawing inspiration for her novels from places as diverse as Winchester in England, Istanbul in Turkey and Troyes in France. A writer of both fiction and non-fiction, Carol lives in London with her husband and daughter. Visit her website at caroltownend.co.uk.

Books by Carol Townend

Mills & Boon Historical Romance

Knights of Champagne

Lady Isobel's Champion
Unveiling Lady Clare
Lord Gawain's Forbidden Mistress
Lady Rowena's Ruin
Mistaken for a Lady

Palace Brides

Bound to the Barbarian
Chained to the Barbarian
Betrothed to the Barbarian

Wessex Weddings

The Novice Bride
An Honourable Rogue
His Captive Lady
Runaway Lady, Conquering Lord
Her Banished Lord

Visit the Author Profile page
at millsandboon.co.uk.

To Kathy and Chris, with love.

Prologue

October 1175—Paimpont Manor
in the County of Champagne

Francesca set her quill aside with a sigh. Her maid Mari was setting logs on the fire, muttering darkly under her breath. Mari had been with her for years and her familiar face was creased with lines. Despite the age gap between them, Francesca considered Mari her friend as well as her maid. 'Mari?'

'My lady?'

'Will you hear what I have written?'

Mari stabbed at a log with the poker. 'If I must.'

'I would appreciate your views.'

Mari scowled and the poker clattered on to the hearth. 'I don't know why you want to read it to me, you will send it to Brittany whatever I say.'

'Be that as it may, I value your opinion.' Francesca's gaze lingered on her signet ring, the ring

Tristan had given her on their wedding day. A lump formed in her throat. Tristan's features remained clear in her mind—the startling blue eyes; the thick, jet-black hair; that firm jaw. Tristan was the most handsome of men, so much so that he was often referred to as Tristan le Beau—Tristan the Handsome. Unfortunately for Francesca, his image hadn't faded with time, she hadn't been able to forget him.

The wrinkles about Mari's mouth deepened as she came to the table and looked sourly at the vellum. 'My lady, if you valued my opinion, you wouldn't be writing that letter in the first place. It's a waste of ink, the man's not worth it.'

Francesca took a slow breath. 'The man, as you call him, is Count Tristan des Iles. He is also presently my husband. I beg you to remember that.' Mari muttered something that might or might not have been an apology and Francesca continued. 'I am not asking you to give your opinion of Lord Tristan, Mari, you have already made your views very plain. I would like your opinion on the letter, not my husband.'

'You want him back,' Mari said. 'My lady, he never replied to your other letters, what makes you think he will reply to this one?'

Foolish hope. Francesca ran her forefinger over

the three cinquefoils stamped on the face of her ring, conscious of a sharp ache in her chest. It was depressing how fresh the pain was, even after almost two years. Tristan. She tried to forget him by day, but each night he returned. He came to her in her dreams, night after restless night. Dark-lashed blue eyes would be smiling deep into hers, strong arms would reach for her and those clever, wicked fingers would work at her lacings and slide her gown aside…

Hoping she wasn't blushing, she looked at Mari. 'What if my letters never reached him? It's possible.'

Mari snorted. 'One letter might go astray, but you wrote several, they can't *all* have got lost.'

Francesca bit her lip. Mari was adamant that all she would hear from her husband was silence, yet Francesca had to make one last-ditch attempt to reach him. Yes, her marriage to Tristan had been an arranged marriage, but she was sure she hadn't been the only one to have felt the shock of delight on their wedding day. Mari had never understood that.

Tristan and I liked each other, we truly liked each other.

Sadly, that liking hadn't had a chance to turn into lasting love, at least not on Tristan's part. First, he had been called away to keep Brittany whole for the little duchess, and then Lady Clare had arrived at Fontaine and Francesca had been ousted as the Fontaine heiress. Francesca had been brought up believing herself to be Count Myrrdin's daughter, only to discover that she wasn't even his distant relation. She was a nobody and she had, albeit unwittingly, married Tristan under false pretences.

Francesca had at one time been certain that the feelings she had for Tristan were genuine. She had been confident that Tristan had liked her because after their marriage he had been the most attentive of lovers. She'd assumed that one day he would love her back. Which was why she was determined to send this final letter. They'd never had a proper chance to get to know each other.

'Mari, if Count Tristan doesn't reply, I shall know beyond doubt that our marriage is over.'

'You said that the last time you wrote to him. He didn't reply.'

Francesca's nails dug into her palms as a deeper fear surfaced. *I never gave him a child. He needs an heir and I failed him.* Was that why he'd never come for her? Did he fear she was barren? 'I need to hear from my lord himself as to his intentions.'

Mari made an exasperated sound. 'You've not seen the man in almost two years; your previous letters went unanswered—what more do you need to know? There is nothing to stop you starting afresh, there hasn't been since you left Brittany.'

Francesca took a deep breath. 'When Lord Tristan and I separated, Brittany was in chaos. The duchy needed him.' She stared at the stick of sealing wax on the table—it was silver to represent the silver field on her husband's shield. 'It needs him still.'

'My lady, he's your husband. He could surely have spared a couple of weeks to make sure you were well?'

Francesca found herself taking her husband's part, even though she knew it would do no good. She and Mari had been over this many times. Mari wouldn't budge from her stance, in her mind Tristan had neglected Francesca.

'Mari, you're forgetting the politics. My lord holds large swathes of land in the duchy and for that honour he is duty-bound to support the duchess. The duchess is a minor—she depends on Count Tristan and other lords loyal to Brittany. Too many noblemen are careless of their responsibilities. Not so Tristan. The duchess and the duchy rely on him.'

Shaking her head, Mari pursed her lips. 'There is no hope, you're besotted. You were besotted when you left Fontaine and you're besotted still. He isn't worth it.'

Francesca pushed to her feet and stalked to the fire. It wasn't easy to speak calmly, but she managed it. 'Until our marriage is actually dissolved, Lord Tristan remains my husband.' Fists opening and closing, she paced back to the table.

'My lady, he should have come for you last year.'

'For heaven's sake, that wasn't possible. The English king had laid waste several Breton counties and the council was relying on my lord to defend the local people.' Francesca stalked back to the fire. The flames were taking hold, licking around the edges of the logs, rimming them with gold. Irritably, she twitched her skirts and turned to head back towards the table.

'Count Tristan left the duchy, or so I heard.'

'My lord went to England on behalf of the duchy. He had Duchess Constance's interests to protect.'

'And his own, I'll be bound. All that man thinks about is politics.'

Francesca was painfully aware that her maid had put her finger on it—Tristan did put politics before all else. Politics and duty. And as his wife, she had failed in her main duty—she had not provided him with an heir.

Sadly, she reached for the vellum and rolled it into a scroll. 'I can see you don't want to help.'

Mari put out her hand. 'I'm sorry, my lady. Please, read your letter.'

'Thank you. Bear in mind this is the last time I shall write him.' Unrolling the scroll, Francesca began.

Right worshipful husband,

I write to you from your manor in Provins.

I pray that you are in good health and that you have suffered no hurt since my last letter. Word has reached us that the skirmishes that broke out between King Henry of England and the rebel lords have come to a satisfactory conclusion. I trust that the negotiations between the King, his son Prince Geoffrey and the rebels will result in a lasting peace and I live in hope that you may at last be relieved of some of your duties.

I would like to ask you about our marriage. You must feel you married an impostor and for that I can only apologise. On my honour, I had no intention of deceiving you. By all that is holy, I swear that I did honestly believe myself to be Count Myrrdin's daughter. Like you,

I believed myself to be heiress to the lands of Fontaine.

Please know that I am anxious to hear your plans regarding our marriage. Is it to continue? Dearest lord, it has long been my earnest wish that our marriage might stand, but since I have not heard from you I can only conclude that you wish our marriage to be annulled. If that is so, please know that I will not stand in your way. You married the heiress of the County of Fontaine, only to discover that far from being an heiress, I am not even nobly born.

Most worshipful husband, I trust you understand that I was not aware of my true status until Lady Clare arrived at Fontaine and proved to be Count Myrrdin's true daughter.

I am not a lady. I bring you no lands and no revenues, save those which may be drawn from an insignificant manor at St Méen. As I mentioned in my last letter, Count Myrrdin and his true-born daughter, Lady Clare, have graciously allowed me to retain it.

My lord, I beg you to inform me if our marriage is to continue.

I will be greatly saddened if you decide on an annulment, but I will understand. Noble lords need to marry ladies who match them in title and estate. However, if you decide to keep me as your wife, let me assure you that although I come to you virtually empty-handed, I bring with me a warm heart. I hold you in the highest esteem.

I beg that you give our marriage—and us—another chance.

My lord, I would be grateful if you would let me know your mind. You are ever in my thoughts.

Your respectful and loving wife,
Francesca

Francesca met Mari's eyes. 'Is it clear?'

'You don't style yourself lady in the letter.'

Francesca stared blindly at the vellum. 'I hold no title in my own right, I cannot presume. If Lord Tristan dissolves our marriage, I will truly be no one.'

'You'll always be a lady to me,' Mari said firmly.

'Thank you.' Francesca gave a faint smile. 'Well? Does this letter pass muster?'

'You will send it whether or not I agree. My lady, Lord Tristan's neglected you for too long.' Mari shook her head. 'In my opinion you're better off without him.'

Francesca felt her expression freeze. 'Mari, please understand, Lord Tristan cannot act at whim, he has the interests of Brittany at heart.'

Mari's mouth twisted. 'Lord Tristan's a man, isn't he? To my mind, it's a crying shame when a man can't put his wife before all else.'

Francesca looked sadly at her maid. 'Lord Tristan is more than a man, he's a count. I knew what I was marrying.' She gripped the letter. 'I only wish he could say the same of me.'

'Send the letter, my lady, it will be good to know his intentions. Where is Lord Tristan at present, do you know where to send it?'

Francesca's chest heaved. 'Not exactly, but if I send it to Château des Iles, it's bound to reach him sooner or later.'

'That may take weeks.'

'Thank you, Mari, I am aware of that.'

Throat tight, Francesca reached for the silver sealing wax. Would this be the last time she used her husband's seal? If Tristan wanted their marriage dissolved, she would have to accept it. She pushed away the memory of those smiling blue eyes. Lord, even now she could actually feel the texture of his dark hair as she ran her fingers through it. Longing was a sharp ache, a spear in her vitals. *Tristan, come for me, please.* Bending over the table, she sealed the letter. Blinking hard, she picked up the quill and ink and crossed to the wall cupboard to put them away.

Tristan would do as he pleased, and if he did not want her, she would have to face it. At least she would know. She would make a new life for herself. First, she would go to the manor at Monfort. Her friend Helvise had asked for advice on running the place and she had agreed to help. Francesca might not have the right bloodlines, but she'd been trained to cope with a castle, a small manor was well within her competence. And after that?

She might marry again, she had always wanted children. There was a chance that with another man she might be more lucky. She shivered. The thought of bedding anyone but Tristan wasn't pleasant.

First, however, her marriage had to be given one last chance. The letter had to be sent. Today. And if the worst came to the worst, if Tristan didn't reply, she would force herself to forget him. She had lived in limbo long enough.

'Mari?'

'My lady?'

'Please ask a groom to saddle Princess. I need fresh air.'

Chapter One

May Day 1176—the market town of Provins in the County of Champagne

Tristan spurred through the Lower Town, his squire Bastian at his side. It had taken them many days to reach his Champagne manor and he'd expected to find Francesca at home when he'd arrived.

Not so. On his arrival at Paimpont, his steward Sir Ernis had told him that Francesca had gone to a revel at Count Henry's palace. A *masked* revel, of all things. On May Day. It could hardly be worse.

Did she have any idea how rowdy the revel might become? How bawdy? Tristan had thought Francesca innocent. Overprotected. It was possible she had changed. These days it was possible she made a habit of attending such events.

With a sigh, Tristan had called for hot water and

a change of horses and he and Bastian had hauled themselves wearily back into the saddle.

Tristan had urgent news for Francesca, terrible news that would knock her back. Count Myrrdin of Fontaine—the man she thought of as her father—was on his deathbed. Count Myrrdin wanted to see Francesca before he died and Tristan had been charged with bringing her back to Fontaine.

Tristan's head was throbbing after so long on the road. His eyes felt gritty and his guts were wound tighter than an overstrung lute. Telling Francesca about Count Myrrdin's illness was bound to be a challenge, he wanted it over and done with. The news was bound to distress her. None the less, the sooner Francesca knew that the man she thought of as her father was on his deathbed, the better. She needed to prepare herself for the long ride back to Brittany.

Would it distress her further when she learned that she must make the journey with the husband she'd not seen in nigh on two years? Impatient with himself, Tristan reined in his thoughts. Since separating from Francesca he'd learned to his cost that thinking about her wreaked havoc with his emotions. She affected his judgement and that he couldn't allow. He was a count with responsibilities. Emotions were dangerous, emotions wrecked lives. Allow strong emotion to take root and good judgement flew to the four winds.

He was here to take Francesca to Count Myrrdin.

He was here to solicit for an annulment. A wife who hadn't troubled to answer any of his letters, a wife who hadn't troubled to reply when he'd invited her to visit des Iles, wasn't the wife for him.

He glanced at his squire. Bastian was young and doubtless worn out. Tristan's territories in the Duchy of Brittany lay many miles behind them, they'd crossed several counties to reach Champagne. 'Holding up, lad?'

'Yes, my lord.'

'You didn't have to come with me this evening, you could have stayed at the manor. One of the grooms could have come with me.'

Bastian stiffened. 'I am your squire, Lord Tristan, it is my duty to accompany you.'

In the Lower Town the market square was clear of stalls, although something of a holiday atmosphere ensured that the taverns were doing a brisk trade. Indeed, the entire population seemed to have spilled out of the narrow wooden houses and into the streets. Men were wandering about, ale cups in hand; girls had braided flowers into their hair. The atmosphere was relaxed. Festive. And all in honour of the ancient festival of Beltane. Tristan knew what that meant, he wouldn't mind betting that every full-blooded male in Provins had one thing on his mind.

He folded his lips together. He'd been told that Francesca had gone to the revel attended only by a groom and her maid. If things got out of hand, would she be safe? His brow was heavy as they trotted through the evening light and made their way up the hill towards the palace. Swifts were screaming in the sky overhead, a welcome sign that summer was on its way, a sign that should have lifted his mood.

Tristan stifled a yawn, Lord, he was tired. His stomach rumbled and his skin itched—that quick wash at Paimpont hadn't done much to remove the dust of the road, he could feel it clinging to his every pore, he was longing for a proper bath.

What would Francesca do when she saw him? She wouldn't be expecting him. *Bon sang*—good grief—he'd left her in Fontaine thinking his service to Duchess Constance would last a couple of months, and they'd ended up being separated for two years. Two years. Francesca was bound to have changed. It was a pity, the girl he had married had been a sweetheart. He gripped the reins as, against his will, his mind conjured her image. She'd been a sweetheart with candid grey eyes and long dark hair that felt like silk. *What is she like these days?* He wasn't sure what to expect or how he would feel when he saw her. Merciful heavens, what did it matter? When she'd fled Brittany without even setting foot in his castle at des Iles, she'd made it plain she didn't see herself as his wife.

The trouble was that now he was on the verge of seeing her again, it was impossible not to think about her. Impossible and painful. By refusing to enter his county, Francesca had, in effect, deserted him. And despite his best efforts, his pretty young wife had managed to occupy most of his thoughts over the past months. In truth, ever since he'd heard that Francesca had been ousted from her position as Count Myrrdin's daughter, he'd had no peace.

Francesca had left Brittany at the worst time. With the duchy infested with rebels, every county had been in a ferment. The council had called on Tristan for support and he'd not been able to go to Francesca. He'd felt bad. Worse than bad. And, given that she had not made any attempt to contact him, far worse than he should have done.

Initially, Tristan hadn't wanted their marriage dissolved. A knife twisted in his gut and he cursed himself for his foolishness. He'd been captivated by Francesca's innocence and apparent liking for him. He'd been overwhelmed by the startling physical rapport that had sprung up the moment they'd set eyes on each other and had clung to the hope that once the dust from the rebellion had settled, they might make their marriage work. He'd ached to see her. Still did.

Tristan had been told that Francesca had fled to his manor in Champagne as soon as she'd learned she wasn't Count's Myrrdin's daughter—his retainers had sent word when she had arrived.

What he didn't understand was why she had chosen to leave Brittany. Francesca loved Brittany, it had been her home. She loved the aged Count Myrrdin, and surely that wouldn't change even though it had been proved she wasn't his daughter?

Had she fled because Lady Clare—Count Myrrdin's true daughter—had made difficulties for her?

Or had she gone because she couldn't bear to live on in her beloved Fontaine knowing it would never be hers?

It had hurt that Francesca had left the duchy rather than wait for him to complete his duties. So many months had passed and she'd not answered a single one of his letters. That hurt too. Theirs had been an arranged marriage, surely he shouldn't feel this way?

Now, with Francesca continually ignoring his

letters, Tristan refused to waste more time. He needed to apply for an annulment. He needed a sound political marriage. He needed heirs.

He hardened his heart. The plain truth was that Francesca hadn't taken refuge in his castle at des Iles as he had invited her to. She had fled the duchy. Her silence was yet more proof that she wanted nothing to do with him. Silence was a form of desertion. And desertion was definitely grounds for annulment.

Somewhere in the depths of his memory a pair of candid grey eyes—Francesca's eyes—smiled back at him. Her smile had been warm and genuine. Or so he had believed. A knife twisted, deep inside.

He set his jaw. It was time to have their marriage dissolved. Francesca wasn't an heiress. Their marriage had brought him nothing but grief—the confusion he'd felt at their parting refused to dissipate. At times it felt very much like pain. Perhaps that wasn't so surprising. He had liked Francesca very much; her lack of response to his letters really rankled.

Bastian was staring at the gatehouse outside Count Henry's palace. 'Is that the palace, my lord?'

'Aye.'

Bastian gave him a troubled look. 'What will

you do for a mask, my lord? Didn't Sir Ernis say a mask was obligatory?'

'Never mind, Bastian, I have the very thing.'

Francesca's mask was green to match her gown. Standing in a stairwell just outside the palace great hall, she held her veil to one side while Mari tied it into place.

'Thank you. Are you ready, Mari?'

'Yes, my lady.'

Giving her veil a tweak to ensure it flowed neatly over the ties of her mask, Francesca stepped into the hall. A wave of noise and heat rolled over her. Unprepared for either the press of people or the warmth, Francesca recoiled so swiftly that Mari—who was following close behind—walked into her.

'I'm sorry, my lady.'

Francesca's eyebrows lifted. 'Saints, half of Champagne must be here. It would be hard to imagine there's room for anyone else.'

A manservant bearing a tray of goblets shot past the doorway faster than she could have believed possible, he nimbly sidestepped a small child playing with a grizzled wolfhound and narrowly avoided an upturned bench.

Behind her mask, Mari's eyes sparkled. 'Oh, my

lady, isn't it exciting? May Day always is the best of the festivals.'

'It's a pagan celebration,' Francesca said. 'It's not an official one, it's not sanctioned by the Church.'

'All the better, we can really enjoy ourselves.' Mari nudged her in the small of her back. 'Well? Don't you think we need a goblet of wine?'

Straightening her spine, Francesca pushed into the throng. The twanging of a lute floated down from the minstrel's gallery. A drum beat softly in the background.

Truth be told, Francesca had no wish to take part in the revel, she wasn't in the mood. She'd only come to please Mari, who had been talking of nothing else since Sir Ernis had so foolishly mentioned there was going to be a masked revel at the palace.

Mari was more of a companion than a servant and, despite her outspoken manner, she was a loyal supporter. It would have been churlish to deny her and Francesca had known Mari wouldn't dream of coming without her. So, despite not being in the mood for frivolity, she'd been persuaded to come.

Mari's mask made her smile. It was a dazzling and complicated arrangement of peacock feathers, gold thread and ribbons. The feathers danced and waved about Mari's face as she squeezed through the press, tickling people as she passed them.

Francesca's mask was far more modest. She had ignored Mari's blandishments that a young lady like herself, one whose husband had clearly given up on her, ought to set about attracting new interest. She had cut a simple mask out of some backing, covered it with a remnant of green fabric from her gown and edged it with some glass beads she'd found rolling about in the bottom of her sewing box.

'My lady, you really must make the most of this revel,' Mari muttered from behind her. 'You need to think about your future. Your marriage is over, and if you want children, you will have to marry again.' Mari glanced pointedly towards the ceiling, where row upon row of knights' colours hung from the beams. 'Look at all those pennons. There are plenty of knights here tonight, you could take your pick.' She lowered her voice. 'Find a new husband.'

'Mari, please.' As Mari's words shivered through her, Francesca was gripped with a horrid suspicion. Had Mari insisted on coming to the revel, not for her own entertainment, but because she wanted Francesca to choose a new husband?

Well, that day might almost be upon her. Her

separation from Tristan was bound to be formalised soon, even so, she wasn't ready to start husband hunting. Not until she had heard from Tristan himself.

The long silence probably meant that she would at any moment receive notice that he had asked the Pope to annul their marriage. Tristan had good cause to do so. She'd failed him in the most damning of ways, she was a nobody, a nobody who had not provided him with an heir.

Determined not to give the knights' colours another glance, Francesca kept her gaze trained on the trestle tables arranged around the walls. She had come here tonight so Mari could let her hair down. As to her future, she had already discussed moving to Monfort with her friend Helvise, she would think more about that another day.

Francesca forged on, heading for a tray of goblets next to the wine racks. Heavens, she'd never seen tables so laden—great platters of venison, mountains of pastries, honeyed almonds… Unfortunately, her stomach felt like lead and she doubted she could eat a bite.

It would help if she could forget how she had enjoyed Tristan's company. The trouble was that every time Mari spoke about Francesca's plans for the future, Francesca found herself dwelling on her brief time with Tristan. Until she had discovered she wasn't related to Count Myrrdin in any way whatsoever, she had been so happy.

My life has been a lie. None of it was real.

Tears rushed to her eyes and the tray of goblets seemed to waver in a mist. Blinking fast, she stiffened her spine. She knew what she had to do. She must step aside and allow Tristan to make a more propitious marriage. With a noblewoman. With an heiress who would give him heirs.

Francesca reached for a goblet and wrenched her mind away from Tristan. 'Count Henry is generous,' she said brightly.

Mari was staring wide-eyed at a stand that was bowing under the weight of so many wine barrels. Her peacock feathers shivered. '*Dieu du ciel*, God in heaven, Count Henry's steward must have raided the stock of every wine merchant in Champagne. That rack will surely break.'

'I am sure the barrels will soon be empty.' Francesca handed the goblet to Mari as one of her maid's peacock feathers flicked across the face of a large man with a shock of white hair. The man sneezed.

Francesca took another goblet. When she turned back, wine in hand, Mari was gone.

'Mari?'

Francesca could see no sign of her. No, wait, there she was, halfway across the hall. At the centre a space had been cleared, dancing was about to begin. The man with the shock of white hair had taken Mari's arm and was drawing her into the crowd. Mari glanced over her shoulder, Francesca saw the glint of her eyes behind the mask. She was smiling.

Returning the smile, Francesca mimed for Mari to join the dance. With any luck, Mari would soon be so engrossed that Francesca could sneak back to the ladies' bower and retire. She really wasn't in the mood for a masked revel. And she certainly wasn't in the mood for husband hunting.

Pensively, she took a sip of wine and skirted round the edge of the hall. She hadn't gone more than a couple of paces before a tall man with untidy yellow hair stepped in front of her.

He gave her a flourishing bow. 'Will you dance, fair lady?' he asked, holding out his hand.

The man's mask was black and Francesca caught a glimpse of blue eyes. Her heart missed a beat and she immediately thought of Tristan. Heavens, this had to stop! She was seeing Tristan in every man she met. It was ludicrous, this man didn't even have the right colour hair.

Was he a knight? Francesca didn't want to dance,

however, if he was a knight, there was a danger she might insult him by refusing. He certainly held himself confidently enough. She dipped into a curtsy. 'I am sorry, sir, I do not dance.'

'*Dommage.* Pity,' he said, easily enough.

A woman squeezed past Francesca, elbowing her in the ribs. 'Excuse me, mistress.' She jerked her head at a wine barrel. 'I can't reach the tap.'

The fair man took Francesca by the arm. 'Come, we are in the way here.' He guided her away from the serving tables. It didn't take long for Francesca to realise that he was making a beeline for one of the corridors—a corridor that at this hour was dark and shadowy and lit by a line of lanterns. Francesca resisted the tug on her arm.

'Sir, if you please. I have arranged to meet a friend in the ladies' solar.'

'All in good time.' Behind the black mask, blue eyes—the wrong blue eyes—gleamed. 'First, we shall step into the quiet and introduce each other properly.' His grip firmed and before Francesca could protest she found herself in the corridor.

From the minstrels' gallery, there was a bird's-eye view of the goings-on in the great hall. This was just as well because Tristan was wearing his helmet instead of a mask. He'd had to put it on before the pages would admit him and the view through the eye slits was somewhat restricted. None the less, he would surely spot Francesca easily from up here. And he would know her, he was sure, even if she was wearing a mask.

After nodding briefly at a lute-player, he turned back to the guard rail. His gaze was caught by a slender, dark-haired lady in a group standing by the hearth. A brief perusal told him it wasn't Francesca, the lady's hands didn't look right. Too many rings. He skimmed quickly over a group of would-be dancers forming in the middle, again, one or two of the women had Francesca's build. None of them had her grace. Next, he studied the revellers by the serving tables as they jostled to reach the meats and the wine barrels. One lady in a crimson gown with a mask to match looked too young; another in a blue gown and heavy silk veil was too small; another— No, none of them resembled Francesca.

His gaze moved on, sliding over more guests until at last, by the door that led into a corridor, Tristan caught sight of a large, fair-haired man pulling a tall, willowy woman in a green gown towards one of the doors. The hairs rose on Tristan's neck. Francesca!

Before he knew it, he was tearing down the twisting stairs.

He hadn't seen her face, she had lost weight and her ebony hair was hidden beneath her veil, but he didn't need the details to know he'd been looking at his wife. Swearing under his breath, Tristan shoved his way unceremoniously through the revellers.

His mind raced. What the devil was she doing leaving the great hall in the company of a stranger?

A name jumped unbidden into Tristan's brain. Joakim Kerjean. His pulse thudded and his mind filled with questions.

Before setting out from Château des Iles, Tristan had learned that a yellow-haired knight named Joakim Kerjean had been enquiring after Francesca in the village. Never having met the man, Tristan had followed up with some enquiries of his own. He'd not got far, all he'd learned was that Sir Joakim Kerjean held title to some land not far from Francesca's manor at St Méen. That in itself was fairly innocuous. What was more worrying was that after Sir Joakim had been told that Francesca was living in Tristan's Champagne manor, he had gone on to ask for precise directions as to how to get there. Clearly, this Kerjean was determined to find her. Why?

If Sir Joakim's manor bordered with Francesca's,

he might be after her land. He might be considering marriage.

Was the man a fortune hunter? Tristan might be considering an annulment, but he had no wish for Francesca to fall into the hands of a fortune hunter. If Francesca were to remarry, it was Tristan's duty to make sure she married someone who treated her with the respect she deserved. Sir Joakim would have to prove himself a decent man before Tristan allowed him anywhere near her.

Tristan shouldered through the throng. That yellow-haired man might not be Kerjean, what mattered at this moment was whether Francesca was going with him willingly.

That man could be her lover. Tristan clenched his fists, filled with an emotion so raw he couldn't begin to analyse it. He was about to petition for an annulment, what Francesca did was no longer his concern. So why in hell did the sight of her walking into a shadowy corridor with another man have him in knots?

'Excuse me, sirs.' Tristan pushed past several knights with barely concealed impatience. The very fact that he'd found Francesca at this revel argued against what he'd believed about her living quietly at Paimpont Manor.

Before Tristan had left her to join the Breton

council in Rennes, he had made a point of telling her how important it was that he proved himself a loyal subject of the duchy. He'd been sure she understood, he had to do his duty.

Tristan had long been aware that of all the duchess's vassals, his hold on his county was tenuous. He held it on sufferance. The trouble was that if he put a step wrong, he'd lose more than his county. Tristan hadn't told his wife that he wanted to make up for the shameful mess that his father had left behind him. That would have felt too much like betrayal.

Before parting from Francesca, he had warned her that he would only be able to write to her occasionally. She had given him one of her dutiful smiles and had said that she understood. He'd been sure she would wait for him. Yet she hadn't replied to any of his letters and here she was, sneaking into a corridor with a stranger at a revel. It was hardly the act of an innocent.

It wasn't what he would have expected of the young woman he had married. *I thought you were daughter of the Count of Fontaine. I thought you were innocent.*

Hell burn it, it wasn't pleasant to have one's illusions ripped away. When they had first married, he'd been beguiled by her innocence. Yet how innocent had she been? He wasn't sure about anything any more. Who was she? What was she? What drove her? He had no idea.

Is that man forcing her? Is it the man who was nosing around des Iles? Is it Joakim Kerjean? Digging his nails into his palms, clenching his jaw, Tristan brushed past an embracing couple and stepped into the corridor.

Candles were burning in a row of lanterns set in wall sconces, the rest was gloom. At the far end of the corridor, he caught the flash of a green skirt.

'Let me go!' Francesca's voice was sharp. Anxious. 'Unhand me, sir!'

'My lady!' Tristan lurched towards her, swiftly closing the distance between them.

A large shadow moved. The lantern light fell on the man's yellow hair as he glanced Tristan's way before bending purposefully over Francesca.

Tristan heard a sharp crack as she slapped the man's face. Relief—this was no tryst—warred with anger. The cur, how dare he molest her! Tristan reached them and all he could think was that he wanted Francesca safe. Her green mask was crooked, her breast heaving.

He forced his way between them and tore off his helmet. It fell to the floor with a clang. He was vaguely aware that he ought to know better than to mistreat a Poitiers helmet in such a way, it had cost a fortune. It wasn't important. Ignoring Francesca's gasp of surprise as she recognised him, he glared at her molester. 'Touch my wife again and you die.'

The man's jaw slackened. His gaze dropped to Francesca and he scowled. 'You didn't tell me you had a protector.'

Francesca lifted her chin and the beads glinted on her mask. 'You didn't bother to ask, sir,' she said. 'And even if I had told you, I doubt whether you would have listened. You may leave.'

The man's mouth tightened. 'There's a word for women like you,' he said, voice surly.

Anger surged, dark and primitive. Tristan felt like pounding the man into the floor. 'Watch your mouth.'

Muttering obscenities, the man shouldered past him. Heavy footsteps receded down the corridor and Tristan discovered that learning whether or not the man was Kerjean had become utterly irrelevant.

Was Francesca unhurt?

A candle flared, spitting and hissing as it guttered and went out. It didn't matter. Tristan wasn't aware of anything save for Francesca standing before him, a door at her back. Her face was in shadow. Her mask glinted.

Francesca dipped into a curtsy even as she whipped off her mask. Her grey eyes were shining with what looked very much like happiness. 'Tristan! How wonderful to see you.'

Tristan found himself returning her smile before he recalled why he was here. Count Myrrdin, the man she thought of as her father, was dying and he had promised to bring her to him.

She touched his hand and every nerve tingled. 'Your arrival was most timely. I thank you.'

Tristan curled his fingers round hers. 'We can talk in here.' Pushing through the door, he pulled her with him into the chamber. He had a dim recollection that it was used as an office by the palace steward, Sir Gervase de Provins. It was cramped and dark. No candles. No matter.

Kicking the door shut with his heel, Tristan felt for the bolt and shoved it home. All he could think was that they were together again. *At last.*

Tugging Francesca to him, he slid an arm about her waist. He had to kiss her. One last kiss. God save him, after their wedding she had tasted so sweet, he had to see if that had changed. One kiss. He touched her face, fingers lingering on her cheek. So soft. Warm. A faint, womanly fragrance reached him—jasmine and roses. She'd always liked jasmine. *Francesca.*

'Tristan.' Her voice trembled. Her body did too.

Lowering his head, his lips found hers. He intended to keep it gentle and brief. He ought to tell her about Count Myrrdin and he would, as soon as they had finished this kiss. This kiss—their first in almost two years—was *everything.*

Feeling engulfed him. Lord, it was almost too much. Finally, he had her in his arms again and her lips were as soft as he remembered. She stood trembling in his arms as he went on kissing her, nibbling at her mouth, waiting—aching—for her to respond. Lightly, lightly. He tasted cinnamon and honey, she'd been drinking spiced wine.

She must feel something, she must respond, she must.

His blood began to heat, yet he held himself in check. They would talk in a moment, but first he had the absurd wish that she should respond in the old way.

It didn't take long. He felt a last shiver run through her body, one moment she was hanging in his arms, apparently nothing more than a bundle of nerves, and the next she gave a small sigh and her body fell against his as it had done in the early days of their marriage. The ache inside him intensified, it became actual pain. *Mon Dieu*, he had missed this—she had him in flames with a touch. He'd never known anything like it.

A couple of heartbeats later, small hands took firm hold of his shoulders. She eased back and her soft murmur reached him through the dark. 'Tristan.'

Triumph flooded every vein. The cracks of light edging round the door were thin, the dark almost absolute. If she was little more than a shadow, then so was he. 'My heart.' The old endearment slipped out before he had thought. And his hand slid round her head, he was unable to stop himself urging her mouth back to meet his. They fell into each other's arms in the old way and went on kissing. The kissing got deeper. Wilder. It was as though Tristan had been dragged back in time and they were newly wed. While they were kissing, Tristan could almost imagine that he had never felt guilty for keeping secrets from her. He could almost imagine that they had never separated, and there had never been this silence between them. His blood pounded in his ears. It was impossible to breathe. There was so much to resolve, but it was drowned by the need to kiss and touch.

With difficulty, he eased back. He had to tell her about Count Myrrdin. Talking was the last thing he wanted to do, he was hard as iron. He wanted to go on touching her; he wanted to keep her close; he wanted to kiss her until they both lost their senses. He was halfway there already. Lord, he would never let her go.

His thoughts blurred and despite his resolution—*I must tell her Count Myrrdin has summoned her to Fontaine*—all he could think was how much he wanted her. He fought the impulse to press himself against her and caught himself wondering if an annulment might, after all, be a mistake. Then the old bitterness stirred. *She never came to des Iles, she deserted me. She never replied to my letters.*

He heard her swallow, her breathing was unsteady. 'Tristan, it is marvellous to see you, but should we be kissing with so much unresolved between us?'

It was on the tip of his tongue to reply that she was his wife and he had every right to kiss her. He had to remind himself that she had fled Brittany and never looked back. 'Probably not. Francesca, I bring news from Fontaine.'

Damn the gloom, he couldn't read her expression, all he could see was her shape. Her very feminine shape, temptingly outlined by the light creeping round the door. Desire coiled inside him, dark and angry. Francesca wasn't the woman he'd thought her to be and their life together had disintegrated into an utter shambles. He needed a titled lady with a spotless reputation. Despite that, he'd never wanted a woman more than this one and he had no words to tell her.

Blindly, he reached for her, but his arms closed on thin air.

Chapter Two

Francesca drew in a steadying breath, stared at the dark shape that was Tristan and tried to analyse the warmth that had flooded every vein. It was heaven to be with him again, pure heaven, so much so that it was almost impossible to concentrate on what he had said. Something about news from Fontaine.

She felt most odd. Light-headed. Dizzy with happiness. Tristan had come for her! He had received her letter and he had come for her. Her heart thumped. Had he decided their marriage would stand? He had acknowledged her as his wife before that bully of a knight—that had to be a good sign.

Unless—Francesca's stomach sank—Tristan was extremely possessive. Perhaps he had come to tell her their union was to be dissolved and he had claimed her only because until their marriage was over she remained his. Sad to say, the decision was in Tristan's hands, she would have little influence. Tristan le Beau was Count of the Isles, she was no one.

Pushing the news from Fontaine to the back of her mind, she cleared her throat. 'Have you called for an annulment, my lord?'

'Not yet.'

'Why not?'

'Why the hurry?'

She gave a quiet laugh and felt the happiness slowly ebb away until there was only the familiar uncertainty. What were his intentions? 'Why the hurry? Tristan, it's been two years since we have been in each other's company, that is hardly a hurry.'

A loud knocking made her start.

The door rattled and Tristan groaned. 'Holy hell.'

Another bang had the door jump on its hinges. 'Who's in there?' It was a man's voice, edged with impatience. 'Open up!'

Tristan made for the door.

'Tristan, a moment, if you please.' Cheeks scorching, Francesca straightened her gown. Heaven help her, she had lost her veil and dropped her mask and the lack of light meant she had no hope of finding them.

'Open this door!'

'Gervase, is that you?' Tristan asked.

'Aye, open up. Open up at once.' The door shook. 'Hurry, or I'll have the guard smash their way in.'

'Calm down, man. It's Tristan, Tristan des Iles.'

'Who?'

'Tristan des Iles.'

'What in Hades are you doing here? I thought you were in Brittany.'

Tristan gave a curt laugh. 'I'll be out shortly. Then you'll understand.'

Francesca dropped to her knees and groped around on the floor, desperate to find her mask and veil. Nothing. The cool flags, the edge of the chamber, the wooden desk leg—it was hopeless. With a sigh, she straightened and smoothed her hair. She could hear more rustling. Tristan was doubtless tidying himself too. She had an unsettling recollection of dragging his tunic free of his belt so she could run her hands over his chest.

Why had he kissed her? He hadn't denied that he needed an annulment. He would need a more propitious marriage. He shouldn't have kissed her!

And she should not have responded.

'Ready, Francesca?'

'Aye.'

The bolt scraped and the latch clicked. Light filled the chamber as Sir Gervase crossed the threshold, a lantern in hand. Glancing over his shoulder—half the palace seemed to be congregated in the corridor—Sir Gervase pulled the door firmly shut. His mouth curled into a knowing grin.

Francesca's heart ached and her cheeks were on fire. It was obvious what she and Tristan had been doing. In truth, it looked as though they had done far more than kiss—her veil and mask lay in a corner and Tristan was adjusting his belt.

Sir Gervase's eyes danced. 'Tristan, you devil.' He gave Francesca a puzzled look. 'Who is this lady?'

'This, Gervase, is my wife, the Countess Francesca des Iles.'

By the time they left the chamber, Francesca had put on her veil and her mask was firmly in place. Tristan's appearance had her mind in a shambles. Not only that, she was mortified, it was obvious that Count Henry's steward thought he had interrupted a passionate tryst. Grateful that the mask would hide the worst of her blushes, she let Tristan take her hand in a firm grip and march her through a boisterous and nosy crowd. Grinning onlookers stood aside to let them pass.

Tristan didn't trouble to replace his helmet, everyone knew exactly who he was. There were several sniggers and, out of the corner of her eye, Francesca saw a lewd gesture.

Someone hissed. 'Tristan le Beau.'

'Aye, but who's the woman?'

'I've no idea.'

Francesca didn't want to hear the rest. It was plain the entire palace thought they'd been making love in Sir Gervase's office. It was beyond embarrassing. Determined not to catch anyone's eye, she stared at the floor as she was swept along the passageway. Only when they neared the entrance to the great hall did she lift her head. And there, leaning against the doorpost, was the yellow-haired knight who had tried to kiss her. He'd removed his mask and was watching Tristan, mouth thin, eyes cold.

Tristan's grip tightened on her hand. The yellow-haired knight unfolded his arms and slipped into the hall ahead of them. At once a ring of dancers encircled him, swallowing him up.

'How have you been, my lord?' Sir Gervase was speaking to Tristan. 'How do matters stand in Brittany?'

'All is well, sir, save for a few loose ends,' Tristan replied absently. He was looking towards the dancers, a deep crease in his brow. 'Sir Gervase, who's the man with the yellow hair?'

'His name's Kerjean, I believe, Sir Joakim Kerjean.'

The men talked as they made their way across the hall towards the stairwell and Francesca found she couldn't tear her gaze from Tristan. It had been so long since she had seen him and it had been too dark in the chamber to see whether he had changed. Saints, he was just as good to look upon as he always had been. In the brightly lit hall he was achingly familiar. So handsome. That raven-black hair was as thick as she remembered; his shoulders were pleasingly broad, and through his tunic she could see hints of the well-honed muscles that she'd felt in the gloom of Sir Gervase's office. As for his eyes, that clear sapphire blue was as beautiful as it was unmistakable. How could she even for a moment have imagined she'd seen them elsewhere? That other knight's eyes were nothing like Tristan's.

'Loose ends?' Sir Gervase was saying, with a puzzled frown. His brow cleared. 'Ah, the trouble in Brittany. I would think there are always loose ends.'

'True enough, there's been trouble for decades. Thankfully, the rule of law has prevailed.'

Sir Gervase grunted. 'That's good to hear. My

lord, what about Prince Geoffrey? Do you think he will make a match of it with Duchess Constance?'

'I believe he will. The prince seems to have the interests of Brittany at heart and he's genuinely fond of our little duchess. I see no reason why they shouldn't marry when she is older.'

'So all is well.'

'Aye.'

Smiling, Sir Gervase gripped Tristan's arm. 'Count Henry will be pleased to hear you attended the revel.'

'I haven't seen him, he's away?'

'Count Henry is dining with a deputation of Apulian merchants.'

A torch was flickering at the foot of the stairs, Sir Gervase waved them on. 'It's at the top, I'm afraid, the very last bedchamber. It's not large.' He grinned. 'If you'd given me more notice, I'd have found you something grander. We're bursting at the seams tonight.'

'I'm sure.'

'Have you just ridden in? I'll send someone up with food and wine, if you wish.'

'My thanks, I would appreciate that. Francesca, are you hungry?'

'No, thank you.'

Sir Gervase looked at Tristan. 'Do you want someone to find your squire?'

'No need, the lad is exhausted, we shall manage very well. Thank you.'

Francesca stepped forward. 'Sir Gervase?'

'My lady?'

'Sir, my maid Mari is in the great hall enjoying the revel. She will worry when she can't find me. I would be grateful if you could ask someone to search her out and tell her I am with Lord Tristan and that I shall speak to her at breakfast.'

'How will I know her?'

She smiled. 'You won't be able to miss her. Her mask is decorated with the longest peacock feathers in Christendom. When I last saw her, she was dancing.'

'Her name is Mari, you say?'

'Aye, Mari de Fontaine.'

Sir Gervase bowed his head. 'Consider it done, my lady.'

'Thank you.'

With a smile, Sir Gervase returned to the great hall.

Tristan glanced thoughtfully at their linked hands. Uncurling his fingers from hers, he stood back. 'After you, my lady.'

Francesca went cold. His voice was curt and he

was no longer meeting her eyes. 'Tristan, what's the matter?'

He looked down at her and gave her a tight smile. Her heart dropped to her toes, his smile was counterfeit and his eyes, those beautiful blue eyes, weren't smiling at all.

'Tristan?'

'After you, my lady.'

Swallowing hard, Francesca picked up her gown and started up the stairs. What was going on? She didn't know what to think. Tristan's kiss had felt like a kiss of welcome. And his voice, the voice that spoke so warmly to Sir Gervase, was utterly changed. She cast her mind back. What had she done? She couldn't think of anything. Had Sir Gervase given him ill news? She thought she'd been attending to their conversation, however, it was possible something had slipped past her, she had been staring at Tristan much of the time.

Pausing halfway up a twist in the stairs, she turned. 'Tristan, have I done something wrong?'

He looked blankly at her. 'I don't know, have you?'

What a strange reply! And to deliver it in that surly tone, it was as though he loathed her. Francesca searched his face, hoping to see a trace of the warmth she thought she had felt in the downstairs chamber. The torchlight shone full on his face, yet it revealed nothing, he might as well be wearing a mask. His blue eyes looked stony. Remote. Had she imagined the warmth? Had she wished it into being in some way?

With a sigh, she continued up the stairs. Brittany was far away, he must be exhausted. 'How long did your journey take?'

'A little over a week.'

She shot him a startled look. 'Saints, you must have galloped full tilt the whole way. Did you sleep at all? When I travelled to Troyes with Lady Clare, we took ages.'

Tristan didn't reply and they continued up the stairs.

Francesca gave a sad, reminiscent smile. Tristan never knew when to stop, he had exhausted himself. She used to watch him in the practice yard at Fontaine, sparring with Sir Brian and the other household knights. He'd dance round his opponent, sword flashing, darting this way and that as though his armour weighed little more than a feather.

Except—she frowned—she'd seen Tristan exhausted many times, yet not once did she recall him being surly. And she certainly didn't remember him using that cold tone on her. What had she done?

She should never have kissed him. That was undoubtedly the problem. He had kissed her and she should have known better than to respond. Before their marriage, Mari had warned her never to forget that she was a lady. Ladies were expected to be quiet and modest, Mari had said. They must remain unruffled. Detached. Even if a lady came to love her husband, she must never tell him. And she must certainly never initiate their joining in the marriage bed.

All of which had sounded so easy before Francesca had met Tristan le Beau. The attraction between them had been overwhelming. She had felt such joy and she could have sworn it was mutual. It would have been easier for Francesca to fly than to pretend a coolness towards her strong and virile husband. She had loved joining with him in their marriage bed. She had loved talking to him long into the night. In short, her foolish sixteen-year-old self had tumbled head over heels in love with him.

No wonder Tristan had never replied to her letters. She had forgotten her training as soon as they married and in so doing had lowered his opinion of her. She'd been too eager. She hadn't been ladylike. And with Lady Clare taking her place at Fontaine, Francesca's true colours had been revealed to the world. *I am not a lady, our marriage is over. I mustn't let a handful of kisses delude me into hoping otherwise.*

And if discovering that she was in truth no lady wasn't bad enough, today she had behaved like a loose woman. The Count of the Isles needed a real lady—one with impeccable bloodlines and lands to bolster his holdings and revenues.

Tristan's kisses meant nothing—he was ambitious, he needed a dynastic marriage.

How stupid she'd been down there in Sir Gervase's office. She'd lost herself in his kiss. A kiss which had made her long for things which were not hers and never could be.

Tristan wanted a real lady. Francesca couldn't excuse herself by saying she'd been overcome by passion, she should know better. She couldn't even claim it had been the sight of his handsome face or his powerful body that had weakened her knees. It had been far too dark for her to see very much. Being in his arms had simply overwhelmed her.

Her mistake had been that she shouldn't have let him know it. Mari would be well within her rights to call her a halfwit. She had forgotten her training and in responding with such heat she'd simply confirmed her lack of breeding. She'd made matters worse.

At the last turn in the stairs, they came to a studded oak door. Leaning past her, Tristan opened the door.

Candles were burning in wall sconces. The bedchamber was, as Sir Gervase had hinted, cramped. There was a decent-looking bed, a long, shuttered window and not much else.

Confirmation of Sir Joakim Kerjean's identity had hit Tristan like a blow to the gut. Shaken by a bewildering combination of fury and anxiety, he'd barely heard anything else Sir Gervase had said.

Sir Joakim Kerjean was the very man who'd been asking after Francesca at des Iles. What had the man been planning when he had pulled her into the palace corridor? Had they spoken before this? Had she become his mistress?

Tristan cast his mind back to the moment he'd come upon them outside Sir Gervase's office. He wanted to believe that Kerjean had lured an innocent Francesca into the corridor. He wanted to think that she had been cornered by an unwelcome and unexpected admirer. She had certainly slapped the man smartly enough. Unfortunately, it might not be as simple as that. Tristan must keep his mind open to all possibilities, however grim he might find them.

Think, Tristan, think. Francesca was still his

wife. Their marriage was in tatters, yet he couldn't help but be fond of her. That kiss had proved—as he feared it might—that their passion for each other wasn't completely dead. And what Tristan was feeling now—the anger, the rush of loathing towards Kerjean, the terrible uncertainly that scattered clear thought—it felt very much like jealousy. Jealousy would not help here.

Think. When Tristan had followed them into the corridor, both Francesca and Kerjean had been wearing masks. The most harmless possibility was that neither of them knew the other's identity, they had met by mere chance. In light of the enquiries Sir Joakim had been making in des Iles, the idea that Tristan had stumbled upon an innocent flirtation seemed extremely unlikely. Sadly, the idea that they had met by mere chance must be dismissed.

Tristan tore his gaze from Francesca as she looked about the bedchamber and forced himself to remember exactly what he had seen from the gallery. Kerjean had taken her by the hand and he'd been pulling her towards that corridor. Had she gone willingly? It might not have been an assignation.

He was starting to feel distinctly queasy. It had certainly been ill-advised of Francesca to allow

Kerjean to lead her away from the safety of the crowd in the great hall. Perhaps what Tristan had witnessed had simply been a mild flirtation on her part, one that had got out of hand.

A far more disturbing possibility was that Kerjean had set out to entrap her into becoming his mistress. What were the man's long-term intentions? Marriage? If Kerjean believed Francesca was alone in the world, he might consider her easy prey.

Think, Tristan, think.

Francesca had slapped Sir Joakim's face. She had been turned away from Tristan, she couldn't have known Tristan was about to interrupt them, yet she had slapped the man's face. Tristan ached to believe that slap was proof of her innocence. Kerjean, on the other hand, had been facing Tristan's way, Kerjean had seen him coming. Suppose the man had *told* Francesca to slap him to make their meeting appear innocent?

Tristan shoved his hand through his hair. What was wrong with him? He felt as though he was losing his mind. This only ever happened with Francesca. She clouded his thoughts in a way no one else ever did. In truth, after they were married, Tristan had feared that he was coming to be ruled by his emotions. He'd feared his judgement was at risk, and when the council had summoned him to Rennes to help contain the rebels, it had almost been a relief. He'd hoped that a separation from Francesca would clear his mind.

And here he was, after scant moments in her company, as confused as ever. It was profoundly unsettling.

Could he be jealous? If so, he was letting it get the better of him. No more. This was Francesca, she would never take a lover, not whilst she was still married. She would never betray him in that way, it wasn't in her nature.

Swearing under his breath, Tristan pushed Kerjean to the back of his mind. *I must tell Francesca about Count Myrrdin and I should tell her without delay.* Tristan wanted to break the news of Count Myrrdin's illness to her kindly. The count had been a father to her and she loved him—news that he was on his deathbed was bound to distress her.

'Francesca?' Tristan gave her a guarded look. 'You'd best brace yourself, I bring ill news from Fontaine.'

Grey eyes met his. Candid grey eyes. Wary eyes that had silver and gold flecks in them. Tristan had been attracted to her eyes from the first, surely she could not look at him in such a way if she was hiding some deceit?

'From Fontaine?' She lost colour. 'What's happened?'

Tristan took a deep breath. 'With your permission, I'll tell you straight. There's no prettying this.'

She swallowed and clasped her hands. 'Please do.'

'It's Count Myrrdin. He is sick, Francesca, mortally sick. He's asked that you and I attend him.' A hand reached towards him and fell back. Swearing softly, Tristan reached for it and enfolded it in his. It was icy, she was in shock. He took her other hand.

'Papa—the count—is dying?' Her voice was faint, a whisper of pain.

'I'm afraid so.' Gently, he stroked her hand.

'How did you hear? Lady Clare?'

'Aye, she sent word to my steward Sir Roparz, it was waiting for me when I arrived at Château des Iles. Francesca, the count is fading fast and it is his dying wish to see you.'

She bit her lip, dragged her hand from his and started to pace. 'I have to go to him. Tomorrow.' Agonised grey eyes held his. 'He wants to see you too?'

'He does.'

'Are you planning on escorting me to Fontaine?'

'Of course, we shall go together.'

'Thank you.' She walked to the bed, stared down at it and heaved a great sigh. 'So this was why you came to Provins. To tell me Count Myrrdin is dying.'

'That is one reason, yes.'

She nodded and said nothing, leaving Tristan to wonder what was in her mind.

'Francesca, once I had the news, I rode as swiftly as I could. I ought to tell you that even if we leave tomorrow, even if we travel lightly and ride like the wind, we might not reach Fontaine in time.'

'We should leave at first light.' Her face was drawn and pale.

'I need sleep, Francesca. As does Bastian.'

'Bastian?'

'My squire. Rest assured though, we shall leave in the morning.'

'Thank you.'

'We will travel light. And fast.'

'I understand.'

Francesca sat on the edge of the bed, watching Tristan devour the bread and meat a servant had brought up. She was curious about the differences between the man she had married and the man she saw before her.

He had altered in some as yet indefinable way,

that much was plain. It had been two years. He had known battle, faced death. He had seen friends slain. And he had also, or so she had heard, become quite the courtier. There was a disturbing edginess to him and she wasn't sure she liked it—a hardness that she hadn't noticed before. Had he always been this way? Had love—no, it had surely been lust that had flared between them, not love—had lust blinded her to his true nature? She didn't love him, she couldn't. To love someone you had to know them and it was becoming painfully clear that she didn't know Tristan at all.

It wasn't going to be easy sleeping with him. Did he really expect her to join him in bed?

'Tristan?'

He looked up from his meal, a handsome stranger with blue eyes that were hard as sapphires. 'Aye?'

'We don't have to share this chamber. I could quite easily bed down in the solar with the other ladies.'

He tore a chunk off the bread and frowned at some cheese on a platter. 'We stay together.'

'Why? Because I am not a lady?'

He narrowed his eyes on her and for a moment she thought she had disconcerted him. Then she realised her mistake—he hadn't expected to be questioned. Doubtless his men obeyed him in a trice. No one would dare question Lord Tristan le Beau, Comte des Iles.

'Don't be ridiculous.'

'Tristan, I assume we are to seek an annulment. If it is unseemly for a man and woman to lie together when they are not wed, surely it is unseemly for a man and woman to lie together when they are planning on dissolving their marriage?'

His expression hardened. 'We stay together.'

'Why?'

'I want to know where you are. I want to know what you are doing.'

She frowned. 'Even at night, when I am sleeping?'

'Even then.'

'You don't trust me, why? Tristan, please tell me what's wrong.'

A muscle flickered in his jaw. He didn't answer, he simply turned his attention to the food, leaving Francesca to her thoughts. Clearly, the kiss he had given her was an aberration. An annulment was obviously what he wanted, she had to free him so he could make a proper marriage. The pity was that he had kissed her before he had told her his reasons for coming to find her. Her foolish heart had soared, for a wild moment she had thought he'd come for her.

What a simpleton, to allow a kiss to affect her so, she should have known better. She shook her head, she must not let him upset her. Particularly when she was planning to move on with her life. It was a pity he'd kissed her though, that kiss merely proved that she was a fool if she thought she'd find it easy to marry someone else.

Tristan had come to escort her to Fontaine because Count Myrrdin was dying. That was what mattered. He would take her to Brittany and after that they would part.

Saints, in the past hour so much had changed. Count Myrrdin was dying and by Tristan's account he might not be alive when they reached him. A lump formed in her throat. Francesca loved Count Myrrdin, she'd always hoped to return to Brittany and she had assumed that he would be there to greet her. From what Tristan had said, it looked as though she'd best pray for a miracle.

Quietly, she rose from the bed and turned her back on her husband as he finished his meal. She placed her mask on a side-table next to a jug of water and a basin. She unpinned her veil and began to undress.

After their marriage, Francesca and Tristan had slept naked, that wasn't going to happen tonight. She was conscious of Tristan's eyes on her as she pushed her shoes under the bed and drew off her gown. She left her undershift on.

She washed quickly, flicked back the bedcovers and got into bed. Rolling on to her side, she presented Tristan with her back and waited.

She heard the clack of a knife being dropped on to the platter. She heard a splash—wine being poured?—no, he was using the water in the ewer. She waited some more.

Clothing rustled. The bed dipped.

'Goodnight, Francesca.'

'Goodnight, my lord.'

Tristan yawned, shifted on the mattress, and the room went quiet.

The hours crept by.

Francesca could scarcely believe she was lying in bed next to the husband she had never expected to see again. One who apparently trusted her so little that he wasn't prepared to allow her to sleep in the solar. She fixed her gaze on a candle, watching as it slowly burned down to a stump before flickering out. The shadows moved in. Tristan was surely asleep, his breathing was low and even and he hadn't moved in an age.

She sighed, carefully rolled on to her back and stared into the darkness. Wary of touching him, she was trying desperately to lie still. He had looked exhausted and was plainly in need of rest. His face was leaner than it had been, and there was a drawn look to it that she'd never seen before.

Sleep came and went in fractured snatches. One moment she was staring into the darkness, listening to Tristan's breathing, and the next a heavy weight was resting on her shoulder. Tristan's head. They had moved together in sleep. His foot was hooked about her calf and his hand was warm on her waist. He was naked. At least she thought he was. She couldn't be sure and exploration was simply out of the question.

Softly, she eased away. More of the night drifted by with her listening to his breathing.

The second time she woke, she was on her side facing him and his breath was warm on her face. This time his hand was on hers, almost as if he were holding it.

With a slight huff, she freed herself and rolled away from him.

On her third awakening, light was creeping round the shutters and the shadows were retreating. She was on her side with Tristan's body wrapped tightly around hers as though he would protect her until the end of time. Yes, he was definitely naked.

Half-asleep, she lay there unmoving. Her undergown had ridden up and she could feel the rough brush of his legs against hers. She could smell him, a musky masculine scent that brought back bittersweet memories—legs tangled in rumpled bed linens; lingering kisses; warm caresses that sent fire shooting through every vein.

Heavens, what was she doing? Their marriage was over.

She knew it, and so too did he.

Chapter Three

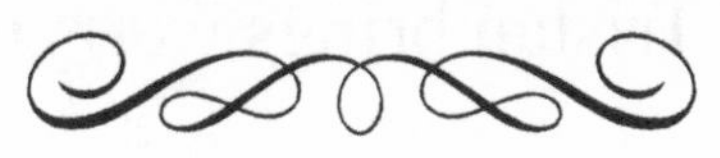

Leaving Tristan to sleep off the rigours of his journey to Champagne, Francesca dressed with a heavy heart and slipped down to the great hall to find Mari. The tables were up for breakfast and Mari was sitting with a group of women at one of the long benches. The peacock mask lay on the table next to a basket of bread, it was a little the worse for wear with the longest feather bent out of true.

'Good morning, Mari.'

Mari jumped to her feet with the energy of a woman half her age. 'Good morning, my lady. I'll fetch some fresh bread.'

'There's no need. Mari, I need to speak to you. I take it you received my message that Lord Tristan is here?'

Mari picked up her mask and moved with her to the side of the hall. 'Aye, Sir Gervase told me.' She gave Francesca a long, assessing look. 'You're not happy—what's happened?'

Francesca took a steadying breath. Mari had spent most of her life in Fontaine; she was bound to be upset when she heard of Count Myrrdin's illness. 'Lord Tristan brings worrying word from Brittany.'

The peacock feathers trembled. 'My lady?'

'Count Myrrdin is gravely ill.' Francesca touched Mari's arm. 'It's so serious that I gather he is unlikely to recover. He has asked to see me. He wants to see Lord Tristan too, we are to journey back to Brittany together.'

'Count Myrrdin is dying? Oh, my lady, that is terrible news.'

'Lord Tristan and I will set out this morning, before noon.' Francesca blinked back tears. 'Do you wish to accompany us?'

Mari gripped Francesca's hand and nodded fiercely. 'Of course. In any case, you will need a maid.'

Francesca managed a smile. 'I should warn you, the journey is going to be rushed and likely very tiring. Sadly, as I understand it, we don't have much time.'

Mari gave her a doleful look and a tear tracked

slowly down her cheek. 'Count Myrrdin,' she murmured, voice choked. 'One of the best.'

Francesca's eyes prickled. 'Aye.' She squared her shoulders. 'Mari, we need to get back to the manor, to pack. We shall be taking one saddlebag each.'

'Just one, my lady?'

'We will reach Fontaine more quickly if we travel light. Come, we should get back to the manor. If you are still hungry, you can eat there.'

'Yes, my lady.' Mari glanced towards the stairwell. 'What about Lord Tristan?'

'He's exhausted. We'll let his squire know what we are doing and they can join us at the manor when Lord Tristan is ready.'

'Very good, my lady.'

Seeing Sir Gervase enter the hall, Francesca moved towards him. 'I'll bid farewell to Sir Gervase and join you in the stables.'

An hour later, Francesca was back in her bedchamber at Paimpont, kneeling before one of three travelling chests that were lined up against the wall. She felt as though she was being pulled in two.

Count Myrrdin was dying. It was hard to accept. The count was getting on in years, so it shouldn't have been such a shock, yet shock it was. All this time Francesca had been fondly imagining that she would return to Brittany and see him again. She'd never imagined that meeting would take place at his deathbed—assuming they got there in time. How horrible, she'd taken Count Myrrdin for granted.

And then there was Tristan, here in Champagne. It was only beginning to sink in.

All in all, Francesca felt utterly dazed. It was only the second time in her life that she had felt quite so stunned. The other time had been when Lady Clare and Sir Arthur Ferrer had arrived at Fontaine bearing news that Francesca was not Count Myrrdin's daughter. Afterwards, Francesca had drifted about in a dream, doubting everyone and everything.

Lady Clare was Count Myrrdin's real daughter. Francesca, despite her upbringing, was no one.

Paralysed by uncertainty, Francesca had no longer known how to behave. Who was she? What was she? She'd been brought up as a lady, but she wasn't a lady.

Enquiries had been made as to her parentage, but every trail was long cold. In the end, she'd had to resign herself to the fact that her background would remain shrouded in darkness. She was no one. In a sense, it would have been better if they had discovered her to be a peasant, at least she would have had parents.

I am no one. Sometimes Francesca had found it hard to string a sentence together. Uncertain what was expected of her, and with no sign of her elusive husband, she had hidden herself away at her manor at St Méen with only Mari for company. It had taken a visit from the new Lady Clare to winkle her out.

Lady Clare had been wonderful. So understanding. The new lady of Fontaine had had a hard life, and she was quick to make it plain that she wasn't going to make difficulties. Lady Clare had asked Francesca to think of her as a sister. And it had been Lady Clare who had urged Count Myrrdin to let Francesca keep St Méen. By rights it should have devolved to Clare as the count's true-born daughter.

Notwithstanding Clare's kindness, Francesca hadn't found it easy to adjust to her change of status. She'd felt wounded. Her mind had been in a tangle. Sensing that she needed to recover somewhere where there were no reminders of her past life, she had come to Champagne.

Heart like lead, Francesca fingered the cold metal edge of the travelling chest. There was no time for shock today, though in truth that was what she felt. She stared blankly at the chests. They contained everything she owned and before the revel she had spent days packing in preparation for her departure from Paimpont.

Having had no reply from Tristan, Francesca had concluded that she was no longer welcome here. She had been ready to leave—if Tristan had brought his news a couple of days later, he would have found her gone.

Some weeks since, after much heartache and soul-searching, Francesca had decided that Judgement Day would come before Tristan deigned to answer her letters. She had contacted her friend Helvise, a friend she'd met in the Provins marketplace, and told her she was ready to go to Monfort. Helvise came from a humble background just as she did, and when Helvise had confessed to feeling overwhelmed regarding the running of a small manor outside the town, Francesca knew she could help. Francesca might not be a real lady, but she had been trained to run a castle and answering Helvise's questions had been child's play. And when Francesca had offered to move to Helvise's manor so she could teach her all she knew, Helvise had jumped at her offer.

Francesca had realised that if she continued to live in Tristan's manor, she would never be free of him. She would for ever be waiting for him to ride into the courtyard. Why, if she had a silver penny for every day she'd caught herself wishing he would sweep her up on to his saddle-bow and carry her back to Château des Iles, she would be a rich woman.

The scales had fallen from her eyes, she had waited long enough. She wanted a real marriage. God willing, she wanted children. It was possible she and Tristan had simply been unlucky. Of course, she only really wanted Tristan's children, but if she couldn't have them with him, much as it grieved her, she'd find someone else. There was no point being married to a man one never saw. Beginning a new life with Helvise had seemed the perfect solution, there was great comfort in being needed.

Helvise must be told of this change in arrangements.

I must repack, and quickly. Count Myrrdin is dying and I must go to him.

Heart heavy, Francesca reached into the trunk and shifted her neatly folded crimson gown to one side. Red fabric was costly and worn only by nobles. The gown wasn't suitable for the ride to Brittany, and even if it had been, these days she didn't have the gall to wear it.

She riffled though the chest. Whatever happened, she must remember one thing—the only reason Tristan had come for her was because he was honouring Count Myrrdin's deathbed wish to see her again. Would Tristan have come to Champagne if not for the count's last request? She doubted it.

Tristan had mentioned the need to travel light. She would need a couple of her most serviceable gowns; a couple of cloaks; a spare veil; a pair of shoes in addition to her riding boots; one good gown; an extra shift…

Mari clumped into the chamber, a saddlebag over each shoulder. 'Ned found these for us, my lady,' she said, as one of the bags slid to the floor with a clunk. 'He suggested that you use that one, it looks fairly new.'

'Thank you.' Francesca pulled the bag towards her and eyed it doubtfully. It didn't look large enough to contain everything she would need, but it would serve. 'You're happy with the other one?'

'Yes, my lady. Here, let me help.'

Francesca waved her away. 'You have your own packing to do, I can manage.'

Mari nodded. Halfway to the door, she sent her a wry smile. 'Will we be returning to Champagne, my lady?'

Francesca sat back on her knees. 'Of course, we can't disappoint Helvise.'

Mari eyed the small pile of clothes Francesca had set aside for the journey. 'Aren't you going to take a few of your good gowns? Won't you need them in Fontaine?'

'Mari, I am no longer the Fontaine heiress, it wouldn't be right. In any case, Lord Tristan insists we travel light. Sir Ernis will look after our things, I am sure.' Thoughtfully, Francesca ran her forefinger along a line of stitching on the saddlebag. 'Mari, we shall have to send word to Helvise that our plans have changed and our visit to Monfort will be delayed. Don't let me forget.'

'Very good, my lady.'

Tristan was in the manor gatehouse, issuing last-minute instructions to Sir Ernis before their departure.

'Ernis, as we won't be a large party, all we shall need in the way of food is a small supply of bread and cheese. Some ale and a couple of flasks of wine—you know the sort of thing. We can't carry much, we simply need something to tide us over in case we don't happen upon an inn when hunger strikes.'

'Of course, my lord. We had chicken last night—

I could ask the cook to wrap some in muslin for your noon meal.'

'My thanks. Have someone give it to Bastian, he will be in charge of provisions.'

A clattering of hoofs drew Tristan to the doorway. Ned was mounted up and heading out of the gate. Thinking it a little unusual that a groom should be riding out alone at this hour, Tristan caught his eye and the lad reined in.

'My lord?'

'You've an errand in Provins?'

'No, *mon seigneur*, I'm headed for the manor at Monfort.' Ned patted his saddlebag. 'Lady Francesca has asked me to deliver a letter.'

'She's writing to someone in Monfort?' Tristan waved the boy on his way and glanced thoughtfully at his steward. It was natural to expect Francesca to have made friends during her stay in Champagne. All Tristan knew about Monfort was that it lay a few miles from Provins, he hadn't been back long enough to name all the landowners. 'Ernis, who holds Monfort?'

'Sir Eric, my lord.'

Tristan leaned on the door frame and folded his arms across his chest. 'Never heard of him.'

'Sir Eric fostered at Jutigny with Count Faramus de Sainte-Colombe. He married the count's daughter, Lady Rowena.'

Tristan drew his eyebrows together. 'And my wife is writing to de Monfort because...?'

Sir Ernis cleared his throat and developed an intense interest in the toe of his boot. 'I...I don't think Lady Francesca is writing to Sir Eric or Lady Rowena, my lord. I expect she is writing to one of his servants.'

Tristan's eyebrows lifted. 'She's writing to a servant?' Ernis looked up. With a jolt, Tristan realised that his steward was deeply uncomfortable. 'Can this servant even read?'

'I have no idea, my lord. Her name is Helvise and I believe she is Sir Eric's housekeeper. My lord, she met your wife in the market and they became friends. I don't know much about it except that Helvise has a child and you know how Lady Francesca loves children.'

Tristan felt a twinge of guilt, he hadn't known. 'And?'

'Lady Francesca was planning to visit Monfort.'

'To help with the child?'

'It is possible. Helvise is unwed,' Sir Ernis said. 'I also heard that Helvise has asked for advice over changing some of the domestic arrangements at

Monfort. Lady Francesca has offered to lend her a hand.'

'It sounds rather irregular.'

'My lord, I do not think there is cause for alarm. I have met Helvise and she struck me as an intelligent, honest woman.'

'That is something, at least.'

'If you are concerned, *mon seigneur*, perhaps you had best speak to Lady Francesca. All I know is that about a week before the revel she asked for her travelling chests to be taken into her bedchamber. She and Mari have been packing for days. I would have told you about this in my next report to Sir Roparz, but since Lady Francesca hadn't actually gone and might change her mind, I saw no reason to say anything.'

Tristan hooked his thumb over his belt. Francesca hadn't mentioned having plans to visit Monfort. However, she and Tristan hadn't been together long, and after he had told her about Count Myrrdin's illness, doubtless everything else had been pushed from her mind. What was she up to? Planning to start a new life in Monfort or—Sir Joakim Kerjean's face flashed into his mind—was she thinking of remarrying?

Dieu merci, at least the journey to Fontaine would get her away from Kerjean.

'Thank you, Ernis, I shall be sure to ask her. Now, about your reports, you may send them direct to me from now on. We shall be riding to Fontaine, where we shall doubtless stay for a few days. After that you may reach me at Château des Iles.'

Sir Ernis smiled. 'I should think you'll be glad to remain in one place after so long in the train of the prince.'

Tristan murmured assent. 'I can't deny it, I've been living the life of a wandering knight and am heartily sick of it. It will be good to have the same roof over my head for more than a week.' His smile faded. What the devil was he going to do with Francesca? With luck, he would soon prove her meeting with Sir Joakim had been mere coincidence.

And then? Back at the palace, Francesca had hinted that she expected an annulment, what would she do after that? If she wanted children, she would need to marry.

He grimaced, there was a bitter taste in his mouth—the idea of Francesca remarrying didn't sit well with him. Why, he couldn't say. She had walked out of his life and was no longer his responsibility. In truth, he'd long ago come to the conclusion that the feelings she stirred in him—so all-encompassing they bordered on the obsessive—lessened him. They clouded his judgement. They weakened him.

Except that now he'd seen her again he realised that he couldn't simply wash his hands of her. This was Francesca, for pity's sake. What was he to do, have their marriage annulled and forget her?

It wasn't possible. He'd thought he could do it and that it would be relatively easy, but that was before he'd seen her with Kerjean, before that surge of jealousy had ripped through him. He couldn't forget her. Not Francesca. He would always want her. The emotions she stirred in him, though unwanted, made him feel truly alive.

Impatiently, he shoved his emotions to the back of his mind. What mattered was that on their wedding day, he had accepted responsibility for her and he wasn't one to shirk a duty. Tristan had felt that way before he knew of Count Myrrdin's illness and now, knowing Francesca would shortly be on her own in the world, his resolve had strengthened. *If Francesca wants to remarry, I shall have to ensure she marries well.*

What would happen to her otherwise? She had no one else to watch out for her and clearly, despite the months that had passed, she remained an innocent. The softness of her lips under his, the way she had melted against him. Lord, it had been a grave error kissing her. He would have to ensure she married well. To a sensible, honourable man. Then, with Francesca safely remarried, he would see to his own nuptials.

It shouldn't be difficult finding Francesca a husband. Yes, he'd find her a husband, it wouldn't take long. After all, she was stunningly beautiful; she had a kind heart; and she was extraordinarily gifted in the bedchamber. Except…

Lord, that rendezvous with Sir Joakim was back in his head. He didn't seem to be able to shake it.

'Sir Ernis?'

'My lord?'

'Have you heard of a Breton knight, name of Joakim Kerjean?'

'Can't say that I have. Why?'

'Sir Joakim was at the revel last night and I was wondering if he was a regular visitor to Provins.'

'My lord, I have no idea. If you wish, I could make enquiries.'

'I'd be glad if you would. Be sure to forward any intelligence about him to me at des Iles.'

'Certainly, my lord.'

Tristan had sworn to protect Francesca, and if Kerjean thought to put himself forward as one of Francesca's suitors after their marriage was annulled, it was Tristan's duty to ensure the man was honourable.

In a sense, it was a pity Tristan couldn't remain married to her himself, that way he could really keep an eye on her.

Of course, he would have to overlook the fact that she'd run away after the revelation that Lady Clare was Count Myrrdin's true-born daughter. That didn't present many difficulties, Francesca had been so young and the circumstances had been unfortunate in the extreme.

What rankled most was her lack of response to his letters. He'd agonised over it, telling himself that likely she was ashamed that the revelations about her birth meant that she brought him the most meagre of dowries. Yet to go on not answering—it was hard to set that aside.

He grimaced. The scales were starting to weigh against her. Had last night been the first time Sir Joakim had met her? He found it hard to believe otherwise, but he couldn't stop wondering. *How well do I know her? Has the charming girl become a calculating woman?*

Tristan gripped his steward's shoulder. 'My thanks for your continuing loyalty, Ernis.'

'You are welcome, my lord. I shall see to it the food is packed and given to Bastian.'

Tristan left Ernis and strode briskly across the yard. He wanted to see the main bedchamber before they set out. He'd not seen it in years and what Ernis had said about Francesca's plans to visit Monfort had roused his curiosity.

As Tristan passed through the hall, he noticed for the first time the polished side-table and the smell of beeswax. He paused to take stock. There were changes since his last visit. Hundreds of miles from his county in Brittany, Paimpont was his most outlying manor. It had always looked rather run-down. Unlived in. Tristan's father had neglected it and Tristan had always intended to make up for that. Yet events had conspired against him and somehow he'd never been able to give Paimpont the attention it deserved. Yet now—the floor was strewn with fresh rushes; the cloth on the trestle table was crisp and white; and a jug of wild flowers sat in the centre, next to a polished silver candle stand. The hall had never looked so welcoming. His mouth went up at a corner. This wasn't the work of Sir Ernis. Clearly, Francesca hadn't been idle.

Upstairs, Tristan pushed through the bedchamber door and blinked at the travelling chests lined up against the wall. They weren't locked. Frowning, he flipped back the lid of one and peered in.

Surely, these were her best gowns? Dropping to his knees, he turned them over. Here was the lavender gown she had worn on their wedding day. And this, surely this was the brocade cloak he had given her? Opening a cream leather pouch, he drew out a silver circlet set with amethysts. He'd given her this as his wedding gift.

Replacing the circlet where he'd found it, he shoved back another lid. Her Bible was tucked in between two other gowns; a coral necklace was wrapped in a woollen shawl. He recalled her telling him that Count Myrrdin had given her the necklace when she'd been a child. He opened the last coffer and found yet more of her treasures. A bone-handled eating knife; a beaded necklace; a scrap of finely worked embroidery. Francesca's belongings, reduced to three travelling chests. His frown deepened.

The trip she'd been planning had been more than any visit, she'd been leaving for good.

Well, not if he could help it, not with so much unfinished business between them.

He rubbed his chin, struck by a strange thought. Perhaps he should shoulder some of the blame for Francesca's disappearance from Brittany. He'd never told her how much he appreciated her. And in not wishing her to be frightened by the dangers posed by the conflict between King Henry and his sons, he'd not explained how vital it was that the duchy had his support.

He'd kept other things from her too, important personal matters. He'd never told her about Esmerée—his mistress before his marriage to Francesca.

Naturally, Tristan had ended his relationship with Esmerée before he'd met Francesca. Indeed, Esmerée was now happily married to Tristan's greatest friend, Sir Roparz de Fougères. None the less, perhaps he should have told Francesca about her. His only excuse was that Francesca had been so young when they'd married. She'd been so innocent. And so adoring. Tristan had never had anyone look up to him in that way and he'd been afraid of destroying it.

Should he have told her about Esmerée? His relationship with Esmerée had been purely physical, there had never been that disturbing sense of recognition and belonging that he'd felt with Francesca. He'd not seen any reason to mention past liaisons to his innocent wife.

He grimaced, he'd been deceiving himself, there had been consequences to his relationship with Esmerée. Esmerée had given birth to Kristina—

his daughter and only child—and the moment she had done so, he should have told Francesca.

I should have told Francesca about Esmerée and I should have told her that I have a daughter.

However, it wasn't that simple. Tristan intended to acknowledge Kristina as his, but the continuing unrest in Brittany had been to blame for his silence. If the rebel alliance had got wind of the fact that the Count of the Isles had an illegitimate daughter, Kristina's life might have been put in jeopardy. Thus far only three people knew the truth—himself, Esmerée and his friend Roparz.

However, with the alliance broken and peace more or less restored, the need for discretion regarding Kristina was no longer so urgent. He was free to tell Francesca about her.

Except what was the point in him telling her? With them both considering divorce, did it matter?

He closed the chest with a thud and swore under his breath. It mattered. For some unfathomable reason he wanted Francesca to know about Kristina.

Obviously, he couldn't tell her immediately, she had enough on her mind with Count Myrrdin's illness. Soon though.

Yes, he would tell her about his daughter after she had bid farewell to Count Myrrdin—Papa, as she called him.

Tight-lipped, Tristan pushed to his feet and went to the top of the stairwell. 'Ernis, are you still in the hall? Ernis!'

Heavy boots sounded on the boards below. 'My lord?'

'Secure Lady Francesca's coffers and have them sent on after us, will you? No need to send them to Fontaine, they can go directly to des Iles with your next report.'

Chapter Four

It was a glorious spring day as Francesca and Tristan clattered on to the highway ahead of Bastian and Mari. A handful of clouds meandered across the sky, the hawthorn bushes were bursting into leaf and the hedgerows were alive with sparrows.

'You're still riding Flint, I see,' Francesca said, glancing at Tristan's raw-boned grey.

'He suits me.' Expression softening, Tristan gestured at Francesca's mare. 'I see you kept Princess. I did wonder. Thought you might have left her behind.'

'She's perfect, I would have been mad to leave her in Brittany.' Francesca folded her lips firmly together. In truth, Tristan had given Princess to her at their betrothal. She was a glossy black and much adored. Francesca was reluctant to reveal exactly how much the horse meant to her. Every time she rode her, which was often, she thought of Tristan.

Tristan gave her a brusque nod, leaving Francesca to wonder whether she had imagined the softness in his expression.

'I'd like to make the most of this weather,' he said, giving the heel to Flint. 'It won't stay dry for ever, and a dry road is infinitely preferable to having the horses slog through acres of mud.'

Francesca urged Princess on. Her heart was heavy. Count Myrrdin had played such a large part in her life. She hadn't seen him in two years and yet he lived in her mind as though they'd spoken only yesterday. For eighteen years she had adored him as a loving and generous father.

The count had many eccentricities—the forgetfulness which seemed so at odds with the way he never failed to revere the memory of his beloved wife, Countess Mathilde; the wildness of his snowy-white hair and beard; his extraordinary mismatched eyes—one grey, one green. Each eccentricity merely served to point up what a quirky, lovable man he was. The day that Francesca had discovered that Count Myrrdin was not her father had been bleak indeed.

Her life had, quite simply, fallen apart. At a stroke, she'd lost a beloved father and she'd lost her place in the world. It had been well-nigh impossible to accept that she had no connections with Fontaine whatsoever. She was a changeling and her standing as a noblewoman was nothing but a lie. She cast a sidelong glance at Tristan—she'd lost the respect of her husband too. With not a drop of noble blood flowing through her veins, she had lost her purpose in life.

However, this was not the time to dwell on her disastrously inappropriate marriage. The man she would always think of as her father was dying.

'Count Myrrdin is the kindest man I know,' she murmured, eyes stinging. 'I pray he isn't suffering.'

She didn't think Tristan had heard her, he was looking over his shoulder at Mari and Bastian. Bastian had a packhorse on a leading rein, other than that they were travelling light as Tristan had suggested.

Following Tristan's gaze, it dawned on Francesca why Tristan had insisted that they wore practical, everyday clothing. No one would take them for the Count and Countess des Iles. The Count and Countess des Iles would surely ride through the land in bright silks and fine linen. They would have a grand entourage—guards and servants to fuss over their every whim. This way, with only Mari and Bastian and a solitary packhorse, they would pass through the towns and villages much faster. There would be no pomp and certainly no ceremony. They were riding incognito. With sackcloth covering Tristan's shield, the three black cinquefoils were hidden from view.

Her gut tightened. Did Tristan want them to travel unobtrusively because he was ashamed of her? His low-born wife. With a shake of her head, Francesca pushed the thought aside. Tristan was a proud man, not a cruel one.

Tristan cleared his throat. 'Your maid Mari is no longer young. Are you sure she can keep up?'

'I'm sure. Mari is livelier than many women half her age, she never keeps still. And her father was a groom at Fontaine, she learned to ride at an early age.'

'That's good to hear. It's safer if we keep together.' Tristan set his face forward and urged Flint on. 'Francesca, I don't think you need worry about Count Myrrdin suffering. I have heard Lady Clare is very competent.'

'Aye, so she is.'

Penetrating blue eyes met hers. 'I wasn't sure how well you knew her.'

'Well enough to know that she wouldn't withhold the poppy juice if Papa was in pain.'

Tristan held her gaze. 'I doubt that poppy juice

will be necessary. Knowing Count Myrrdin as we do, I think we may safely assume he is more likely to have fallen into one of his deep abstractions.'

Eyes misting, Francesca stared straight ahead. 'I pray so.'

Leather creaked as Tristan reached across to briefly squeeze her hand. 'Our main concern will be whether he is able to speak to you when we reach Fontaine.'

Francesca's throat closed. Tristan meant well, bless him, he was warning her that they might arrive too late. Blinking hard, she nodded and Tristan lifted his hand from hers.

'I shall do my best to ensure we get there as swiftly as humanly possible.' He paused. 'Francesca?'

'Aye?'

'What happened when Lady Clare came to Fontaine to claim her inheritance?'

Francesca felt herself go rigid. Shame. Hurt. Bitterness. However, Tristan's blue eyes were kind. Thoughtful. 'Tristan, I am sure you have already been given a full account.'

'So I was, but I'd like to hear your version of events.'

'Very well. Lady Clare's arrival was most unexpected, she arrived without any fanfare—with only one knight as her escort.'

'Sir Arthur Ferrer, yes, that much I knew. How soon did she reveal her identity?'

Chest tight, Francesca stared down at her hands. 'She didn't have to. The moment Papa set eyes on her he saw Countess Mathilde in her.' She shook her head. 'As did half the retainers. Lady Clare has red hair. But the most telling thing is her eyes, they are mismatched.'

'One is grey and one green?'

'Aye, they are *exactly* like Papa's.'

Tristan grunted. 'Count Myrrdin's eyes are certainly exceptional.'

Francesca's saddle creaked. 'When you see them together—' her voice broke '—*if* you see them together, you will realise there is no doubt. Papa was as shocked as I was, but he was quick to recognise her as his legitimate daughter.' She gripped the reins. 'Tristan, I am truly sorry you married me under false pretences. If I had known, I never would have agreed to marry you.'

Tristan made a sound of exasperation. '*Bon sang*, Francesca, I would never think that of you.'

Her throat closed and her eyes misted. 'Thank you.'

He grunted. 'Francesca, all your life you've been

thought of as Count Myrrdin's daughter. Did anyone try to find out how such a terrible mistake might have been made?'

'Yes, indeed, Papa did investigate and the castle priest, Father Alar, came forward. He had, years before, heard the confession of one of the villagers.'

Tristan leaned towards her, a slight pleat in his brow. 'Priests do not generally reveal what is said in a confession.'

'That is true, but given the lapse of time since the confession, and the importance of what was at stake, Father Alar told Papa that one of the villagers had confessed that her sister had stolen a child and run off with it.'

'A villager stole Lady Clare from her cradle?'

'So it seems.'

'And then? How was it that no one noticed the difference between you and Lady Clare?'

Francesca sighed. 'To answer that question we venture into the realm of speculation, I'm afraid. Countess Mathilde died giving birth to Lady Clare and Papa was grieving so much I don't think he had much time for a baby.'

Tristan nodded. 'That fits, my own father was out of his mind when my mother died.' His gaze sharpened. 'With regard to you, the wet nurse must have known she was nursing a different child. She must have been in on it. Is she still alive?'

'Sadly not. Though I agree she must have known. I can only suppose she panicked when Lady Clare vanished and I replaced her. Father Alar told Papa that he'd had no confession from the wet nurse.'

'If the wet nurse did substitute you for Lady Clare, likely she would have been too terrified to admit it. Francesca?'

'Aye?'

'Where did you come from? What about your real parents? Did Count Myrrdin learn anything about *your* background?'

She lowered her gaze. 'No. Apart from that one confession about the stealing of Lady Clare, we know nothing. I'm sorry, Tristan, my background is a complete mystery. I am truly no one.'

'Lord, it's not your fault. Francesca, I want you to know how much I regret that I wasn't at your side when Lady Clare rode into Fontaine. Was there much awkwardness between the two of you when it became clear who she was?'

Francesca shot him a startled glance. With her mind on Count Myrrdin and his illness, she hadn't expected an apology from Tristan. And she certainly hadn't expected all these questions. She fixed her gaze on a vineyard to the right of the highway. The vines were pruned and staked, bright curls of green were unfurling from the rootstocks. 'Lady Clare is very warm-hearted. I like her, everyone does.'

'Were you angry?'

'Not for a long time, I think I was in shock.'

'That's understandable.'

'At first I couldn't believe she was Papa's daughter, even though the evidence was there every time I looked at her.'

'Your father's eyes; Countess Mathilde's hair.'

'Exactly. Tristan, when you meet her, you will see it is impossible to question Lady Clare's parentage, she is the Fontaine heiress. She was kind to me. She seemed to understand my confusion, and when she said she was following Sir Arthur to Troyes, I decided to accompany her.'

Tristan's gaze was watchful. 'I was surprised when Roparz sent word that you had taken up residence in Paimpont. I was up to my neck in duchy business at the time, keeping a sharp eye on Prince Geoffrey.'

'That must have been a challenge.'

'It was like walking on eggshells. King Henry didn't trust the prince—Lord, no one trusted anyone. I was sent to England for a time.'

Francesca gave him a sharp look. 'How long were you there?'

Francesca had always wanted to know more about the extent of Tristan's involvement in Breton politics and this was the first time he'd spoken openly of it. In the past he'd been tight-mouthed about his work and she'd hated it. Hated that he'd kept things from her; hated that so much of his life was out of bounds to her. She had fallen in love with him and, naively, she'd thought he would open up to her.

How strange that he should choose to start talking when their marriage was in shreds.

'Roughly a year—I was sent there on account of the revolt against Henry of England.'

'The Princes' Revolt.'

Francesca knew a little about it. King Henry's sons, wanting more in the way of land and revenues than their father was prepared to grant them, had rebelled against their father. Henry's Queen, Eleanor, had even been implicated. However, the princes and their mother had not prevailed and King Henry's punishment had been swift and sure. Queen Eleanor had reportedly been carted off to England, where she had been incarcerated; and the rebel lords who had supported the princes had also been punished—King Henry's army had laid waste huge tracts of land in Brittany.

Tristan gave a rueful smile. 'Aye. King Henry wanted to keep an eye on Prince Geoffrey, so he summoned him to England. And since I was keeping an eye on the prince—on behalf of the duchy—I had to go too. In the end, settlement with the king and his sons was reached at Montlouis. Later, the treaty was confirmed in Falaise.'

'Sir Ernis told me that after the revolt, the duchy was ready to fall apart.'

Tristan grimaced. 'That's putting it mildly. There was a complete breakdown of law and order. Disgruntled lords and self-styled knights with no pretensions to chivalry jumped at the chance to grab what they could. Every knight with a half-baked claim to the meanest acre fielded a minor army to bolster his claim. It was chaos.'

Slowly, Francesca shook her head. 'I heard rumours, of course, but I didn't realise the extent of the trouble.'

Something was niggling away at the back of her mind. Her breath caught. Her letters! Had they gone astray? With Tristan moving hither and yon, it was easy to see that they might have got lost. Meeting his eyes, she watched carefully for his reaction.

'Tristan?'

'Mmm?'

'Did you get my letters?'

He must have jerked on the reins, for his horse jibbed. 'What letters?' His expression was puzzled, other than that it was unreadable.

'Tristan, you have to know I have been writing to you. I sent you several letters, long ones, the last in October.'

'Where did you send them?'

'Château des Iles.'

Tristan's gaze burned into her—he was watching her as closely as she was watching him. 'I received no letters. When I was in England, I left instructions for Roparz to forward me my correspondence. I never got anything from you.'

'That can't be right.'

'I received no letters from you.'

Francesca ached to believe him. Their life together had been short and her knowledge of Tristan's character was limited, but she'd never known him to lie. She made her voice light and managed a small smile. 'I suppose that might explain why you never replied.'

'Francesca, I couldn't reply to letters I never received, but I did write to you.'

Francesca lost her breath. 'You did?'

'Don't tell me—' his voice was flat '—you never got them.'

She shook her head.

'They couldn't have been lost,' he said. 'Not all of them.'

She frowned. 'How many did you write?'

'Four, I think. Yes, four.' He paused. 'I would have written more, except your lack of response made me think I was wasting my time.'

'Tristan, what could have happened?'

He searched her face. 'Let me get this straight. You wrote to me. I wrote to you. We both wrote several times and none of our letters was delivered.' Blue eyes bored into her. 'You swear you wrote?'

'Many times.'

Tristan swore. 'What the hell has been going on? In the past two years I received several reports from Sir Ernis. Not a word from you.'

Francesca twisted the reins round her forefinger. 'I can't understand it.'

'Nor can I. You sent all your letters to Château des Iles?'

'Yes, Ned took them. He told me he delivered them safely.'

'Ned is a good lad, I can't imagine what has gone wrong.' Tristan stared thoughtfully at the road ahead. 'Francesca, Roparz is my steward at des Iles and he told me— Well, never mind. That is in the past. Francesca, I swear not one of your letters reached me.'

As their journey along the Paris road continued, Tristan felt Francesca's gaze rest thoughtfully on him, although whenever he looked her way, she was frowning at Princess's glossy black mane. When Francesca's frown deepened, Tristan decided it could do no harm to repeat what he had told her earlier. 'Francesca, I did not receive your letters.'

Silence.

Tristan couldn't be certain Francesca believed him and it irked him not to be believed. Guilt sat heavy in his heart. This was largely his fault, he should have done more to prevent their relationship deteriorating so badly. In focusing on politics and fighting, he'd seriously underestimated Francesca's importance to him. Worse, he had used duty as an excuse to keep unruly emotions safely locked away. Their marriage had begun so well, she hadn't deserved his neglect.

The wind lifted her veil so it billowed out behind her. With a sigh, she reached back over her shoulder and dragged the veil forward, deftly twisting it into a rope to make it more manageable. Another woman would have had to rein in to complete such a manoeuvre, not so Francesca. He watched her tuck the veil efficiently beneath her cloak, and a simple phrase repeated itself over and over in his head.

Francesca wrote to me. Francesca wrote to me.

Tristan would give anything to know the content of those letters. That they hadn't reached him would have to be investigated later, but in the meantime her question—*Did you get my letters?*—changed everything.

When Tristan had responded to the call to arms, he'd left behind a wife who viewed the world through innocent eyes. He would be the first to admit that they hadn't really known each other. It hadn't seemed to matter. Francesca had been young and fresh and Tristan had found her guilelessness unexpectedly appealing. He'd never come across someone as uncomplicated. It had been extraordinarily refreshing and very flattering. Her face would light up if he so much as looked her way.

He had no doubt that Francesca's delight in the joys of the marriage bed hadn't been feigned. It wasn't predicated on the fact that he was one of Brittany's greatest lords, it had nothing to do with his wealth, or the power and standing Francesca would have as his countess. There was an astonishing spark between them and it had been as delightful as it had been unexpected.

Back then, Francesca hadn't hidden a single emotion. When they had married, they had known each other only a week, and she had come to their marriage bed as eager as he. Her untutored sensuality was as exciting as it was beguiling.

It had taken three days of marriage for her to tell him that she loved him. It would have been impossible for her not to tell him, he realised. She had been the most straightforward, honest person he had ever met.

Another week of their marriage had passed before Tristan realised that he was in danger of becoming seriously besotted himself. He didn't tell her. He couldn't, he simply wasn't a man to wear his heart on his sleeve. He'd sworn fidelity and he'd meant to honour that vow. He'd sworn to cherish her too. He'd been confident that Francesca would understand how he felt, his body spoke to hers in bed and hers responded. She understood.

Or so he had thought. When Esmerée had been brought to bed with Kristina, Tristan had naturally returned briefly to des Iles to ensure she was being cared for and to meet his daughter. That was when the secrets had begun.

Guilt sat heavy in his gut. He really should have told Francesca about Esmerée and he should have told her about Kristina. He hadn't done so because of the rebel alliance, it seemed safer that way. If the alliance had found out that Tristan had a daughter, Kristina's life would have been in danger. An innocent child might have been used as a bargaining chip.

So, instead of trusting Francesca with the truth, Tristan had lied to himself. He'd told himself it didn't matter that he was putting barriers between them. He'd convinced himself that his marriage to Francesca wasn't a matter of the heart, it was a political arrangement designed for the benefit of the Counties of Fontaine and des Iles and as such he had no need to tell her about Kristina.

In reality, there was more to it than that. He hadn't wanted anything to spoil the extraordinary rapport he'd found with his wife. Knowing that Roparz was caring for Esmerée had given Tristan the excuse to relegate his former mistress and his daughter to the back of his mind. They were part of his past, Francesca was his future. He hadn't wanted her altered in any way. Kristina and Esmerée hadn't been mentioned.

And later, when Tristan had been summoned to Rennes to the service of the little duchess, he'd been confident that his guileless, adoring and innocent wife would be waiting for him when he returned.

I took Francesca for granted. I thought she would keep all that shiny innocence.

Tristan hadn't liked leaving her, the extent to which he'd felt torn in two had surprised him. After all, he was used to being separated from his family. As a boy, his father's long silences when Tristan had been sent to foster with Lord Morgan had taught him to tamp down his emotions. And after what had happened with his father— Briefly, Tristan closed his eyes.

Emotions were messy and complicated and not for great lords—it was a lord's duty to focus on politics—battling enemies, holding land. That was a piece of advice he recalled his father, Count Bedwyr, giving him shortly after his mother had died.

Unfortunately, his father had not heeded his own advice—with tragic consequences. Tristan had learned from his father's tragic end. Emotions must be dominated, they must be controlled.

Even so, after Tristan had left Fontaine to serve the duchy, he'd been astounded at how he'd longed to hear from Francesca. Her silence had cut him to the quick, although it hadn't really surprised him. His father had never written to him whilst he'd been growing up under Lord Morgan's eye, why should Francesca?

But now…

She *had* written to him. He studied her profile—the sweet curve of her nose and the pretty pink of her mouth. The long, dark eyelashes. A curl of desire twisted inside. He wanted her. From that first meeting before their wedding, he'd wanted her. That had not changed. He'd wanted her in Sir Gervase's office, he would always want her.

If only they could go back in time and recapture some of the joy of their early days together. Was that possible?

Tristan had often tried to imagine what it must have been like for Francesca, believing she was a high-born lady, only to discover that she was nothing of the kind. As he had waited in vain for her to write to him, it had never occurred to him that she in her turn might be waiting for letters from him.

Had she waited? Had she longed to hear from him?

If waiting for her letters had driven him mad with uncertainty, what had his apparent silence done to her? In losing what she believed to be her birthright, she had reason enough for bitterness.

Add to that two years of what she must think was neglect and carelessness from him. No wonder she expected an annulment.

A blinding flash of insight had him freezing in the saddle. He didn't want to let her go. He wanted what he had never had, space to get to know her. *I want to give our marriage a chance. I don't want an annulment.* Sir Joakim's face swam into his mind and Tristan gritted his teeth. He certainly didn't want Kerjean to marry her.

I want to keep her. Tristan's heart jumped and his blood quickened, the thought of persuading Francesca to remain his wife was most enlivening. And not a little unnerving.

He would make the most of this journey to Brittany. He would explore every facet of Francesca's character. He would give her a chance to trust him again and at journey's end he would ask her to stay with him. And if she really didn't want him, he would do his utmost to see her happily settled before finding himself a second wife.

Noticing him watching her, she gave him a faint smile. 'I'd forgotten what it is to ride so fast.'

Tristan took the change of topic in his stride. 'You haven't been galloping through the Champagne vineyards?'

'Certainly not. I have lived a quiet life—too quiet.'

Which chimed in with what Sir Ernis had told him. Francesca was shy, Tristan realised with something of a start. It was an aspect of her personality he had not marked until now, mainly because the passion between them had ignited so swiftly. It had never occurred to him that Francesca might be shy with other people. Acting as Count Myrrdin's steward, he hadn't had much chance to observe her outside Fontaine, where, before the arrival of Lady Clare, she had naturally felt entirely at home.

Tristan had first met Francesca a week before their marriage. They'd done their courting as they rode along the tracks and paths that criss-crossed the woods above Fontaine Castle. One of the first things that Tristan had noticed about her was that she was an excellent horsewoman. Princess had been the obvious betrothal gift and Francesca had kept her in good condition, the mare's flanks gleamed like polished ebony. Francesca looked stunning on her—a dark-haired beauty on a delicate black mare. Tristan's gaze caught on Princess's bridle as a round harness strap gleamed softly in the light—a silver-strap ornament complete with an enamelled black cinquefoil.

He'd given Francesca a set of strap ornaments as

a Christmas gift and it would seem she still used them. Her large grey eyes were full of shadows, she was thinking about Count Myrrdin. Likely it didn't help that she was wary about being in Tristan's company. *We have been apart too long. She has learned to mistrust me.*

There was no doubt that the girl Tristan had married was gone. That gorgeous, shiny naivety was no more. Sadly, he was pretty certain that the lost letters were only part of the story. He too was to blame, he had taken her for granted when he had left to serve the duchy and this was the result. His sweet, beautiful, adoring wife had changed. She was, in some invisible way, scarred. He wasn't sure if he could mend matters between them, but by God, he was going to try.

He gave her a direct look. 'You don't believe I wrote to you.' Tristan's belly tightened as he paused for her reply. He could delude himself no longer, he didn't want an annulment. All the while he had waited to hear from her, he had held on to the hope that she would one day welcome him back. The silence lengthened as he endured her careful scrutiny.

'I am not sure, my lord.'

My lord. Her use of a more formal mode of address didn't escape him. She was wary and was using formality to keep him at a distance. Very well, he wouldn't push it. Yet. 'We shall discuss this further when we stop to rest the horses.'

A lock of Francesca's ebony-coloured hair streamed in the wind. 'As you wish, my lord. However, if you say you didn't receive my letters, then of course I must believe you.'

A village passed in a blur of movement. They slowed down to trot over a bridge and spurred on again. Tristan looked back. He was glad to see that Mari and Bastian were only a couple of horse-lengths behind. It would be the packhorse rather than Mari that slowed them down.

Irritably, he rolled his shoulders, instinct was telling him that someone was following them. He looked past Mari to the road they had covered. There was nothing there, just Mari and Bastian and the packhorse. The feeling remained—a slight prickle of unease running down his spine. Surely Kerjean wasn't foolhardy enough to be following them? Having warned him off in Provins, it seemed unlikely.

Nevertheless, the prickle down his spine persisted. Someone was following them and sooner or later they would reveal themselves.

As the field strips flashed by, Francesca's face was tight with concentration. That line between her eyebrows remained, a line that warned Tristan that despite her words, she had reservations about him and was holding herself aloof.

'We won't be keeping up this pace for ever,' he said.

'No, indeed, we'd lame the horses.'

'I aim to reach Melun tomorrow.'

'We are staying at the castle?'

Tristan made a negative gesture. 'I think not. Melun is a stronghold of the French royal domain, and if Lord Ursio is in residence, he will press me for information on Breton relations with the English king and Prince Geoffrey. I'd like to avoid that if I can. We'll stay at St Michael's Abbey—their guest house is second to none.'

'And tonight? Where do we stay tonight?'

'There's an inn at La Chapelle, it's midpoint between here and Melun. The lodgings are clean and the food's tolerable.'

'Very well, I shall rely on your judgement.' Her voice was cool, her eyes remote.

Tristan glanced at the silver-strap ornaments on Princess's bridle and hid a smile. With luck, it wouldn't be long before he made Francesca's face light up in the old way.

Chapter Five

They stopped to rest the horses halfway to La Chapelle and reached the inn by nightfall. Francesca wasn't used to so much riding and sight of that torch-lit stable yard was welcome indeed. Stiffly, she dismounted, surreptitiously stretching tired muscles as Bastian led the horses into the stable.

Tristan offered her his arm. 'Aching?'

'A little.' She grimaced and allowed him to lead her into the inn. 'I am not used to spending the whole day on horseback.'

Tristan's mouth crooked up at one corner. 'It's only been half a day, we didn't set out till noon.'

'Nevertheless, I confess I can hardly walk.'

The inn was busy, this being a regular stopping point for travellers heading to Paris or Chartres. Tristan gave her a brief smile and saw her settled at a bench in a corner. A tallow candle stood on the table, the surface of which was spotted with candle grease.

'You'll be warm enough here while I see about food and lodgings?' he asked.

'Yes, thank you.'

Tristan squeezed past the tables to reach the serving hatch, hair gleaming like jet in the candlelight. A serving girl appeared out of the shadows and Francesca leaned her chin on her hand and watched him as he spoke to the girl.

She liked looking at Tristan, she always had. His dark, masculine features were undeniably attractive and that hadn't changed. Tristan laughed at something the girl had said before turning and making his way back to her.

'We're in luck,' he said. 'They have a small chamber under the eaves that is sometimes used as a bedchamber. We shall take that. Mari and Bastian can sleep in the common room.'

Francesca managed to hide her dismay. It was dispiriting not to be trusted and clearly he was not prepared to let her out of his sight. She forced a smile. 'I could sleep for a month and I am sure you are about to tell me that we will set out at first light.'

His lips curved as he took his seat. 'How well you know me.'

She held his gaze. 'Do I? I don't feel I know you at all.' Apart from the conversation as they had set out, they had hardly spoken. Most of today's ride had been completed in silence.

The bench creaked as he turned to study her. 'You wish to know more about me?'

Tristan's question startled her. He'd always been reserved and she'd often wished she knew more about him. These past couple of years, she had been building an image of him in her head, an image she was beginning to see might be entirely wrong.

'I believe I would.' If Tristan had written to her, she had misjudged him. Of course, even if she had misjudged him, she would still have to step aside to allow him to make a more propitious marriage. None the less, it would be good to have the chance to understand him better.

When they had met, Francesca's fascination with Tristan had been entirely carnal, she'd been too young to realise she should have taken time to learn more about the man. His reputation for being highly ambitious had made her wary of asking too many questions. Back then, she had been in awe of her handsome husband, she'd been certain he wouldn't welcome curiosity from a green girl who knew nothing of the world of politics and power.

This was her chance. He might not trust her, but that didn't stop her wanting to know everything about him. 'I am sorry I was silent earlier.'

'You were thinking.'

'Aye.'

A pot-boy approached with a flagon of wine and two clay cups. 'The meat won't be long, my lord.'

The boy moved off and once again that warm blue gaze was focused on her. 'Please continue, Francesca. I am yours to command.' Tristan picked up the wine flagon, filled the cups and slid one towards her.

The wine was rich and heavy and steeped with spices. Francesca sipped thoughtfully. She wanted to know how Tristan had passed the last two years. It couldn't have been easy maintaining good relations with a wayward and wilful prince. Given that such a task was more diplomatic than military, both Baron Rolland and the English king must think highly of him.

Noting how busy the inn was—Mari and Bastian had been forced to take a table some distance away—Francesca leaned towards Tristan and kept her voice low. 'With the tavern so full, I don't suppose I can ask you about your business of the past two years? I'd love to know what Prince Geoffrey is like.'

Tristan glanced about the inn and his mouth twitched. 'That might not be wise,' he murmured, dark head touching hers. 'The people here look like farmers and merchants, but appearances can be deceptive.'

She murmured assent. She was painfully aware that whilst she did want to hear about Tristan's business for the duchy, she was far more interested in what had lain in his heart. Had he thought of her often? Had he been saddened when his letters had gone unanswered? Had he decided to cut her out of his life for good?

Had he been faithful? Had he?

With an effort, she chose another question. 'You never talked much about your parents.'

He drew back and his broad shoulders lifted. 'There's not much to tell, I barely knew them. I was sent to foster with Lord Morgan de Vannes. I was there when my father sent word of my mother's death.'

Francesca blinked. 'Count Bedwyr sent you word? He didn't come and tell you himself?'

Tristan gave her an odd look. 'Of course not. Lord Morgan told me, Father was busy with the funeral rites.'

Of course not. How strange. 'You went to the funeral though?'

Face a mask, Tristan shook his head. 'Father thought it best that I remain with Lord Morgan at Vannes.'

Francesca found herself struggling to understand. She had been told that Count Bedwyr had worshipped his countess, and that after her death he'd been struck down with grief. Surely he had loved his son too? It was hard to fathom him abandoning Tristan in such a way. She opened her mouth to express her disapproval of Tristan being left to grieve alone in an alien household, when Tristan covered her hand with his.

'Francesca, I can see what you are thinking and you are wrong, very wrong. Lord Morgan is the kindest of men and his wife, Lady Renea, is a good woman, I wasn't neglected.'

Francesca stared at Tristan's hand lying on hers. It was so much larger than hers, and so strong. Those long warrior's fingers could be gentle. Loving. His thumb moved—Francesca wondered if he even knew what he was doing—gently caressing the back of her hand. Her gut ached, sweet and agonising. Tristan's touch—Saints—he still had the power to melt her.

Raising her eyes to meet his, she swallowed and found words. 'If you say so, although I can't help thinking your father treated you harshly.'

'Francesca, it is common practice for the sons of noblemen to be fostered in other households. It's supposed to teach self-reliance.'

'I know, I know. But I've never warmed to the idea of fostering.'

With a jolt, Francesca realised that in a sense both she and Tristan had been fostered. Of course, their cases were entirely different—she had grown up believing Count Myrrdin to be her father; whilst Tristan, knowing his father, had been sent to train in another lord's household. The difference between them surely was that she had grown up knowing what it was to be loved. Could the same be said of Tristan?

'Tristan, did Lord Morgan knight you?'

'Aye.' A muscle flickered in Tristan's jaw. 'As it happened, I consider it a blessing I was sent to Vannes when I was. With my father dying a year after my mother, it was probably just as well I'd come to know Lord Morgan.'

'It made the blow easier to take?'

'If you like, although as I said, Father was always a distant figure. He named Lord Morgan my guardian. Lord Morgan ran des Iles until I was old enough to take over myself.'

Strangely moved, Francesca stared at their hands and fought the impulse to link her fingers with his.

'Lord Morgan didn't come to our wedding, why was that?'

'Lady Renea was ill.'

Francesca waited, frowning when he said nothing more. How like Tristan to tell half the tale. 'Really, Tristan, you can't leave it at that. Lady Renea—did she recover?'

'Aye, she recovered well.'

'That is good to know.' She took a deep breath. 'Tristan, I don't care what you say, to my mind, your father treated you shabbily by making you miss your mother's funeral. Papa—Count Myrrdin, that is—would never have behaved in such a way.'

Broad shoulders lifted. 'As I told you, I didn't know my father well. However, as far as I could judge, Count Myrrdin was very different. That might be something to do with his age.'

Francesca hesitated. As Count Myrrdin had grown older he had begun to suffer from periods of vagueness which increased as the days went by. 'You are referring to Papa's dreaminess?'

'Not at all.' Tristan's thumb moved softly over her skin, back and forth, back and forth. It was both soothing and distracting. 'If you must have it, I was thinking of Count Myrrdin's generous character. The way he welcomed me when I arrived at Fontaine, I shall never forget his warmth.'

Francesca relaxed. 'He likes you.' She stared at Tristan's hand, enjoying the warmth of his touch more than she should, given that Tristan was likely planning their annulment. It was very confusing. Gently, she drew her hand from his. 'Should you be doing that?'

'What? Oh, my apologies.'

She watched, bemused, as dark colour ran into his cheeks. Tristan? Flushing? He looked slightly bewildered, which was most strange.

An awkward silence fell and Francesca toyed with her wine cup. When the silence drew out, she lurched into speech. 'Count Myrrdin wasn't always otherworldly. He used to be extraordinarily clear-headed.'

'And well known for his prowess at arms—he was quite the warrior in his youth.'

'So I hear.' She sighed. 'Tristan?'

'Aye?'

'Papa withdrew from the world of power politics long before our betrothal. It occurs to me that his lack of interest in anything that happened outside Fontaine had its effect on me.'

'Oh?'

She ran her finger round the glazed rim of her wine cup and gave a small smile. 'Whenever I questioned him about duchy business, he would change the subject.'

Tristan's eyes were full of sympathy. 'He was old and his mind was tired. I've seen it happen to others—their world begins to shrink and they lose interest in what is happening elsewhere.'

'I know he couldn't help it. Papa lost interest in the world outside the castle long before you and I were married. I suspect his world began to shrink after Countess Mathilde's death. My main regret was that every time I asked him about Breton affairs, he would lose the thread of his thoughts.' She gave him a small smile. 'It was almost impossible to unravel what he was saying.'

'That must have been frustrating.'

'That is an understatement. I wanted so much to be able to converse intelligently with you. You must have found me very uninformed.' A lowering thought came to her. Was that why Tristan had kept her in bed in the early days of their marriage? Had he thought her too ignorant to be taken seriously?

He smiled, eyes gleaming in amusement. 'You do yourself a disservice. Francesca, I enjoyed being with you. It was restful beyond anything I had experienced. You brought me no petitions, you made no demands.'

'I suspect Papa knew he was at fault for not tutoring me better. One of the reasons he chose you for my husband was because he respected your acumen and trusted your judgement. However you look at it, I was too ignorant to marry a count. I must have been a grave disappointment.'

Tristan pressed his thigh against hers—the movement was subtle and, she thought, deliberate.

'Far from it.' His mouth curved, he was staring hungrily at her mouth and her stomach swooped. 'As I recall, after the wedding there was never enough time for talking.'

Her face scorched and she looked swiftly away. 'That's true.'

They'd spent too much time in each other's arms. Although they had talked, endlessly, it had been about inconsequential domestic topics such as how soon they might enlarge the stables at St Méen so as to accommodate more of Tristan's horses. They discussed the decoration of the manor solar—how many cushions Francesca should embroider with Tristan's colours. Why, he'd even given her his opinion on her design for the wall-hanging.

When she glanced his way again, Tristan was still staring at her mouth as though he wanted to devour it. Inevitably, their eyes met and for a moment she lost her breath. That look made bittersweet memories rush back at her—rumpled bedsheets; the softness of raven-dark hair as she sifted it through her fingers. That look, Saints, it was altogether too carnal for a quiet supper in a tavern.

The candle flickered—the pot-boy stood at Tristan's elbow, a wooden platter of lamb in one hand and a basket of bread in the other. 'Here you are, *mon seigneur*,' the boy said, placing the platter in front of them with a clunk. 'If you would carve off as much as you and your lady need, I will take the rest of the joint to your friends over there.' He jerked his head towards Mari and Bastian.

Tristan took up the carving knife and Francesca realised she would get no more out of him until after they had eaten.

Holding his candle clear of a draught, Tristan approached the bedchamber. The landlord had told him there was only one bed and, given how Francesca had pulled her hand from his when she'd realised he was caressing it, Tristan was concerned. Hoping to forestall an argument, he'd taken the precaution of asking the landlord to escort her upstairs as soon as she'd pushed her empty plate aside. That had been a good half hour ago. If she had been going to object about sharing a bed with him, she would surely have done so.

Tristan could have asked for a pallet to be brought in. He hadn't, he wanted to sleep with her. Nothing would happen, he was determined on that. He wanted her close, he enjoyed her company. It was undoubtedly a weakness, Francesca was his Achilles' heel. He'd enjoyed holding her hand before supper. Until she had noticed. It had been oddly warming to watch those large grey eyes fill with fellow feeling as he told her about his mother's death. Lord, his own eyes had prickled. More weakness. Sympathy always made him uncomfortable. It was such a novelty, he hardly knew how to react. As he had told Francesca, he'd been with Lord Morgan so long he barely remembered his mother. He couldn't account for that prickle of tears. Francesca got under his guard in a way no one ever had. She was his weakness.

He knocked on the bedchamber door and waited.

'Tristan, is that you?'

'Aye.'

'Come in.'

She was sitting in bed with the bedcovers drawn up tightly under her chin. Her expression was wary and it seemed safe to assume she was wearing an undergown as she had on the previous night. Not that he should be thinking of that. Nothing was going to happen between them.

Calmly, he set the candle on a wall shelf. 'There's no need to look at me like that,' he said softly. 'I won't take advantage of you.' He placed his sword by the bed, knowing from experience it was best to have it to hand when sleeping in an unfamiliar place.

Under the bedcovers her breast heaved. 'It doesn't seem right, our sleeping together, Mari agrees with me.'

Tristan had had nothing from her maid except scowls. He swallowed down the reply that Mari loathed his guts, so naturally she would disapprove of their sleeping together, and said, 'We sleep together until I am sure of you.'

Her chin went up. 'What exactly do you mean by that?'

With a shrug, he turned away and began to strip. He heeled off his boots and hung his clothes on a wall peg—leather gambeson, shirt, braies…

'Tristan, if you are sharing this bed with me, you ought to put that shirt back on.'

There was an edge of panic to her voice. Tristan's lips curved, he knew she didn't fear him. 'Afraid you won't be able to resist me, my heart?'

She made an exasperated sound. 'It's not seemly when we don't intend to stay together.'

Fully naked, he turned to face her.

With a squeak, she dived beneath the bedcovers. 'For heaven's sake! Tristan, blow out the light.'

Pinching out the candle, he felt his way to the bed, climbed in and gave a languorous sigh. 'Goodnight, my heart.'

'You shouldn't call me that,' she said, in a muffled voice. 'It's not appropriate.'

'Is it not?' Folding his arms behind his head, Tristan smiled into the dark. The mattress wasn't large and by rights he should feel her lying beside him. He couldn't, which had to mean that she was balanced on the edge of the mattress. He wondered how long she would be able to perch there without falling out of the bed. 'Sleep well.'

Francesca huffed. She lay still for some time and then shifted. And shifted again. Each time she shifted, her body worked its way inexorably closer to his. It wasn't long before he could feel her body heat.

'Relax, Francesca,' he murmured. 'We slept in the same bed last night. What harm can another night together do?'

Finally, she lay still. When her breathing evened out, Tristan allowed himself to close his eyes. Really, he felt astonishingly content. The lamb had been tender and plentiful and his belly was full. He hadn't felt so at ease in years. He yawned, he was pleasantly tired—not exhausted as he had been the previous night. Tristan had enough self-awareness to know that his contentment had nothing to do with the exercise he had taken or the tenderness of the lamb. It was Francesca. Being in her company again was an unexpected blessing.

Realising that she had written to him during their separation changed everything.

Rolling on to his side, Tristan breathed in her scent. He was smiling when sleep claimed him.

Some while later, a loud thud woke him. He snatched at his sword. The door rattled, faint light was shining through a crack at the bottom—someone was stumbling about on the landing. A man gave a choked laugh and hiccoughed and the noise moved off.

Francesca sat up. 'What's happening?'

'Someone with a jar too many inside him is falling up the stairs, I imagine,' Tristan said, replacing his sword under the bed. 'You are quite safe, such things are to be expected in a tavern like this.'

Francesca scooted back under the bedcovers.

Tristan was wide awake and so, it seemed, was she. The mattress rocked as she shuffled this way and that. The bed ropes groaned. She pushed the covers away. She dragged them up again.

It was full dark in the chamber. It made no difference, Tristan didn't need light to visualise her. Silken skeins of night-black hair would be working loose; her undergown would be slipping off one shoulder; her legs…

Mon Dieu. Tristan gritted his teeth against the urge to draw her into his arms and stroke her hair. She used to like him holding her in that way. *Soon*, he told himself. Not tonight. He ought to tell her about Esmerée and Kristina first, and much as he longed to, it didn't seem right when she was worrying herself sick over Count Myrrdin.

Francesca had much to come to terms with. If he wanted to win her, he had some rough ground ahead of him.

'Can't sleep?' he murmured.

The bedclothes rustled and he felt warm breath on his arm. 'I am sorry, Tristan, I know I am disturbing you. I can't help wondering how Papa is.' Her voice cracked. 'I should be with him. I love him so much, and if we arrive too late, I won't be able to tell him. I didn't thank him for looking after me so well and I should have done.'

'You were planning to return?'

'Yes.' She paused. 'No.' Another pause. 'Saints, Tristan, I don't know. I was confused when I left Brittany, the world had turned upside down and every instinct was screaming at me to get away.'

'You wanted to discover who you were away from the trappings of Fontaine. It's understandable.'

'Is it? It was a mistake to stay away so long. It was selfish. I know Papa loves me, whoever I am—' She broke off and a heavy sigh filled the air. 'It was just— I didn't feel I belonged there any more. I wanted to know who I was, who I truly was.'

The words slipped out before Tristan realised. 'My wife?' *My weakness.*

'We hardly knew each other. You told me you wanted an heir and we worked most diligently to that end, in truth we did little else.' She gave a soft sigh. 'I failed you there too. I came to you empty-handed and I failed to give you an heir.'

Tristan grimaced. He never would have imagined that their sensual compatibility would come back to haunt him, yet that was what seemed to be happening. He wasn't about to deny the pleasure they took in each other though—not when they had scandalised half the Fontaine household with their reluctance to leave the bedchamber. 'Francesca, don't speak of yourself as a brood mare.'

'Well, that is what I was. A brood mare who failed to give you an heir.'

Tristan found her hand and gently linked his fingers with hers. 'That never concerned me, you were young and I hoped we would have a lifetime together. You were far more to me than that.'

'Was I?'

'You know you were.' Not wanting to push the point, Tristan leaned thoughtfully against the pillows. Their relationship was changing fast. Discovering their letters had gone astray had begun the process and where it would end he couldn't say. What he did know was that as far as he was concerned, Francesca's lack of lineage was unimportant. Despite the inconvenience of the emotions she evoked, despite the way she clouded his judgement, he was coming to understand that he'd be happy with her at his side to the end of his days. His thumb caressed her palm.

It was too soon for him to declare his intentions. His belated confession concerning Kristina wasn't all that stood in his way. Francesca had kept her hurt inside her for two years, she needed time to adapt to their altered circumstances. The frost had to melt. Much as he wanted to, he couldn't rush her. Too much change, too soon, and she would be sure to baulk. He had to take this slowly. He would use logic, dismantling her objections one by one.

He would begin by accepting the blame for not taking her fully into his confidence before he left to serve the duchy. He would try to do what he'd spent his life avoiding. Even though it went against the grain of everything his father had taught him, he would attempt to be open about his feelings. His secretive nature had pushed her away.

'I should not have left Fontaine without telling you how much you meant to me.' Tristan toyed with her fingers and, as he measured their length in the dark, he felt a ring. His thoughts scrambled. Surely this was the ring he had given her on their wedding day? Yes, she was definitely wearing his gold signet ring. 'You're wearing my seal.'

She freed her hand and an instant later she pressed the ring into his palm. 'I'm sorry, it slipped my mind. I knew I would have to return it.'

He flinched. 'Good grief, Francesca, I'm not asking for it back. Wait until we are sure what we want.' He recaptured her hand and pushed the ring back where it belonged.

Somewhere in the inn, a door slammed.

'Tristan, you need to make a proper alliance.'

'Ours is a proper alliance.'

'No, it isn't. You need a titled lady with a dowry, a lady with influential relatives who will become your allies. I am no one.'

'You are my wife.' He nudged her shoulder with his and leaned towards her. The bed ropes creaked.

He found her cheek and kissed it. Tension was coming off her in waves and he made himself pull back. 'Francesca, I will have no more nonsense. We shall travel to Brittany and see if we might recapture some of the pleasure we found in each other after our wedding. If we do, it is my earnest wish that you should remain my wife.'

'Pleasure,' she murmured in a sad voice. 'Tristan, you don't need me, you need a high-born lady.'

'You are all the lady I need.' He lowered his head and nuzzled her shoulder. Finding that her undergown had indeed slipped, he managed to kiss bare skin. The scent of jasmine wound through his brain—*Francesca*—and his pulse jumped. Lord, what was he doing? He had just told himself not to rush her, and here he was, pressing his attentions on her like a lovesick boy.

'You mean this?'

'Of course. You are my wife.' Before he could stop himself, he had wound his arm about her and brought her to his chest. 'Relax, Francesca. I am simply holding you.' He put warmth in his voice. 'I am planning to win you back.'

Her body stiffened. 'No kisses. You mustn't kiss me.'

'You see? You fear my kisses, and it isn't because you mislike them, it's because you like them too much.'

She shook her head and a strand of hair whispered across his shoulder. Tristan's skin tingled and he gritted his teeth against a rush of desire. *Mon Dieu*, lying with Francesca was proving to be a test of will that had to be of the devil's devising. He held in a groan and tried not to remember the times her limbs, long and lissom, had tangled with his.

'You, my lord, are the most arrogant man I have ever met.'

Her tone wasn't angry, although Tristan couldn't quite read it. Doubtful? Hopeful?

'On my honour, there will be no more kisses.' Tonight, at least.

Praise be, she took him at his word. Releasing a long sigh, she laid her head against him and slid her hand about his waist.

Progress. At least Tristan hoped it was progress. With Francesca, one could never be certain.

Chapter Six

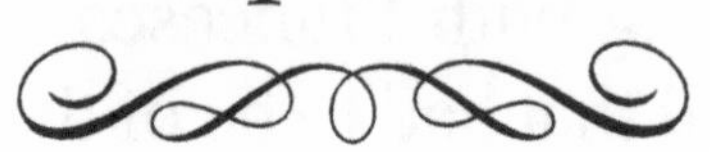

The next day their party followed the road west. A light drizzle was falling and everyone, Francesca included, hunched under their hoods. Tristan had told her that with luck they would reach St Michael's Abbey at Melun in the evening. They would bed down at the abbey before setting out again the following dawn. As the morning progressed and the rain became a steady downpour, Francesca found herself praying that they would fare better on the morrow.

The road ahead was pockmarked with puddles, mud splattered and the wet seeped through her cloak and gown. Her thighs felt damp. Itchy. Large raindrops blew into her eyes; they hung like jewels on Princess's mane before being flicked away by the wind.

As the morning progressed, the idea of drying out before a large guest house fire became ever more alluring. Abbey guest houses were renowned for their hospitality towards noblemen, and even though they were travelling without fanfare, Francesca had no doubt that Tristan, Comte des Iles, would be warmly welcomed.

He was sitting easily in the saddle, his face obscured by the fall of his hood. He tipped back his head, studied the clouds and turned to her as she was surreptitiously easing her wet gown away from her thighs.

'No need to look so glum, my heart. I doubt the rain will last, it's brightening in the west. We should be dry in a couple of hours.'

'I hope so. Tristan, please don't call me my heart.'

'Very well, if it makes you uncomfortable.'

'It does.' Francesca lowered her eyes to her gloved hand, the hand that still wore his seal. What was he doing? Flirting? Toying with her to amuse himself on the ride to Fontaine?

In the bedchamber last night he'd said he was planning to win her back. He'd told her that she had once meant much to him. Yet if that were true, why had he never mentioned it before this? In the past, they'd made love countless times. She distinctly remembered telling him that she loved him and not once had she had an answering response. Reassured by his passionate nature—how young she had been, how naive—she'd been certain that he would tell her eventually. He never had.

And then last night he had announced he intended to win her back. He'd pushed his ring back on her finger. He'd cuddled her. Did he truly mean to keep her?

Half of her longed to believe him, whilst the other half, the half that had wept bitter tears at the drawn-out death of their marriage, was afraid. Loving Tristan had come so easily, and it had turned to ashes equally easily. Could they really start again?

Francesca believed him when he said he'd written to her—Tristan could not be a bare-faced liar. But they'd had two years to grow apart. Two years in which Tristan had followed his political heart and had done what he loved most—forging vital connections with a prince of England. The prince who would one day wed Duchess Constance. All Tristan ever thought about was politics and power. Love had no place in his life. He was toying with her feelings because he needed heirs, and he—being both honourable and sensual—wanted a woman in his bed whose company he relished.

She wasn't sure she could open her heart to so much pain. She'd done it once on his behalf, she didn't think she would survive a second round.

Tristan's saddle creaked as he twisted to look behind them, a frown between his brows. Francesca followed his gaze. Mari and Bastian were riding side by side, apparently deep in conversation. Behind Mari and Bastian, faintly visible through a shifting curtain of rain, another group of travellers was headed their way.

'Tristan, if you are worried about Mari, you needn't be. I told you, she won't fall behind.'

He gave her an abstracted look. 'Hmm?' His face cleared and his mouth went up at a corner. 'Yes, I can see Mari is quite the horsewoman. But I like to check up on her every now and then.'

'Oh?'

The smile turned into a full-blown grin. 'Your maid looks on me with such adoration, I fear she would pine away if I didn't let her see how often I think of her.'

She laughed. 'Really, Tristan, you are ridiculous.'

He sent another look over his shoulder. 'Be honest, Mari loathes my guts.'

Francesca lifted an eyebrow. 'She is very loyal.'

'To you, perhaps. As far as I'm concerned, she's the grumpiest woman alive. For my sanity, you might tell her I wrote to you.' He peered over his shoulder. 'I swear her eyes are burning holes in my hide.'

'I told her about the letters.'

'Don't tell me—she didn't believe it.'

Tristan wiped the rain from his face with the back of his hand. Francesca had to smile. Against the grey backdrop of the sky, his eyes seemed bluer than ever. And very warm.

'You're right, she didn't.'

'And you? Do you believe I wrote to you?'

She couldn't look away. 'I believe you.'

His face lit up. 'Thank God. I will win you yet, my heart.'

Francesca's heart missed a beat. Fear? Unfortunately for her sanity, she didn't think so. She rather suspected it was the old excitement—the excitement she used to feel when in Tristan's company. Telling herself she was older and wiser than she had been, far too old and wise to remain susceptible to a pair of shining blue eyes and a winning smile, she seized on the first topic that came to mind.

'Tristan, you have never really talked about your father. I am sure he would have been proud of all you've done for Brittany.'

Tristan's face went cold. Francesca blinked, not quite believing how swiftly his smile had gone. Her stomach tightened, yet she persisted—she'd always wanted to see into his heart, where better than to start by talking about his father?

'Tell me about Count Bedwyr, Tristan.'

'There's not much to tell.' His tone was clipped. Dismissive.

She had heard him use that tone when chastising an undisciplined trooper. It came to her that he used it as armour, to keep people at bay. Well, he wasn't going to keep her at bay, not any longer. If he wanted to save their marriage, he needed to be more open.

'How much did you see of Count Bedwyr after your mother's death?'

His blue eyes narrowed and at first she thought he wasn't going to answer. Then he glanced swiftly away, a muscle jumping in his jaw.

'Not much. I remember Father scarcely better than my mother. As I've told you, he was a distant figure. At his last visit to Vannes his expression was as dour as your maid's.'

'You exaggerate, I am sure.'

Tristan shook his head and a scatter of raindrops flew out from the edge of his hood. 'I don't think so. It's hard to recall him exactly, the turning years have all but erased him from my mind.' His mouth tightened. He was focused on the rain-soaked highway ahead. 'Ask me about Lord Morgan, if you wish. I have clearer memories of him.'

Francesca followed his lead and they continued on their way with her doing her best to learn more about the man she had married. *How old were you when you won your spurs? Did you form close friendships when you were fostered at Vannes?*

Tristan answered those questions easily enough, but the warmth had gone from his eyes. He had withdrawn the moment she'd asked him about his father and there was more to it, she was sure, than the usual distance between a father and a young son who had been sent to live in another lord's household. That cold dismissive tone he used when he wanted to hold someone at arm's length—had he learned it from his father?

Certainly, something about Count Bedwyr made him deeply uncomfortable. Watching Tristan's set face as they rode through the wet towards St Michael's, Francesca feared he wasn't really going to open up to her any time soon. Perhaps he never would. Perhaps all they had was that dazzling flare of physical passion. If that were to die away, what would be left?

Francesca held down a sigh and tried to ignore the regret twisting her insides to knots. Deep down, it was beginning to look as though they were completely incompatible.

The rain had stopped and the bell for evensong was ringing when St Michael's Abbey hove into view. Tristan spurred towards the abbey walls with a sigh of relief.

All day Francesca had shown far too much interest in hearing about his father. She'd been extraordinarily inventive. Every blessed topic had deftly been linked back to Count Bedwyr. Tristan had no idea how she'd managed it.

They had talked about horses and Francesca got in a question about whether he had got his interest in building up his stables from his father. Tristan reminded her he didn't have much to say about his father and, thinking that would be the end of it, swiftly changed the subject. They'd talked about food and wine and before he knew it Francesca was asking if Count Bedwyr had kept a good cellar at des Iles. She could be a stubborn wench when she chose to be. Another change of subject—this time it had been his foray to England with Prince Geoffrey—and there she was enquiring if his father's interest in politics had matched his. Had his father visited England? Stubborn wench indeed.

There was a small, shuttered window in the

abbey wall and a bell rope. Riding up to the window, Tristan kneed Flint closer and pulled the rope. As the bell rang, geese honked on the other side of the wall. After a brief pause, the shuttered window slid back to reveal a round face and a tonsured head.

Tristan smiled. 'Brother Simon, I assume?'

'Aye?'

'Tristan des Iles at your service. You are expecting us, I believe.'

Brother Simon nodded. 'Certainly, my lord. I shall open the main gate and let you into the lodge.' The monk looked past Tristan. 'There are just four of you?'

'Aye, this is my wife, Lady Francesca, and her maid.' He gestured at Bastian. 'My squire will look after the horses. I have business in the village and will return later. Brother, we are all somewhat damp because of that rainstorm, I would be grateful if you could set a large fire.'

'Very good, my lord.' The shutter closed with a clack.

Tristan waited, tapping the pommel of his saddle whilst the gate was unbolted. He made the mistake of looking at Francesca, who was studying him, a pleat in her brow.

She lifted her chin. 'Business in the village, Tristan?'

'Aye.' His voice emerged more curtly than he intended. 'I shouldn't be long. However, don't hold supper on my account.'

Francesca nodded, mouth tight. Tristan wheeled Flint about, turned his head towards the village and trotted away.

Tristan had noticed the party of riders behind them.

Under the guise of watching Mari, he'd kept looking back and through the rain he'd imagined he'd seen a shock of fair hair. Of course, he could be mistaken, the visibility had been appalling. None the less, those riders made him uneasy. Particularly if one of them turned out to be Sir Joakim Kerjean. Surely it was too much of a coincidence that Kerjean should be returning to Brittany at precisely the same time that they were? Several possibilities presented themselves, none of them palatable. The most obvious one was that Kerjean might be foolish enough to consider that Francesca remained easy prey. If so, he was about to learn otherwise.

Tristan had lost sight of the other travellers just before the village. He was retracing his steps, praying that he was wrong about the identity of the man with the yellow hair. Sir Joakim Kerjean was not the only man in the world with hair that colour, it might not be him. However, if it was Kerjean, he was about to receive a warning. Francesca was out of his reach.

And if it wasn't Kerjean—well, no harm done. Tristan jabbed Flint with his heels. At least he would have a breathing space from Francesca's gentle and insistent probing about his father.

Tristan loathed talking about his father, he was too ashamed. His father had committed a great sin, a mortal sin that would shock good Brother Simon and the other monks. Indeed, Count Bedwyr's sin was so terrible that if the Church knew what he had done, it would not have allowed his body to be buried in hallowed ground.

Count Bedwyr of the Isles had committed suicide.

There was no proof, or none that had survived. Lord Morgan had made sure of that. And only a handful of people knew the shocking truth—Lord Morgan, Tristan and Roparz. Roparz had been a squire at des Iles, indeed poor Roparz had had the misfortune to find Count Bedwyr's body.

My father hanged himself from a hook in the stables and Roparz found him.

Roparz had had the sense to run straight to the castle steward, Sir Izidor. Sir Izidor had acted swiftly, removing Count Bedwyr's body to his bedchamber. He had summoned Lord Morgan and the two of them had made sure that word of Tristan's father's mortal sin never got out. Tristan prayed it never would. Sir Izidor had died some years since; Lord Morgan wouldn't dream of saying anything; and Tristan would trust Roparz with his life.

Even though not a whisper had escaped, Tristan discouraged all mention of his father. It was too painful. How could he have done such a thing? To be sure, he must have been wretched after the untimely death of his lady. But suicide? To deny life in that way, to have turned his back on his many heavy responsibilities? How could he have done it? Why? His father must have had reasons, but whatever they had been, suicide was surely a cowardly solution.

The trouble was that Tristan recognised that if he was going to save his marriage, he must be more open with Francesca. And he was being open, at least about their relationship. He had told her that he wanted their marriage to stand and he meant it. He just wasn't prepared to talk about his father.

It occurred to him that as far as Francesca was concerned, not talking about his father had become a real struggle. Part of him longed to tell her. Something about her made him want to bare his soul to her. Which was impossible. If she found out his father had killed himself, she was sure to be appalled. And if anyone else were to find out…

A shudder went through him. No one must know. He couldn't afford to make a slip, his father's bones had been resting next to his mother's in the family grave for over a decade and there they must stay.

Tristan set his jaw. No one, not even Francesca, must know of his father's sin.

Jerking irritably at his damp cloak, he fixed his gaze on the wretched-looking inn they had passed earlier. Blast this wind, his skin was covered in goosebumps.

The inn's roof was thatched and sagging. At either end, by the eaves, grass was sprouting. A tattered inn sign moaned as it swung in the wind, the image on it so battered and blurred by the turning seasons that all Tristan could make of it was a pale splotch of paint. The White Swan? The White Hart? He didn't really care, he just wanted this over. He wouldn't rest easy until he had confirmation that the man he'd seen on the road today—the one with the yellow hair—was *not* Joakim Kerjean.

Sight of that yellow hair had been deeply unsettling. Why had Kerjean gone to Provins? Had meeting Francesca been his main purpose? If so, what did he want from her? Was marriage to Francesca his aim? Another possibility was that Kerjean could be planning to use Francesca as a means of putting pressure on Tristan. If so, to what end?

A horrible thought came to him. *Mon Dieu*, was it possible that the rebel alliance might flare back to life? Was that was this was about?

Tristan and Baron Rolland had been battling against unruly barons and their rebel alliance for months, and up until this moment Tristan had been confident that the alliance was a spent force. A few suspects had vanished, scuttled into hiding, no doubt. Naturally, both Tristan and Baron Rolland had known there would be stragglers on the loose. It was only to be expected, the day would never dawn when every miscreant was under lock and key.

Knowing stragglers were at large was one thing, a possible revival of the alliance quite another. Could that be what was happening here?

Tristan had long known the alliance made use of the trade routes to carry messages to supporters further afield. Kerjean's appearance in des Iles and later in Provins made his involvement a distinct possibility. Normally, Tristan would be inclined to give the man enough rope with which to hang himself. Yet with Francesca involved, that was impossible, she must be protected at all costs.

When he had set out for Champagne, Tristan hadn't bargained on the effect that Francesca would have on him. Her safety was paramount. The last thing he wanted was for her to be dragged into Brittany's struggles against outlaws and rebel barons.

Tristan rolled his shoulders, pushed inside and headed for the warmth of the fire. A tired-looking serving woman appeared out of the gloom. Her hair was drawn back in an untidy braid and her dress was as faded and grey as her face.

'Can I fetch you some ale, sir? Maybe you'd like wine?'

'Ale, if you please.' Tristan doubted this place would serve anything approaching wine. Choosing a bench by the fireside, he unwound his cloak from about his shoulders and draped it on the bench.

As he sat down to watch the door, steam rose gently from his hose. He knew he wouldn't have long to wait and he wasn't wrong, the woman had only just brought him his ale when the door opened.

Sir Joakim Kerjean walked in.

Tristan's every sense sprang awake. Lord, what a nightmare, it *was* Kerjean. What the hell was the man up to? Keeping his face free of expression, Tristan rose to his feet. 'Good evening, Kerjean.'

Sir Joakim checked before smoothly continuing towards him. 'Count Tristan, I didn't think to be conferring with you so soon. I thought you would be at St Michael's with your beautiful wife.'

Tristan stiffened. *I didn't think to be conferring with you so soon.* A threat? It certainly sounded like one. Tristan gestured at the table, saying drily, 'I would be honoured if you would join me.'

Sir Joakim peeled of his gloves and tossed them down. 'Didn't think you'd noticed us.'

Us? So the men Kerjean had been riding with were in some way linked to him. Interesting.

'Spotted you some miles back.' Tristan shrugged. 'Couldn't be sure it was you, you kept your distance. Ale? Wine?'

Sir Joakim combed his yellow hair with his fingers, hooked out a bench with his foot and sat down. 'Ale, thanks.'

Tristan narrowed his eyes. Sweat was beading Kerjean's brow, the man wasn't as cool as he pretended. Catching the serving woman's eye, Tristan signalled for another ale. 'You're a fair way from home. What took you to Provins?'

Kerjean's smile was suggestive. 'Had a mind to

find myself a new mistress and thought the May Revel was a good place to find one.'

Rage gripped Tristan and he found himself wrestling with the urge to go for the man's throat. Thankfully, years of training stood in good stead and he kept his seat. He wouldn't learn anything if anger took over. Lifting an eyebrow, he picked up his ale mug. 'Weren't the Breton ladies receptive?'

The serving woman brought Sir Joakim his ale. Gripping the mug, he downed it in one and wiped his mouth with the sleeve of his tunic. He leaned towards Tristan, eyes cold. 'Heard there was an especially pretty lady in Champagne who was looking for a new home. Heard her husband had neglected her.'

The blood rushed in Tristan's ears. An image flashed before him—Francesca in that corridor just off the palace great hall, lifting her hand to slap the man's face. The image helped him keep his calm.

'So you admit you knew she was my wife. You deliberately sought her out. I did wonder.'

'I thought I would test the waters, thought she might be getting lonely.' Kerjean leaned back and grinned. It was an infuriating grin, blatantly designed to make Tristan lose his temper.

'If you're trying to anger me, it won't work,' Tristan said.

'I am not so sure.' Another infuriating grin tested him further. '*Mon seigneur*, I am thinking you are fond of that girl despite your neglect.'

'You might try to be civil. That girl, as you insolently name her, is currently my wife. I would prefer it if you gave her the respect she is due as Lady Francesca des Iles.'

'If you say so. Certainly, I wasn't the only one to ride a long way to see her. Did you miss Lady Francesca while you were darting about all over Christendom? Were you thinking of patching up your marriage, my lord? Or do you plan to keep her—around—whilst you hunt for a real heiress?'

Tristan took a draught of ale to help him hang on to what was left of his temper. What was Kerjean up to? Unfortunately, Tristan knew next to nothing about him. If he knew more, he'd perhaps understand Kerjean's sudden interest in Francesca.

Kerjean's mistress-seeking didn't hold water. Had the man even met Francesca before the May Revel? Why wait until now to seek her out? Was he after her manor? Did Kerjean have cronies—his fellow travellers, perhaps—who were planning to use Francesca as a weapon against him?

A ball of ice settled in Tristan's gut. To think

that he had at first thought to send someone else to escort Francesca to Fontaine. Thank God he'd come for her himself. Although it would seem he'd made a grave mistake riding to Champagne with a single squire for company. *If Kerjean is planning something dark—Francesca's abduction, for example—I need men to back me up.*

Conscious that every muscle was tight as a bowstring, Tristan forced himself to relax. 'Lady Francesca is my wife, Kerjean. And as long as she is, she is out of bounds to you.'

Sir Joakim lifted his ale mug in a mocking salute. 'As you wish, my lord. Far be it for me to stand between a man and his wife.'

The door opened to admit a rush of damp air. Half a dozen burly men, swathed in dark cloaks, swaggered in. They were all wearing swords and they made a beeline for the serving hatch. The word 'mercenary' sprang into Tristan's head.

'Friends of yours, Kerjean?'

'Travelling companions. Merchants.'

Tristan raised an eyebrow. 'Rough-looking merchants.'

Sir Joakim gave a thin smile. 'Merchants need to be strong these days, particularly if their route takes them away from the jurisdiction of the

Guardian Knights. Not every highway is as safe as those in Champagne.'

Tristan's skin crawled as his suspicions hardened. Kerjean didn't support the new peace in Brittany. He was siding with men who believed a faction-ridden duchy offered rich pickings. Did he think to use Francesca to force Tristan into negotiations? Tristan could feel his anger building. He doubted that Kerjean was ready to go as far as an abduction, but he wasn't prepared to take the risk. For Francesca's sake, he must ensure Kerjean believed her welfare meant little to him.

Tristan gave a casual shrug. 'You won't have to wait long, in a few weeks you may press your suit. It makes more sense for me, politically, if my marriage is dissolved.' Which was, Tristan reflected, true enough. That didn't mean he was going to allow that to happen.

Sir Joakim studied him. 'It seems damned odd that you tramped all the way to Champagne to collect a woman you are preparing to divorce.'

Leaning back against the plaster, Tristan crossed his legs at the ankles. His spurs chinked. 'Family matters, Sir Joakim. I am merely fulfilling an obligation to Count Myrrdin.'

'Oh?'

'You haven't heard? Count Myrrdin is ill. Frankly,

he's not long for this world. Likely you will know that he thinks of my wife as his daughter. He's asked to see her.'

A blond eyebrow shot up. 'You're acting as Count Myrrdin's envoy?' Sir Joakim's lip curled. 'Must be something of a comedown to someone used to consorting with kings and princes.'

'It's called loyalty, not that I can expect you to understand. Count Myrrdin was good to me after my wedding.'

Kerjean let out a bark of laughter. '*Jésu*, the man foisted some peasant's get on you, and you run about for him like a servant?'

Tristan's hand curled into a fist. 'I advise you to think before you start hurling insults. Lady Francesca remains my wife, and until such time as our marriage is annulled, you will refer to her by her title.'

'She's a pretty wench. Perhaps I'll have her as my mistress when you're done with her.'

Like hell you will. Tristan took a deep breath and hoped he looked more careless than he felt. 'I wish you luck with that, though from my observations in that corridor in the palace, things don't look good for you. For the present, Lady Francesca goes with me to Count Myrrdin. You can press your suit after the divorce.'

'Des Iles, you can't fool me, you don't want a divorce. At the palace, Sir Gervase told me he'd housed the two of you together in a tower bedchamber. The innkeeper at Melun told a similar story.'

Tristan yawned. 'Believe what you like.'

'So your interest is merely to get her to Fontaine?'

Another yawn. 'Quick, aren't you?'

A muscle flickered in Sir Joakim's eyelid. 'I can wait.'

'See that you do.'

Coming to the conclusion that he wasn't likely to get any more out of Sir Joakim, Tristan abandoned the pretence of finishing his ale and reached for his cloak. He would deal with Joakim Kerjean later. In the meantime, he would push on to Fontaine with as much speed as was humanly possible.

Tristan wasn't sure what Kerjean wanted with Francesca. He did know that the sooner he had her safely behind the walls of Fontaine, the better he would feel.

Chapter Seven

At the guest house, Francesca, Mari and Bastian changed out of their damp clothes and hung them to dry on a rack by the fire. They ate supper and Tristan's portion was covered and placed by the hearth to keep warm for when he came back.

Leaving Mari and Bastian at the table murmuring quietly to one another, Francesca found herself exploring the guest house hall, wondering why she felt so very ill at ease.

Her disquiet had nothing to do with their lodgings. St Michael's guest house was one of the finest in Christendom. Long and narrow and built of stone, it had a generous hooded fireplace. At either end of the chamber, thick wool curtains were looped back behind great iron hooks. When drawn across, the curtains would act as screens for people to sleep behind, it was all very civilised. She stalked to one of the looped-back curtains, turned and retraced her steps to the other.

No, her disquiet had nothing to do with the guest house. She couldn't stop thinking about Tristan. Why had he gone back to that ramshackle-looking inn? Surely he should have told them what he was doing? He was keeping something from her. Again. She let out a sigh, here was yet another barrier to drive them apart.

Without doubt, she had irritated him when she'd kept asking about his father, but she hadn't been able to stop. Tristan's reluctance to talk more openly with her was surely a root cause of what had gone wrong between them.

It wasn't simply that he had abandoned her to fulfil his duty to his beloved Brittany—every lord in the land had responsibilities. Count Myrrdin hadn't taught her much about local politics, but Francesca understood how the feudal system worked. The lords held land from their overlords, and for that privilege the lords had many obligations. They must attend endless council meetings and, most importantly, if their overlord needed men to bolster his cause, he called on his lords to supply them.

Loyalty was the foundation stone upon which the entire system rested. Currently, King Henry of England was Duke of Brittany, so theoretically the

Breton lords should be loyal to him. After Francesca and Tristan had married, Tristan had been quick to answer the council's call to arms. Some noblemen had schemed and plotted against the king, questioning his right to be Duke of Brittany. Not so Tristan. He was the most loyal of men. The most principled. Francesca recalled him saying that if they could only win peace, everyone in Brittany would benefit. It made complete sense.

No, Tristan's duties had not caused their difficulties.

Neither had those lost letters.

Nor, if Francesca could believe what Tristan had said to her last night about hoping their marriage would survive, had the difference in their status. Yes, Tristan was a great lord and she had turned out to be a nobody, but if that didn't concern him, then surely it need not concern her?

She bit her lip. Perhaps there was hope for them. Hope. Her stomach churned. Hope, she was learning, was extremely unsettling. She wrapped her arms about her middle. What a fool she was. If Tristan did the sensible thing, he would set her aside and find a well-dowered noblewoman.

She marched up and down. She had no grounds for confidence. Not whilst Tristan kept things from her. That lay at the root of their problems and therein lay her greatest challenge.

He was so used to giving orders, he expected everyone to jump to do his bidding. He wasn't in the habit of confiding in people and he hated being questioned. His pride, she supposed.

Still, he had made a start by telling her about his mother's death. It wasn't enough, he didn't fully trust her. She scowled at the lodge door. Why had he gone back to that horrible-looking inn?

She bit on a fingernail, realised what she was doing and stalked to the airing rack. Irritably, she twitched at their clothes, turning them so they would dry more quickly.

The latch lifted. Flames rocked in the fireplace and the door banged. Tristan. He tossed his cloak on the bench.

'My lord, does Flint need bedding down?' Bastian asked, smothering a yawn.

'Relax, lad, I've done it.'

'Wine, my lord?' Rising, Bastian went to drape Tristan's cloak on the airing rack.

Tristan glanced at Francesca. 'It's palatable?'

'It's very good.' She tipped her head to one side. 'Did you dry out properly? Tristan, that rain—'

'I sat by the inn fire.' Noticing the ewer on a side-table, he went to wash his hands. 'I'm starved.'

Francesca felt a smile form. 'Of course.' Taking up a cloth, she collected the dish from the hearth and took it to the table. 'Here, it should still be hot.' She lifted the lid.

Tristan took a place at the table as she reached for the ladle. 'What is it?'

'Fish stew. Eel mostly.'

He grimaced. 'Must be Friday.'

'You don't like eel? There's bread and cheese and—'

'I could go to the refectory and see if the monks have anything else, my lord,' Bastian said on another yawn.

'This will be fine. Get to bed, Bastian, for pity's sake,' Tristan said. 'We've another early start tomorrow.'

'Yes, my lord.' Bastian hesitated. 'My lord?'

'Aye?'

Bastian shuffled his feet and his ears went pink. 'Are you and my lady— That is, I was wondering— I haven't organised the sleeping arrangements yet, my lord.'

'Lady Francesca and I will take that end of the room, you and Mari may take the other.' Tristan looked at Mari. 'I take it that is acceptable?' It was clear from his tone that he expected no argument.

'Yes, my lord,' Mari said, meek as a lamb.

* * *

Later, when Tristan had finished eating and the fire had been banked up for the night, he and Francesca carried candles to their sleeping space behind the woollen curtain. Two pallets had been dragged together—presumably by Bastian before he'd gone to bed. Francesca hadn't noticed him do it.

As soon as the curtain fell into place, Tristan took her candle from her and placed it on a shelf on the end wall. A golden fringe of light glimmered around the edge of the curtain—fire glow and a lantern they'd left burning by the hearth. His dark hair gleamed in the candlelight. His eyes were unreadable and his expression thoughtful.

'Come here, if you please.' He tugged her towards him and slid his hand about her waist, not holding her tightly, but gently, as though he was waiting for her to object. After a moment, Francesca felt warm lips on her neck and the slight scrape of his growing beard.

Hands on his shoulders, she shifted back. 'Tristan, what happened at the inn?' Mindful of Mari and Bastian sleeping behind the curtain at the other side of the hall, she kept her voice to a whisper. 'Why did you go back?'

A large hand cupped her face as he stared into her eyes. 'Francesca.'

'Tristan, what happened? What's the matter?'

He swallowed, there was a hint of vulnerability in his eyes. Yes, something was definitely troubling him.

'Francesca, you remember what I told you last eve? About our marriage?'

'You said you hoped to save it.'

'Aye, that. I would ask you—do you still want an annulment?'

'Tristan, I never *wanted* an annulment.'

'You didn't?'

Smiling, she shook her head and tightened her grip on his shoulders. 'You surely need a better marriage though, a wife who brings you more lands will secure your position in Brittany.' Reaching up, she placed a swift kiss on his cheek. 'What happened at the inn?'

Tristan released her and began readying himself for sleep—sword belt, tunic, gambeson—without giving her an answer. Sighing, Francesca followed his lead. She was slipping beneath the blankets, having given up on further conversation, when he snuffed out the candle and joined her on the pallet. Again, he pulled her to him. Again, she let him. He was naked, of course, it was useless to pretend otherwise, Tristan always slept naked. And she had to admit it gave her a *frisson*, he was all masculine muscle. Disturbing and comforting. He felt so warm and tempting, she was hard-pressed to resist the urge to cuddle and stroke.

'I saw someone behind us on the road,' he murmured.

'The other travellers? I saw them too. What of them?'

'I went back to the inn because I needed to know who they were.'

'And?'

'The knight you were speaking to at the revel was among them.'

'The man who dragged me into the corridor? How odd.'

'Francesca, I need to know, what did he say to you?'

'Nothing much. Tristan, you saw it all. He tried to kiss me, then you appeared and—'

'You swear he said nothing else? Nothing about me?'

'Tristan, what is going on?'

'I have to say I am concerned. Francesca, the man who accosted you at the revel is Breton, one Sir Joakim Kerjean. He has a manor at Léon.'

Francesca found she was holding her breath. Could it be that Tristan was opening up to her?

On a matter of politics? Her pulse gathered pace. 'You think he sought me out deliberately?'

'I know he did.'

'But I was wearing a mask when he found me.'

'He must have had you pointed out to him. Francesca, Roparz told me Kerjean had been seen in des Iles. The man had been asking about you, he went to Provins specifically to meet Lady Francesca des Iles. Back there at the inn, he claimed he was angling for you to become his mistress.'

'There's no chance of that, I took him in great dislike.' Francesca leaned her head on Tristan's chest and tried to ignore the pleasure it gave her—the scent of his skin, the slight abrasion of chest hair. 'Something else is troubling you.'

'I'm beginning to suspect Kerjean thought to use you in some scheme, perhaps to force my hand in some way. I am not sure how, and in any case I believe his plans are unformed. Clearly, he didn't expect me to suddenly appear in Provins whilst he was trying to seduce you.'

Francesca gave a soft laugh. 'I have to tell you, he is not that good at seduction.'

Tristan caught hold of a length of her hair and gave it a gentle tug. 'I am glad to hear that, my heart.'

He started to play with her braid and after a

moment she felt him unbind it. When they were first married, Tristan used to unwind her hair as a prelude to lovemaking. As he combed his fingers carefully through her hair, her scalp warmed. If only everything could be as it had been. She took a deep breath. 'Tristan, what shall we do?'

'We proceed to Fontaine as planned. Kerjean is travelling back to Brittany with a group of men he tells me are merchants. To my mind they look like mercenaries.'

Her breath caught. 'Mercenaries?'

'There's no need for alarm. I can't prove who they are or what they're up to, but our party is small and I am not putting you at risk. I've taken the precaution of speaking to the abbot. He has agreed that a deputation of monks might travel with us.'

Francesca's jaw went slack. 'The abbot permits his monks to act as guards? I thought monks couldn't bear arms.'

A soft laugh warmed her cheek. 'It is unusual, although I have to say that these men are not quite monks, they have yet to take their vows.'

'Surely the shedding of blood, even by a novice, remains a sin?'

'I am no theologian, Francesca. All I can say is that a sizeable donation to abbey coffers helped win us our escort.'

'I see.' Francesca frowned thoughtfully. Tristan must be worried to have, in effect, recruited bodyguards. 'Monks against mercenaries?' His fingers stroked through her hair, soothing and sensual. Gently, he began massaging her scalp. 'Tristan, do you really think we might be attacked?'

'Not any more, the men the abbot is lending us were not bred for the Church. He tells me that among the novices he has four retired knights, one of whom was a champion-at-arms, and a blacksmith. They are all brawny men. Francesca, I doubt the men travelling with Kerjean have had a day's real training in their lives, there's no way they will attack with four knights in our train.'

'You really think we're at risk without the novices?'

'I couldn't say, but I won't put you in danger. Once in Brittany, you'll be safe at Fontaine.' His arms tightened about her. 'We can discuss the future after you've seen Count Myrrdin.'

Faint sounds reached them through the woollen curtain—the crackle of the fire, the soft rattle of the door as it was buffeted by the wind.

'Tristan, you did bolt the door?'

He ruffled her hair. 'Aye, don't worry, we are safe in here. The monastery walls are high and in good order, and if anyone did scale them, the abbot's wolfhounds would raise the alarm. Not to mention the geese.'

Francesca closed her eyes and turned her head slightly to give Tristan the gentlest, most surreptitious kiss on his chest. She hadn't thought he would notice, but a slight hitch in his breathing pattern told her that he had.

'Everything's changing,' she murmured. 'You think the world will go on as it has always done and suddenly it changes.'

'Count Myrrdin has reached a fair age. He can't live for ever.'

'I wasn't thinking of Papa.'

Tristan angled his body towards hers. 'Oh?'

'I was thinking of you. Of us.' His chest rose and fell steadily under her hand. Strong and achingly familiar. This was their third night together after far too long a separation. She didn't think she could bear it if they were separated a second time.

'I left Fontaine because I was ashamed of my heritage, or rather my lack of it. At least I thought that was why I left Fontaine, I see now that wasn't the whole of it. Tristan, the other reason I left Fontaine was because—' she picked her words with care '—because I didn't think we could ever be truly close.'

He cupped her head with his hand. 'Francesca,

I found great joy in our marriage. Far more than I believed possible. I missed you and I regret not having told you how much you meant to me.'

'I wanted you to open up to me. I was eager to know everything about you—your hopes, your dreams, everything.'

Silence. Tristan's breath warmed her cheek. 'You were very young, my heart.'

Catching his chin, she pressed a light kiss on his mouth. 'I was sixteen and appallingly ignorant. Papa had overprotected me. In part, because he was getting old and his mind was no longer as sharp as it was.'

'This isn't news.'

'Tristan, sometimes all it takes for someone to grow up is to have someone trust them. As you have trusted me with your confidence tonight.' She kissed his mouth again, drawing back when he would have pulled her more tightly against him. 'Finally, things are changing and I, for one, am glad. You're talking to me at last. I know how hard you find it.'

'Hard?' His voice was tinged with surprise. 'Talking is easy, it's picking your friends that's hard.'

Francesca wasn't fooled. Her handsome husband normally remained tight-lipped. With his upbringing, it was hardly surprising. He'd been fostered so young, and then his parents had died before he'd been able to win his spurs and return home. Her throat tightened.

'You would call Sir Roparz a close friend?'

'Certainly.' His voice was warm. 'He's my right-hand man at des Iles. He's more than a friend, he's my steward there.'

'And you tell him everything?'

'Francesca, what's this about?'

'Does Sir Roparz know why you hate your father?'

He went rigid. 'What can you mean?'

'I'd like you to talk to me as intimately as you would talk to Sir Roparz.'

A warm hand ran with slow deliberation up and down her shoulder. 'I've been far more intimate with you, Francesca.'

'That's not what I mean and you know it. There's something about your father you won't tell me, something that angers and distresses you.'

Silence.

She kissed his cheek. 'You can confide in me. Tristan, whatever happens in the future, I won't betray your confidence. Tell me about your father.'

He lay still as stone before sucking in a great breath. 'How did you know?'

'It's obvious that something is very wrong, you turn every question. Tell me. Please.'

She felt his fingers in her hair and his soft sigh on her face. 'I don't hate my father, you are wrong about that.' She heard him swallow. 'However, it's not a pretty tale and it will be quickly done. Mother died, as you know, of sickness. In under a year my father followed her, this you also know. However, my father's death wasn't natural. I'll be blunt, Father killed himself.'

Francesca's breath left her. Count Bedwyr had killed himself? She made to speak and he stopped her with a light touch on her mouth.

'I'm nearly done. Roparz was Father's squire back then and it was he who found him. The castle steward, Sir Izidor, and Lord Morgan dealt with it. They covered up the manner of my father's death and swore never to breathe a word of how he had really died to anyone. Roparz, bless him, did the same.'

'Oh, Tristan.' Francesca hugged him to her and tried to imagine how he must have felt. 'I am so sorry.'

He pulled back. 'Suicide is a mortal sin, you can't tell anyone.'

'As if I would!'

'Father was buried at my mother's side, he would lose his right to rest in hallowed ground if the Church discovered what he had done.'

She gave him another hug. 'I understand.'

'It's a secret that's been well guarded. Sir Izidor went to his grave without telling me what had really happened.'

'It was Lord Morgan who told you how Lord Bedwyr died?'

A slight movement told her Tristan was shaking his head. 'Roparz told me. We were fifteen. Lord Morgan was furious with him, but I—well, I've always been grateful Roparz told me the truth.'

Heart twisting for the sorrow Tristan had hidden for so long, and for the shame he undoubtedly felt, Francesca wound her arms tightly about him. 'Thank you for trusting me with this confidence, I feel truly honoured.'

'Sleep, Francesca.'

Nodding, Francesca closed her eyes, though she knew she wouldn't sleep for a while, Tristan's revelation had shocked her to the core. Count Bedwyr had killed himself. What a burden to lay upon his son.

Against the odds, it wasn't long before she felt Tristan's body relax. It would be good to think that unburdening himself to her had given him some ease.

The warrior monks, as Francesca came to think of their new escort, kept themselves to themselves. They were going to be Benedictines and it was strange seeing them with swords belted about their dark habits. Two of the novices rode in the vanguard, ahead of Tristan and Francesca, whilst the other three brought up the rear, behind Mari and Bastian. They were most diligent, their heads were constantly turning this way and that as they studied the passing countryside. She assumed they were watching out for Sir Joakim and his companions. They rarely spoke, except to Tristan. In many ways they acted as though they were on retreat.

A little over a week later, they were riding along a forest bridleway in this manner when Francesca looked about her with a dawning sense of recognition. Her pulse quickened, they were in the heart of the Brocéliande. This path led directly to Fontaine Castle.

Here, the trees were gnarled and twisted and as old as time. Above them, the spring sun sent bright shafts of light through the greening canopy. On the path, a thick layer of beech mast softened the clip of the horses' hoofs to a muted thud. Streams bubbled up out of the ground, rushing and splashing as they twisted in and out of the trees before vanishing as suddenly as they had appeared.

The last time Francesca had ridden along this bridleway it had been in the opposite direction. She'd been part of Lady Clare's entourage, on the road that had led eventually to Tristan's Champagne manor. She'd been dazed with shock and very distressed.

Francesca was distressed today, albeit for a very different reason—Count Myrrdin was ever in her mind. Soon she would be saying farewell to the kindest man in the world. She knew she wouldn't be grieving alone, of course, he was a lovable man and his death would bring sorrow to many. Knowing that did nothing to lessen the pain. Her eyelids prickled and she turned her head so Tristan wouldn't see the glaze of tears in her eyes.

If it wasn't for Tristan's calming presence, she would doubtless be undone.

These last few days had revealed Tristan in a gentler light. It had also given her space to think, to attempt to sort through the confusion she always felt when in his company. A confusion that was born out of a deep and insatiable attraction to his person. It was an attraction she must repress for Tristan's sake. She needed to think and she needed to think calmly.

Which was impossible to do at night. Each night,

Tristan insisted that they share a bed. It had been the same at every stop on their route—Chartres, Nogent, Laval, Rennes… There was no rest for either of them until he had pulled her into his arms, and she couldn't think rationally with Tristan's body warm and tempting against hers. His musky masculine scent—familiar and impossibly seductive—invaded every dream. No, lying in Tristan's arms wasn't conducive to rational thought.

Which meant that Francesca tried to do most of her thinking in daylight, as they covered the miles to Count Myrrdin's castle. Her thoughts were circuitous. In short, her days were almost as frustrating as her nights. The more she thought, the more confused she became.

Tristan's declaration that he would keep her as his wife was breaking her heart even if it wasn't entirely surprising. Tristan had a highly developed sense of honour. However, he must see that as far as their marriage was concerned he wasn't doing himself any favours by prolonging their association. Over and over the thought came back to her, Tristan le Beau, Comte des Iles, should marry as befitted his station. Keeping her as his wife couldn't be in his best interests. Nor was it in the best interests of his county. She couldn't understand why his political interests seemed to weigh less with him, at the time of their wedding they wouldn't have done. Or would they? Had she misjudged him?

Back then, he'd been aloof, a proud lord driven entirely by political ambitions. He hadn't appeared to have a sentimental bone in his body. Or so she had thought. Now, with his confession about his father's tragic death echoing through her mind, she was coming to terms with the fact that she had misread him badly. Tristan was deeply affected by the way in which Count Bedwyr had died. He was profoundly ashamed and the turning of the years had erased none of the shame. Tristan loved his father, she was sure of it—why else would the manner of his death still give him grief?

She had misjudged him. Tristan was neither cold nor distant, he simply wasn't used to allowing people close. His friend Sir Roparz might be the exception, although with Tristan away from des Iles for most of the last two years, he can't have been much in his company.

Lord, she'd been a poor judge of the man she had married. Furthermore, it would seem she'd been equally wrong about him cutting her out of his life without a thought. He had written to her.

A cold man, a man with no emotions, wouldn't have bothered. He had said he would honour his wedding vows.

If only she had more to offer him than one small manor.

If only she had given him a child. That would have made all the difference, she was sure. She bit her lip. Was she barren? It was possible they had simply been unlucky. Perhaps—if they resurrected their marriage—she could yet give him an heir.

'We're almost there,' Tristan said, drawing rein to peer through the budding trees. Their monkish escort kept close.

In the depths of the wood a cuckoo called. Francesca affected not to have heard it, though the sound had her fingers stiffening on the reins. When the cuckoo called a second time, she flinched. She glanced sharply at Tristan, saw him hide a grimace and knew that she wasn't the only one who had heard the cuckoo. Worse, that grimace told her that Tristan knew about the name-calling she'd had to endure after Lady Clare appeared in Fontaine.

She lifted her chin. 'People call me that, you know. I am your "cuckoo countess".'

Another grimace. 'I heard the whispers,' he murmured. 'Hoped perhaps you hadn't.'

She gave a wobbly smile. 'Whispers travel a long way, they got as far as the market at Provins.'

His hand reached for hers and squeezed lightly. 'Ignore them.' Releasing her hand, he gestured down the track. 'Look.'

Between the trees, the lichen-encrusted walls of Fontaine Castle were starkly visible. Solid and heavy, they appeared to grow out of a forest clearing. A castle planted in the depths of the Brocéliande. Like the forest, it looked as though it had been there for ever.

A fist formed in Francesca's stomach as she stared at the towers and ran her gaze over the guards stationed on the walkway. 'It's been two years and it hasn't changed.'

The glint of a helmet caught her eye, a guard was marching along the walkway in the direction of the gatehouse.

Tristan tracked the guard's progress and cleared his throat. 'This is strange for me too. The last time I was here, I was steward.'

Francesca stared at him, she'd been so lost in her thoughts that she'd forgotten that returning here wouldn't be easy for Tristan either. As Count

Myrrdin's steward, Tristan knew the castle inside out, from the cellars to the topmost turret. He'd assumed that one day Fontaine and all its lands would become his.

Tristan glanced meaningfully at her. 'Count Myrrdin's standard is flying,' he said, nodding in the direction of the gold-and-green flag which hung limply from one of the towers. 'That surely is a good sign, he must yet be alive.'

Casually, he dragged off the piece of sackcloth covering his shield. Francesca stared at his insignia—three black cinquefoils on their silver field. Her throat closed, clogged with so much longing and pain she almost moaned aloud. If only everything could be as it had been before, when she and Tristan were newly wed and Count Myrrdin was in good health.

Tristan signalled to Bastian, who unclipped a staff from his saddle. No, not a staff, Bastian whipped a cloth casing from one end and Tristan's pennon slowly unfurled.

Once again, the cuckoo's call floated through the trees. A chill ran down Francesca's spine as, tense in every muscle, she turned towards the gatehouse. Their arrival had been noted and Tristan's colours recognised. The portcullis lifted. Sergeant Léry stood under the arch, a grin of welcome lighting his dour features.

Two warrior novices spurred towards the draw-bridge. Francesca gathered up her reins and urged Princess after them.

Chapter Eight

Hooking up her skirts, Francesca hurried up the winding stairs to the landing outside Count Myrrdin's bedchamber.

Tristan had been dreading this moment. Were they too late? Sergeant Léry had muttered, for Tristan's ears alone, that the village priest, Father Alar, had been summoned. Which meant that it could only be a matter of time.

Tristan held in a sigh, he'd been praying that reports of Count Myrrdin's frailty had been exaggerated and he sensed Francesca had been doing the same. Sadly, it appeared their prayers weren't going to be answered.

The door was slightly ajar, Francesca pushed it open and paused on the threshold. The man she called Papa was lying in a large canopied bed propped up on a bank of pillows. White hair straggled in every direction. Behind the snowy beard, the count's face was shrunken and his skin as pale as parchment. His eyes were closed, and the veins on his eyelids looked like blue threads. Tristan caught his breath. They were too late, surely they were looking at a corpse? Then he marked the slight lift and fall of the count's chest. Count Myrrdin lived, although not, Tristan thought, for long.

A man and woman sat on either side of the canopied bed. The woman must be Lady Clare and the man her husband, Sir Arthur Ferrer. Lady Clare had her head buried in her hands and Father Alar stood to one side of her, head bowed in prayer.

Sir Arthur got to his feet, he was tall and well built with dark hair. Silently, Tristan gripped the man's arm before transferring his attention back to the bed.

Lady Clare had Count Myrrdin's gnarled hand fast in hers—she was stroking it, apparently trying to straighten fingers which had curled into a claw. A wisp of red hair peeped out from beneath a snowy veil.

Seeing that Francesca had eyes only for Count Myrrdin, Tristan met Lady Clare's enquiring look with a quiet smile. 'Lady Clare?' He bowed his head. 'Tristan des Iles, at your service.'

'Count Tristan, thank you so very much for answering our plea and bringing my sister home. It is good of you.' She gently touched Francesca's hand and Francesca managed a nervous smile.

Tristan moved to the foot of the bed. 'I left for Provins as soon as your message reached me and we rode with all speed. How is he?'

Lady Clare's veil trembled. 'It varies, my lord, but then that is how he has been for some time.'

Tristan made a non-committal sound, he knew exactly what she meant. Even when in full health, Count Myrrdin's later years had been marked by periods of lucidity, interspersed with periods of what a charitable man might call vagueness. 'He is changeable.'

'That's it exactly. He rallies occasionally, but overall he's fading.' Lady Clare went on stroking her father's hand. 'Today is not a good day. Papa hasn't woken and we cannot rouse him. Another day he might open his eyes; he might take a little sustenance. Sometimes he speaks. Sadly, those days are becoming rarer.'

Lady Clare went on talking. Something about being thankful that she had had a chance to get to know her father before his illness had become worse.

Tristan stepped closer and as Clare smiled bleakly at him he could study her eyes for himself.

They were extraordinary—one was grey, one was green. He had been warned what to expect and he knew he shouldn't be staring, except he couldn't help himself. He glanced swiftly at Count Myrrdin and then back to Lady Clare. Tristan had only once seen eyes like that in his life and the sight of them removed any doubts he might have had as to her parentage. Count Myrrdin had the same rare eyes, he was unquestionably her father. And as for the red hair tucked beneath Lady Clare's veil—Count Myrrdin's countess, Mathilde, had been famous for her flame-coloured locks. Sitting in front of him was unquestionable proof that Francesca had never had any right to the Fontaine lands.

A wave of sadness swept over him. Seeing Lady Clare in person gave him new insight into how distraught Francesca must have been. *If only I had been here to help her.*

Lady Clare went on talking, referring to Francesca as her sister, which was good of her. She seemed a kind woman. Francesca had mentioned liking Lady Clare, and from what he had seen, Tristan agreed with her judgement. Had it helped Francesca when Lady Clare had been sympathetic? Or had that merely made matters worse? Francesca must have been deeply wounded by the injustice fate had meted out to her. In her shoes, Tristan would have been livid. It was never easy discharging anger against someone one liked, Lord, Francesca must have been utterly confused.

He glanced at Francesca, whose face was, if anything, paler than her beloved Papa's. This was likely to be a trying vigil. Francesca was so focused on Count Myrrdin, he doubted she had even seen Father Alar. When she did, it would knock her back, for she would realise how close Count Myrrdin was to his end. Tristan was glad to be on hand.

Count Myrrdin's chest lifted. Up and down. Another breath. Another. The breaths weren't forced or strained, though they were undoubtedly weak. Praise God, Count Myrrdin didn't seem to be struggling. During Tristan's tenure as steward of Fontaine, he had come to know the count well. For all his eccentricities, he was a warm-hearted, likeable man. He didn't seem to be suffering and for that Tristan was relieved.

Tristan's own father had died in very different circumstances. Alone in the stables. Tristan could picture him fighting for breath. What had been going through his father's mind at the end? Irritably, he pushed the question aside—it was irrelevant and unanswerable. He forced himself to hold Lady Clare's gaze. 'My lady, I am truly sorry to see your father so ill.'

'Thank you.' Lady Clare seemed to recollect herself and gestured at the tall knight. 'Count Tristan, this is my husband, Sir Arthur Ferrer.'

Tristan and Sir Arthur withdrew a little and exchanged greetings. Sir Arthur was personable and had an easy manner, Tristan liked him on instinct. When the introductions were over, Tristan saw that Francesca was deep in conversation with Father Alar.

She was white as a sheet. Tristan strained to hear what they were saying, and when he heard the priest utter the dreaded words 'last rites', he moved to join her. She was twisting her fingers together. Gently, Tristan took her hand. She didn't react, Father Alar had all her attention.

'Have you offered him the last rites, Father?' she was asking.

'Yes, my lady.'

She seemed to sag. 'It will be soon, then.'

Father Alar's smile was sad. 'I fear so.'

Tristan guided her to the nearest stool and she sank on to it.

'Father Alar, you are certain?' Francesca's voice trembled. 'How do you know?'

'My lady, I have witnessed many people go to God.'

'Will it be tonight?'

The priest spread his hands. 'One can never know exactly, it will be as God decides.'

Francesca's eyes were dry, she had yet to shed a tear.

Lady Clare came round the bed and Tristan stood aside to allow her to put her arm about Francesca's shoulders. 'It is good to see you, Francesca,' she said. 'I have missed you.'

Francesca's face relaxed and she reached up to squeeze Lady Clare's hand. 'It is kind of you to say so, my lady.'

Bemused, Tristan shook his head at the obvious affection between the two women. If he hadn't seen it for himself, he wouldn't have believed it. Francesca had told him that she liked Lady Clare and he'd thought she was deluding herself. Yet here they were, embracing with what appeared to be genuine warmth. Women. He'd never understand them. How could you feel liking for someone who had effectively robbed you of your birthright? Yet here they were, exchanging kisses.

'I mean it, Francesca,' Lady Clare said, shaking her head. 'I'd hoped to see you before now.'

Francesca's grey eyes were trained on Count Myrrdin. 'I am sorry, it was hard to come back.'

'Well, I am glad you have arrived, Father has been asking for you.' Lady Clare straightened, crossed to her husband and put her hand on his arm. 'Come, Arthur, Lady Francesca and Lord Tristan will wish to say their farewells in private.' At the door, she looked back. 'Father Alar? A word, if you please.'

As the door closed softly behind them, Tristan sat on the stool on the other side of the bed, opposite Francesca. Her eyes were bright, shiny with tears that had yet to fall.

'Tristan, you don't have to stay.'

He cleared his throat. 'Yes, I do.'

And then it happened. Count Myrrdin took a deep breath, a muscle twitched in his wasted cheek and his eyelids lifted. 'Tristan? Tristan, my boy, is that you?' His voice was faint, like the whisper of dry leaves.

Tristan leaned forward. 'Yes, my lord, I'm here.'

Francesca's eyes filled. Her mouth was working and she had her hand to her throat—she was probably too choked to speak.

'Tristan, my boy, I must see Francesca, will you fetch her for me?'

'She's here, my lord,' Tristan said. He felt pretty choked himself, Count Myrrdin was the only person ever to have called him 'my boy' in that manner, his father never had.

Francesca reached out to take the count's hand. 'I'm here, Papa.'

'Where have you been?'

'I am sorry, Papa. If I'd known you were ill, I would have come sooner.' A large tear trickled down her face.

Eyes stinging himself, Tristan stood abruptly. 'If you need me, I'll be outside.'

Francesca leaned forward to adjust the count's pillows, he doubted that she heard him. When he left the bedchamber, she was carefully smoothing the count's straggling white hair.

Dawn.

Two throne-like chairs had been found for Lady Francesca and Lady Clare and hauled up to the bedchamber. Cushions were piled on to the chairs and there they passed a restless night, taking it in turns to hold Count Myrrdin's hand when he was asleep. Whenever he was awake, they tried to encourage him to drink. It was a losing battle.

'Papa? Would you try some ale?' Time and time again, Francesca held a cup to his lips.

Time and time again, the white head turned away.

She bit her lip. 'Some wine, perhaps?' Francesca's stomach cramped, the count's face was so drawn he had to be thirsty. She would swear new wrinkles were forming in his aged skin even as she watched. 'What about milk? A posset of some kind? Papa, you ought to drink something.'

All was to no avail, Count Myrrdin simply shook his head. Though he refused to drink, his aged face lightened whenever he looked her way.

Francesca did her best to hide her anxiety. She kept a smile on her face and made it as bright as possible. Occasionally, she caught Clare's gaze and saw her own worry mirrored back at her.

'He's tired,' Clare murmured. 'Perhaps he will drink tomorrow.'

Count Myrrdin closed his eyes and seemed to fall instantly asleep.

'Perhaps.' Francesca yawned.

'You should rest,' Clare said. 'You must be exhausted after so many days on the road.'

Francesca stretched and shifted a cushion to a more comfortable position. 'I'll rest here, I don't want to leave him.'

As she reached to take the count's hand again, she noticed how still he was. His fingers felt cold, so cold. She started to chafe them when something in the quality of his stillness caught her attention. Her eyes widened and she stared at his chest, waiting for it to rise.

Nothing. No movement. No breath. Nothing.

'Papa?' Her fingers shifted to his wrist and she searched for a heartbeat. 'Papa?' The back of her neck prickled. Aghast, her gaze met Clare's.

Tight about the mouth, Clare pressed her fingers to the pulse point on the count's throat. 'Oh, no.' She held the palm of her hand before his mouth. Slowly, she sat down.

Francesca's heart thudded as she and Clare looked at each other. Francesca forced out the words. 'He's gone.'

'Aye.' Clare's throat convulsed. 'God bless him, he's gone.'

It had been a sad and wearisome day, one made even more wearisome because hardly anyone in Fontaine had had any sleep. Tristan spent much of it in the chapel, supporting Francesca as she and Lady Clare took turns to stand vigil over Count Myrrdin's body. The rest of the time he passed at the high table in the great hall, waiting for Francesca to emerge from the chapel.

Tristan found himself in the unusual position of being an onlooker in a castle where he had once stood in command. A man of action, he wasn't comfortable in the role of an observer, he wasn't used to it. He drummed his fingers on the table and stared gloomily at a platter of bread and cheese. Lord, he felt restless. He could see Bastian at the far end of the hall, the lad seemed to have befriended one of the castle grooms.

Tristan glanced at the doorway that led to the chapel. He should have asked Francesca how long she would be. He hoped she wasn't planning on staying in there all night, she was exhausted.

It was odd how events had turned out. After their wedding, everyone had expected that Fontaine would one day be his. He'd never imagined he would be sitting in the hall watching Sir Arthur Ferrer command the Fontaine knights.

Tristan didn't begrudge the man his advancement. Clearly, Sir Arthur—shortly to become Count Arthur—knew what he was about. It was obvious from the easy way Count Myrrdin's retainers deferred to him that they trusted Sir Arthur's judgement and that he was popular here. Good. Fontaine needed a sound man at the helm.

Tristan watched Sir Arthur despatch envoys to Rennes with news of Count Myrrdin's death and nodded his approval. The succession of Fontaine had been rearranged after Count Myrrdin had acknowledged Lady Clare as his true-born daughter, and it was vital that Baron Rolland ratified Sir Arthur's appointment as Count of Fontaine quickly.

A clear line of command had to be established. Tristan didn't think there would be any objections. Given that Count Myrrdin had been ailing for some time, Sir Arthur was, to all extents and purposes, already in command.

Messengers came and went. Candles were lit. Logs were thrown on to the fire and more knights gathered by the hearth, muttering to each other. Muted conversations were taking place all over the castle. Servants with long faces flitted back and forth with food for the grieving household. Every last soul in the household was grieving, there was no doubt of that. Tristan had always known that Count Myrrdin had been liked by his people, but watching the downcast faces, he realised he'd not known the half of it. The people of Fontaine had loved their eccentric lord. It was something of an accolade. Tristan doubted his own father had been held in such high esteem. He caught himself wondering what the retainers at des Iles thought of their present lord and shook his head in impatience. What did it matter? His role was to do his duty and do it well. His heart ached.

A maidservant approached, a jug in hand. Her cheeks were red and splotched with tears. 'More ale, Lord Tristan?'

'Thank you, but no.'

The girl took the jug to the knight sitting next to him on the next bench. 'Ale, Sir Brian?' Her voice cracked.

Count Myrrdin's death was hardly unexpected, yet it was clear that everyone here was grieving.

Tristan was on the point of returning to the chapel to insist Francesca took herself to bed when the door to one of the stairwells opened and Mari came in. To his surprise, she hurried over and bobbed him a curtsy.

'Lady Francesca has finished her vigil, *mon seigneur*. I took the liberty of ordering supper to be taken to your bedchamber. She won't eat. I thought you might like to know.' Mari drew closer and lowered her voice. 'Lady Francesca hasn't cried either. I doubt she will sleep. If you could get her to eat, then she might sleep. She needs sleep more than anything.'

'Thank you, Mari, I shall do my best.'

They'd been allocated a bedchamber just off the solar. It wasn't large, yet it was luxury compared to the chambers they'd slept in on their journey from Provins. The mattress was filled with feathers; two candles stood on a side-table which had been polished to a high sheen; and the walls and ceilings were covered with a repeating pattern of blue flowers.

Francesca must have been washing her face, for she had taken off her veil and was sitting on the edge of the mattress when he entered, folding a drying cloth over and over. Tristan drew her to her feet and wrapped his arms about her.

With a sigh, she leaned against him. He rubbed her back and said, 'My heart, I am so sorry.'

She nodded and they stood there silently until at length Tristan recalled what Mari had said about Francesca needing to eat. He drew back and eyed the tray on the table. 'Someone has brought supper.'

'I am not hungry.'

'It looks like duck—your favourite. You should eat something.'

'Tristan, I couldn't.'

Mari's words echoed in his mind. *She needs sleep more than anything.*

Francesca remained by the bed—her face was bone white and her mouth pinched, she was in the grip of deepest misery. Sensing that she was hardly able to keep to her feet, Tristan removed the drying cloth from her grasp and made her sit with him on the bed.

'Try a little food,' he murmured, sliding an arm about her waist. 'It smells tempting to me.'

'Tristan, I couldn't.'

He touched her cheek. 'Something to drink?'

Francesca stared at him, her beautiful grey eyes so blank with grief that it tore his heart. 'I should have been here. Tristan, all these months—'

'You can't blame yourself, you didn't know he was ill. In any case, guilt is pointless, you can't alter the past.' His thumb shifted, a small caress that brought the tiniest softening to the muscles about her mouth. And was he imagining it, or was she leaning into his caress? Heartened, he stood. 'I'll pour some wine, I believe Mari has had it spiced for you.'

She needs sleep more than anything. Tristan found himself hoping that Mari had included plenty of soothing herbs in the mix. If anyone needed soothing tonight, it was Francesca. Even if there were no soporifics in it, wine would surely help her relax. 'Take it from me, my heart, it will dull the edge of your pain. In any case, you have to drink it.'

She stiffened. 'Have to?'

Tristan smiled. 'I have strict instructions from Mari, who tells me you must be made to eat and drink. If I fail, she'll have my head on a platter.'

Some of the bleakness left her eyes and he went to the side-table to pour the wine. When he held out the goblet, she took it from him. Hiding a sigh of relief, he resumed his place next to her on the bed and waited until she had taken a small sip.

'Good?'

'Aye.' She looked at him over the rim of her goblet. 'You are winning her over, you know.'

'Mari?' He snorted. 'I wouldn't be too certain.'

'Oh, I think you are, she wouldn't be bossing you otherwise.'

Some colour was returning to Francesca's cheeks and her mouth was more relaxed. *She needs sleep more than anything.* At least he was distracting her, already she looked a thousand times better than she had when he'd crossed the threshold.

With a sigh, she set the goblet aside. 'Thank you, Tristan.' She gave a weak smile. 'I should like to retire now.'

'Very well. Here, I shall see to your lacings.'

The tiniest of frowns creased her forehead and he couldn't help but notice how her gaze flickered briefly to his mouth. Gently, he turned her so he could reach her lacings. For some reason his fingers turned into thumbs. He untied the bow.

She needs sleep more than anything. Sleep? Tristan hid a smile, remembering the first time he had unlaced her. They'd become lovers, the best of lovers. Francesca had slept well back then, there had been no tossing and turning, no lying in bed staring wide-eyed into the dark for hour upon hour.

Seduce her. The words popped unbidden into his head and he froze.

Hmm… Could he? His heart thumped. His mouth dried.

Carefully, gripping her by the waist with one hand, Tristan continued unlacing her gown. He didn't hurry, he was too busy thinking. Wondering. She was his wife and he didn't want that to change. Yet to seduce her whilst she was grieving?

It wouldn't be ethical. It would be wrong.

Yet the thought wouldn't leave him. And to make matters worse, the nape of her neck looked exactly as it had always done, eminently kissable. Swallowing hard, he held himself in check. He wouldn't kiss her, not unless he was certain that she wanted him to.

It would help her sleep though, he was sure of that. A pulse throbbed, his blood began to heat.

She looked over her shoulder at him. Her eyes were dark. Impossibly seductive. He held in a groan. That look, if she did but know it, was pure invitation.

She turned away again and slowly, methodically,

he worked down the lacing. She was grieving. It would be wrong.

Fabric sighed as the back of her gown slowly fell open to reveal her linen undergown. Tristan allowed his fingers to slide up to the warm, creamy skin at the nape of her neck. He skimmed his fingertips along the sweet curve, searching for the small black curl of hair that had always lain just beneath her braid. Ah, there it was.

His gut ached. That creamy skin was calling to him. He burned to kiss her. He wanted to lie with her flesh to flesh, he wanted…

She twisted around. 'Tristan, what are you doing?'

He swallowed hard and his thoughts blurred into one another. He had never felt so confused in his life; he had never felt so much heat, so much wanting. He would die if he didn't have her. They would die. 'It would be wrong,' he managed. 'It used to help you sleep, but it would be very wrong tonight.'

'Tristan, what are you talking about?'

Chapter Nine

Tristan was unlacing her gown so sensuously Francesca's pulse quickened. Her skin tingled where he touched it, exactly as though they'd stepped into the past. What was he doing? When she turned to give him a searching glance, she learned nothing—with the candles on the side-table behind him, his face was in shadow.

'Tristan?'

He pushed up from the bed and scrubbed his face with his hand. 'Forget it.' He cleared his throat and lifted his shoulders. 'Your beauty hasn't faded and my mind ran away with me. Let us simply say it has been a long time.'

Once, Francesca would have basked in the blatant flattery. However, something far more interesting than flattery caught her attention. 'It has been a long time?'

Her gaze followed him as he went to the side-table and pinched out a candle. His hand was shaking. Shaking. And his voice—husky with desire—betrayed him. *He wants me. And I want him.*

She tipped her head to one side. They desired each other just as they had always done, that wasn't news. Yet Tristan seemed to be implying there was more to it than that. He was saying he had been faithful to her. Could it be true? In Provins, she'd waited and waited for letters that had never arrived. Convinced he would like nothing more than to forget his low-born wife, she had lived in dread of his dismissal. She had assumed he would take lovers.

It had been horrible imagining Tristan with another woman and she'd tried not to dwell on it. It had been hard though. Tristan wasn't a monk, she knew he'd had lovers before their wedding and, whilst Francesca had not heard of him having any once they were married, he had proved himself the most eager of bedfellows. A vigorous, physical man like Tristan would be certain to find chastity a challenge. In truth, she would have thought he'd find it impossible.

She bit her lip. They'd been swept back into each other's lives so quickly and in the past few days much had happened to change her opinion of him. She now knew she'd judged him too harshly over the letters. Her assumption that there had been other women during their separation might also be wrong.

She twisted her fingers together. 'Tristan, are you saying that you have kept our wedding vows?'

Francesca had been faithful to Tristan, of course. It had been easy. She'd loathed being separated from him and her skin crawled if she so much as thought of sharing her body with anyone else. She'd thought herself in love with him. He, however, had made no such confession, there had been no answering love binding him to her. She had been certain he would have found other willing bedfellows. Had she been wrong? She held her breath as he stepped in front of her. His tall, broad-shouldered form blocked out the light of the remaining candle. His gaze drifted down, and she realised that with the lacings loosed, the front of her gown was gaping. Catching the fabric, she held it to her chest.

'You and no other,' he muttered. 'Since our marriage so it has been. Francesca, I have not broken our wedding vows.'

Her mouth went dry.

Tristan had been faithful to her. She felt herself smile—praise the Lord, he'd been faithful. Recognising he was waiting for her response, she held out her hand.

'I too.' She swallowed. 'I have been faithful to you.'

Warm fingers closed on hers and her heart thumped. He turned her hand over and placed a soft kiss in her palm. As he slowly drew her to her feet, the light fell full on his face—the heat in his eyes was plain to see.

He gave her a careful smile, set his hands on her shoulders and turned her about. 'Come, my heart, you need to sleep. I have my orders.' He tugged at her gown and peeled it from her shoulders, easing it over her hips so it dropped to the floor. 'Bed.'

Leaving her gown where it had fallen, Francesca clambered into bed. She was conscious that before Tristan had entered the bedchamber, she'd been drowning in misery. His presence—overpoweringly male, overpoweringly attractive—was just the distraction she'd needed.

I want him. He wants me. Perhaps, for a time, he can help me forget.

Pensively, she watched him undress, allowing her gaze to slide over his perfect male shape. There was a small scar on his left hip, she remembered that scar and it appeared he had collected a few more. There was a new one on his left forearm and another on his ribs. She studied his strong warrior's shoulders. Tristan was all lean, toned muscle. A glance had her yearning to recapture all they had lost. Shamelessly, she let her gaze follow the way that dark hair on his chest arrowed down. Her cheeks burned, he couldn't deny that he wanted her.

He looked her way. There was a hint of colour on his cheekbones that might be desire. Or it might be embarrassment, though why he should feel embarrassed at confessing fidelity, she couldn't fathom. There was a wistfulness in his eyes that she'd not seen before. He cleared his throat. 'You prefer that I leave the candle lit?'

Francesca shifted, she was absurdly conscious of how much she wanted him. Would it be as good as ever, or might their separation have killed the passion? 'I don't mind.'

'I'll leave it alight, then. It looks safe enough.'

He joined her in bed and she waited for his arms to wind about her.

Nothing. Tristan lay on his back, apparently staring at the blue flowers painted on the ceiling.

She frowned. 'Aren't you going to hold me?'

An arm came out. 'If you wish.'

She rolled closer and nestled against him. 'I

want more than that.' She kissed his chest. 'And so do you.'

'I won't deny it.' His mouth twisted as he stroked the top of her head. 'Francesca, you're grieving, it wouldn't be right.'

'Not even if I want to?'

'I won't take advantage of you.'

She kissed his chest and allowed her hand to drift across his waist. Her fingertips eased towards his abdomen. She heard his sharp intake of breath and smiled. 'You are too chivalrous. Consider this—what if I want to take advantage of you?'

She slid her hand down a little further and closed firmly over him. *Tristan has said he wants to keep me as his wife, even though I bring him so little. If I bore his child, his heir, I would be giving him something of real worth. Saints, I was mad to think I could marry someone else, there is only one man for me.*

'Tristan?'

'Mon Dieu.' A strong hand clamped on hers. His voice was strained. 'Francesca, you test me beyond endurance.'

'I need you, Tristan.'

He shook his head, breath ragged. 'It would be wrong, too much is unresolved between us.'

Francesca squeezed gently, sensuously. 'It doesn't

feel wrong to me.' Slowly, she ran her foot down his shin and a sigh of pure want escaped her. 'It feels—you feel—perfect.'

He tipped her head up, the blue of his eyes burned bright. 'Francesca, you're not thinking straight, you're grieving. You—'

'I know I want you, I always have.' She moved her hand on him, a subtle, teasing, intimate caress. He jumped in her palm, and when his body angled towards her, she knew she almost had him. She smiled. 'Mari would recommend it, I am sure.'

'Like hell she would, that woman loathes me.'

'I am not so sure,' she murmured. She kissed his chest. 'It would help me sleep. Tristan?'

A large hand cupped her face. He toyed with her earlobe and sparks of excitement raced all over her body—breasts, belly, toes. Her limbs went lax, and she melted against him. She could tell he was weakening. His darkening eyes betrayed him, as did the heightened colour on his cheekbones. His breathing was flurried.

With a groan, he pushed her back into the pillows and slid his leg between hers. Gently, he lifted her hand from between them, pressing his entire length against her as he kissed her fingers and meshed them with his.

'Not yet, my heart, or it will be over before it

begins.' He held her gaze. 'You had better not regret this.'

As if I would.

His smile was crooked. 'The things I do to get you to sleep.'

He lowered his head. Francesca strained to reach him even though there was no need and his lips covered hers. He kissed her slowly, teasingly, as though he had all the time in the world. It was far too slowly for her. Hungry for more, she opened her mouth to invite him in. Their tongues met and her senses narrowed, and then it was as it had always been between them.

He turned her into a wanton, a wanton with no thought in her head but bedding with Tristan le Beau. There was no bedchamber painted with blue flowers, there was no bed. There was only Tristan, the most desirable man in the world.

He drew up the hem of her undershift, removed it completely and dropped it over the side of the bed. He sighed as his palms closed on her breasts. His mouth was firm, tempting her in the old way, making her ache with want, making her writhe against him.

His scent, musky, masculine and heart-rendingly familiar, twisted through her consciousness. All she wanted was the feel of skin against skin. His skin against hers. The palms of her hands stroked up and down his flanks, seeming to drink him in. Emboldened by his groan, she wound her arms about his neck and kissed his chin, his cheek, his mouth. She kissed him everywhere she could reach. She had a lot of kissing to make up for, and for this night at least, she knew Tristan felt the same.

She gripped his buttocks. Her hands roamed hungrily over every inch of him. She sucked at his neck and won another sensuous groan.

He nudged her legs apart. His hands, it would seem, were as hungry to touch her as she was to touch him.

The bedchamber was lost. There was just Tristan and Francesca and a world of hot sighs and disjointed phrases.

'Do you still like this?'

'Oh, yes.'

'And this?'

'Please. More, yes, more.'

Finally, when she was in a frenzy of want that had wound so tight she was sure she would explode, he pushed into her.

A moment of stillness fell upon them. Warm hands cupped her face. 'Francesca.' His voice went deep, to the core of her being. 'I have missed this with you. Lord, how I've missed it.'

Heart too full for words, Francesca let her hands and body speak for her. She caressed his broad shoulders and kissed his neck. She slid her hand about his waist and hugged him to her. She gripped his buttocks and tilted her pelvis and the world exploded into movement again.

The rhythm hadn't changed, they found it on an instant. It made her whole, it turned two into one.

It was over far too quickly. Tristan reached between them—one careful, knowing stroke, two—and a blinding flash of bliss sent her to heaven. An instant later, he was with her.

The mood in Fontaine Castle was understandably subdued. Francesca had agreed to spend the morning in the solar with Lady Clare, helping with the arrangements for Count Myrrdin's funeral. Tristan didn't expect her to find it easy. Lady Clare was a nice enough woman, but there was no denying that she was, in effect, standing in Francesca's shoes. Whichever way you looked at it, it was an impossible situation.

Aware of the difficulties Francesca would face, Tristan had arranged for her to meet him by the stables at noon. When the hall door opened and she stepped out into the bailey, he breathed a sigh of relief. He was desperate to escape the confines of the castle and Francesca must surely feel the same. She needed respite from the gloom and complexity. Had Château des Iles been reduced to this state of abject misery after his father's death? Tristan grimaced, it was odd how he couldn't remember. He pushed the thought away—what had happened after his father's death had no bearing here.

Francesca's face was strained as she walked towards him, though it was pleasing to see her eyes soften when she saw him. Tristan felt himself relax. The barriers between them were breaking down. All morning he had been reliving their love play, praying that she would not regret it. He could see no trace of regret, thank God.

Smiling, Tristan met her halfway across the yard as the portcullis lifted and a patrol clattered in. He was further heartened when she held her hand out to him. He bowed over it and kissed it. 'All is well?'

'As well as can be expected.'

'The funeral arrangements?'

'Papa's funeral will be held in three days' time.' Francesca sighed and twined her fingers with his. 'I probably shouldn't say this—in some ways it is worse than I expected being here again. I…I hardly know how to behave and my presence confuses the servants—they don't know who to defer to, me or Lady Clare. It's very awkward.'

This was exactly what Tristan had feared might happen. 'You need fresh air,' he said. 'Bastian is saddling the horses. I thought you'd like to ride out to St Méen, we might inspect your manor. If all is in order, we could stay there until after the funeral. It might make things easier.'

Her fingers squeezed his. 'Thank you, that sounds like an excellent idea.'

They had mounted up and were clattering towards the gate with Bastian when a groom ran up, a bundle under his arm. 'Lord Tristan?'

Tristan drew rein. 'Good day. Conan, isn't it?'

'Yes, my lord.' The incoming patrol were milling about near a water trough, Conan jerked his head towards it. 'I was in that patrol, my lord. I think you should know I found this in a ditch by the gatehouse.'

He passed the bundle up to Tristan. Fabric of some kind, it was heavy with damp, as though it had been gathering dew all night. Mindful not to startle Flint, Tristan opened it out and his eyes widened. He was staring at his coat of arms, carefully embroidered on what had once been a wall-hanging. Several slashes cut right across his shield.

His gut tightened and swiftly he rolled it up again. He wasn't swift enough.

With a gasp, Francesca reached across. 'That is my work! Let me see.'

Silently, Tristan passed it to her.

'Tristan, I made this after our wedding. It hung on the solar wall in St Méen.'

'I remember.'

Her brow knotted as she looked at Conan. 'Where did you find it?'

'In the ditch by the road, my lady. A few yards beyond the gate.'

'You saw nothing else?'

'No, just the hanging. Count Tristan's colours caught my eye.'

Francesca folded the wall-hanging. 'Thank you, Conan. Would you please show it to Sir Arthur and ask if he will permit a troop of household knights to accompany Lord Tristan and myself to St Méen? We shall wait here for his reply.'

We? Tristan's muscles tightened. Francesca could not be allowed to go to St Méen, not now. Clearly, the place wasn't secure. He frowned at the wall-hanging. He was loath to alarm her, but this had to be Kerjean's handiwork. Their monkish escort might have prevented Kerjean and his cronies attacking them on their way here, but clearly it hadn't prevented him from following them to Fontaine.

Kerjean had broken into Francesca's manor. Who else could it be? By leaving the tapestry in the ditch outside the castle, where he surely knew it would be found, Kerjean was sending Tristan a message. No, not a message, a threat. Sir Joakim was telling him that Francesca wasn't safe, not even in Fontaine.

Kerjean had to be attempting to revive the rebel alliance. *It's a message. A message for me.*

Francesca bit her lip as she tracked Conan's progress towards the great hall. 'Someone has broken into St Méen.'

'So it would seem.'

'Papa promised that it would not be left unguarded.' Her fingers tapped Princess's neck. 'Where are those knights?'

Tristan could have groaned aloud. He didn't want to put their fragile, reawakened passion at risk by upsetting her, but Francesca had to be made to see that she could not go to St Méen. 'Francesca, I agree someone has to go to St Méen. You must understand that it cannot be you.'

She stiffened. 'It's my manor, it's my responsibility.'

'No one is disputing that it is your manor. My

heart, someone has broken in and there is no telling what we may find. I will not permit you within a mile of the place until I know it is safe. It needs to be secured.'

Her eyes grew stormy. 'You bar me from visiting my own manor?'

'When I know it is secure, you may visit it then.'

Her gaze sharpened. 'There's something you're not telling me.'

Tristan hesitated, he was certain the theft of the wall-hanging was Kerjean's handiwork, but admitting as much would surely be a mistake. Francesca had enough to deal with without learning that a band of outlaws had decided to use her to further their cause.

Damn Sir Joakim Kerjean, damn him to hell. Francesca wasn't safe in Fontaine. And if she wasn't safe in Fontaine…

'Francesca, until I have assessed the state of St Méen for myself, you're not going anywhere near it.'

At St Méen, Tristan stood in the solar with the manor steward at his side, examining the marks on the whitewash and the empty hooks on which Francesca's carefully wrought work had hung.

'Sir Nicolas?'

'Mon seigneur?'

'You knew this tapestry had gone?'

Sir Nicolas ran his hand round the back of his neck. 'Yes, my lord.'

'And you didn't think to inform Sir Arthur that my lady's manor had been broken into?'

Sir Nicolas flushed. 'I only noticed the tapestry was missing this morning. My lord, I don't check the solar every day. As you know, we're off the beaten track. It is quiet here. We keep only the minimum of retainers and there had been no sign of a break-in.'

Tristan lifted an eyebrow. 'None?'

'None.'

Tristan stared at the empty hooks. Despite the fact that he was looking at a faint outline—like a shadow—of where the tapestry had been, the hanging was bright in his mind. It was a wonderful, clever work—knights and ladies feasting in a woodland setting. Great oaks arched over a damask-covered table; hunting dogs played among the flowers. Francesca had given the wall-hanging a silver border, like the field on his shield, and she had emblazoned the margins with black cinquefoils. And now it was a soggy mess, slashed beyond repair. 'I liked that tapestry.'

'Yes, my lord. I am very sorry.'

'Why the devil didn't you report the break-in as soon as you had discovered it?'

'I was going to, *mon seigneur*, except it didn't strike me as urgent,' Sir Nicolas said. 'We had only just received word of Count Myrrdin's death, God rest him.'

Tristan ran his hand over his face. 'Yes, I can see the loss of a tapestry pales into insignificance beside that.'

'Quite so. And in any case, nothing else has been touched, my lord.'

'You're certain?'

'Lord Tristan, when I saw the hanging had gone, you may be assured I checked St Méen from vault to roof. A full inventory has been done and everything else is as it should be.'

Tristan ran his fingers over the plaster and homed in on some marks—slight indentations, as though something had been scratched on the wall. He bent to take a closer look and swore under his breath. 'Sir Nicolas?'

'My lord?'

'What do you make of this?'

Sir Nicolas squinted at the wall. '*Mon Dieu*, I didn't notice that. It's very faint, but it looks like a knight's shield.'

'So it does. Do you recognise the insignia?'

'I am not sure. It could be a cauldron or a kettle, my lord. I think it's a kettle.' Sir Nicolas rubbed his chin. 'I can't call to mind a knight who uses a kettle as his device.'

'I can,' Tristan said grimly. Sir Joakim Kerjean had a kettle on his shield. If there had been any doubt in his mind that the theft of the tapestry had been intended as a warning, seeing this shield dispelled it.

Kerjean had been poking about in Francesca's manor. He had then walked out entirely unscathed. St Méen wasn't safe for her any more.

Tristan rubbed his forehead. What did Kerjean think he was doing? Surely he must realise that by threatening Francesca directly, Tristan would simply redouble his attempts to keep her safe? Did he think to wring money out of Tristan by threatening Francesca? Money that would rebuild the alliance? If so, the man was a fool. *He must know that I can't let this slide, Sir Joakim's manor must be watched. I shall ask Sir Arthur to lend a few men—men capable of discretion. I have to know what Kerjean is up to.*

Tristan glowered at the marks on the wall. He must alert Baron Rolland—outlaws were at large and there was a strong possibility that the rebel alliance was not a spent force. It looked as though a second set of envoys would shortly be setting out for Rennes.

A pair of long-lashed grey eyes filled his mind. *Where do we go from here?*

Without question Francesca would have to accompany him back to des Iles. For her safety, she was going to have to miss Count Myrrdin's funeral.

It was far from ideal, she would be devastated when he told her. Lord, what a mess.

On first seeing Francesca in Provins, she had mentioned annulling their marriage. Back at St Michael's Abbey, Tristan had got her to confess that she had never actually wanted an annulment. It was progress of a sort, but until Francesca abandoned the idea that he would be better off making a dynastic marriage, he couldn't let his guard down. What was in her heart? After what had happened last night, Tristan couldn't be sure.

He'd ridden to Provins on a mission of mercy, to collect Francesca so she could pay her last respects to the man she had known as her father. This morning, he'd had it in mind that after the journey had come to its sad and inevitable conclusion, he and Francesca would either be reconciled or he would leave Francesca at St Méen and return to des Iles.

This morning, reconciliation seemed a real possibility and Tristan was wary of rushing her. He had thought to win her back gradually. He had hoped that if they lived together at St Méen, they might recapture some of the early magic. Last night had been promising, but Francesca had been grieving, and he couldn't be sure that he'd been more than a distraction. They might have come to a fuller understanding of each other if they'd been able to live quietly together at St Méen. Sadly, Kerjean's interference meant more drastic measures were needed.

Francesca couldn't be allowed to return to her manor, she wouldn't be safe. It wasn't practical for Tristan to watch her every moment, and even if he put her under guard, he couldn't be sure Kerjean would be kept at bay. Tristan's skin chilled. No, St Méen really was out of the question. Kerjean had broken in once, he could do so again. Tristan wouldn't have a moment's peace for worrying about her.

He must take her to Château des Iles, she would be safe there.

Des Iles—bounded by the sea on three sides—was practically impregnable. An outright attack—particularly by a lone knight and a disreputable band of outlaws—was out of the question. Kerjean couldn't field enough men. Yes, Francesca would have to go to des Iles, and the sooner the better. Tristan scowled at the shield scratched into the limewash.

It wouldn't be easy. At des Iles there were serious obstacles to any reconciliation—Esmerée being the most obvious.

How would Francesca react when she discovered that the woman who had once been his mistress was living there? Would she demand that Esmerée be sent elsewhere?

As to any further confessions, revealing his deep and most precious secret—his daughter—that would have to wait. He had no option but to take this step by step. Tristan rubbed the bridge of his nose. He had no idea what to expect if Francesca discovered that he and Esmerée had a daughter. Heaven help him, only Esmerée and Roparz knew that Kristina was Tristan's child. Tristan had hoped to confess all to Francesca, but with the alliance apparently reforming, his hands were, once again, tied.

Hell burn it, last night's truce between Francesca and himself was far too fragile to be put to the test, yet for Francesca's safety, that was exactly what he must do.

Francesca must be taken to des Iles, he had to get her out of harm's way. And whilst he might be able to delay telling her about Kristina, she would have to know about Esmerée.

Tristan nodded at Sir Nicolas and made for the door. On the threshold he looked back. 'It's clear you need reinforcements.'

Sir Nicolas shuffled his feet. 'I am truly sorry, my lord.'

Tristan waved the apology aside. 'Lady Francesca and I will be returning to des Iles shortly. As soon as I get there, I'll send you extra guards. In the meantime, I shall ask Sir Arthur for his assistance.'

Sir Nicolas bowed his head. 'Thank you, my lord.'

'Go back with you to des Iles? Heavens, Tristan, when?' It was later that evening and Francesca was sat up in bed, combing her hair.

Tristan leaned his shoulder against a bedpost. 'We'll be leaving in the morning.'

Francesca felt herself go still. 'Are you mad? We must wait until after Papa's funeral.'

Tristan studied the toe of his boot. 'I'm afraid that is no longer possible, we leave for Château des Iles at first light tomorrow.'

'Be reasonable, Tristan, I can't possibly go tomorrow.' Francesca fought for calm. *I can't miss*

Papa's funeral! She shoved her comb on a shelf by the bed. 'If urgent business is calling you to des Iles, you will have to go alone. Everyone will understand if you miss the funeral. You must see that I can't miss it.'

He set his jaw. 'You're coming with me.'

'Tristan, I will attend Papa's funeral.'

Blue eyes looked her way, so hard and determined they were almost unrecognisable. 'No, you won't.'

Francesca found herself scowling at the torn tapestry which was folded neatly at the bottom of the bed. The tapestry had been aired and the worst of the mud had been brushed off, ready for later inspection. If it hadn't been damaged beyond repair, she intended to mend it.

Glancing back at Tristan, she met that hard, unrecognisable gaze. *He is worried.* 'Tristan, what happened at St Méen? What did you find?'

'Nothing, it is as I have already told you. A minor break-in. Sir Nicolas assured me that nothing was disturbed save the wall-hanging.'

'It seems very odd that someone should steal into a manor and only take a tapestry. Which they then leave by the side of the road. Tristan, there has to be more to it than that. Once again, there's something you're not telling me.'

Expression stony, Tristan pushed to his feet. 'You're coming with me to des Iles.'

Francesca narrowed her eyes. This was a side of Tristan she wasn't familiar with—Tristan at his most intransigent. The great lord and commander who overrode all argument. Her throat ached as she stared at him. It was hard to believe that last night he had softened enough to give her such comfort, whilst tonight he was denying her the chance to attend Count Myrrdin's funeral. 'You, my lord, are a boor. I need to mourn Papa.' Her voice sounded hollow and her eyes prickled, tears weren't far away. 'It will help to attend the funeral.'

He shrugged, apparently entirely unmoved. 'You can grieve at des Iles as well as anywhere.'

'And if I refuse to go with you?'

'You'll come if I have to bind you hand and foot.'

A hot tear ran down her cheek and she averted her head before surreptitiously wiping it away.

The mattress dipped and he touched her hand. 'Francesca, we don't need to quarrel.' His voice softened. 'It grieves me too that we must miss Count Myrrdin's funeral, but miss it we must. I need you to trust me. You are not safe here.'

She glared at him through a haze of tears. 'It would be easier if you would tell me what's worrying you. I am not stupid, I know there's more and I know it's connected to your visit to my manor.'

'I didn't want to alarm you.' Sighing, he brushed a strand of hair from her face. 'I suspect I know the identity of the man who took that tapestry.'

'How so?'

'We found faint marks scratched on the solar wall—exactly where the tapestry hung. The marks are in the shape of a knight's shield and the device is remarkably similar to Sir Joakim Kerjean's.'

'Sir Joakim took the tapestry? That blond oaf? Why?'

Tristan's hand shifted back to where hers was lying on the coverlet. His gaze was steady. 'Kerjean is warning me, he wants me to know that he can get to you, even when you are in your own manor.'

Her brow furrowed. 'To what end?'

His mouth twisted into a wry smile. 'Damned if I know, perhaps he thinks I care about you.' His expression sobered. 'Francesca, I don't believe he means to court you.'

She shivered. 'No, that was definitely a lie.' She gave him a straight look. She'd never been to des Iles and at almost any other time she would be curious to see it. But to miss Papa's funeral? 'Would you really bind me hand and foot to get me to go with you?'

'If I need to.'

There was a pause. She looked sadly at the ripped tapestry and made up her mind. 'There'll be no need for that. I will trust that you have your reasons. I won't fight you, I'll accompany you to des Iles.'

He squeezed her hand. 'Thank you, my heart. I shall do my utmost to make sure you don't regret it.'

She swallowed. 'Have you told Bastian we're leaving Fontaine?'

'Aye.'

'And Mari?'

His lips twitched. 'Naturally.' He glanced at their linked hands and all humour left his expression. 'Francesca, before we leave, there's something I must tell you.' Tristan's voice was calm, although something in his manner lifted the hairs on the back of her neck.

Whatever he had to say, she wasn't going to like it.

Chapter Ten

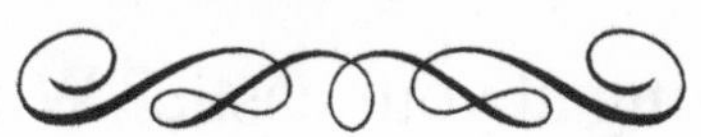

Tristan's blue eyes were so troubled, Francesca's breath stopped.

'I have a confession to make,' he said. 'Before we married, I had a mistress.'

'Tristan, this doesn't surprise me.' Her lips curved. 'Many young lords have mistresses and, innocent though I was, I could tell you'd had experience.'

Hot colour washed into his cheeks. 'I should have told you about her. I should also have told you that she lives at Château des Iles. When we get there, you're bound to meet her.'

Francesca blinked, she was going to meet Tristan's former mistress? His fingers tightened on hers, and if what he was telling her hadn't been so outrageous, she could almost believe he looked regretful. A stone settled in her gut.

'What...what is her name?'

'Esmerée.'

Esmerée. 'Tristan, you told me you have kept our marriage vows. Is your relationship with her at an end?'

'Of course it is, it ended when you and I were betrothed.'

'Yet she's living at your castle? Why? Is she hoping you will take her back?'

'Far from it. Esmerée has married my friend Roparz. He is besotted with her and they're disgustingly happy.' Tristan cleared his throat and stared at the wall behind her. 'Esmerée is expecting her second child.'

Francesca's eyes widened as she struggled to take in what she was being told. Tristan's former mistress was married to Sir Roparz? 'She's a knight's daughter, I assume?'

He shook his head. 'Esmerée's father was a merchant.'

'Yet Sir Roparz married her? Your steward?' A knight ranked higher than a merchant, and generally it would be expected that a knight would marry into his class. It was most unusual for a knight to choose to marry below him. 'Her father was rich?'

'Actually, he wasn't. Roparz simply wanted her, no one else would do. As soon as it became clear that my relationship with Esmerée was coming to an end, Roparz came forward and asked for her hand.' He grimaced. 'I admit to being all kinds of a fool. Roparz confessed he'd wanted her for an age. I'd never noticed, more's the pity.'

'You would have let her go sooner if you had?'

'Of course, my relationship with her was purely a business arrangement.'

'A business arrangement,' Francesca murmured. He made it sound so cold. So distant. Worse, lurking in the back of her mind was the lowering thought that her marriage to Tristan had also been a business arrangement. One that had become worthless the moment Lady Clare was declared heiress to the County of Fontaine. Up until then Tristan had believed that Count Myrrdin's lands would one day be added to the list of his holdings. He'd acted as steward for Count Myrrdin; he knew his way about Fontaine blindfold.

And now? With Count Myrrdin dead, was Tristan regretting the loss of those lands more keenly than ever? Francesca tried to ignore the lump in her throat. Tristan would have to be a saint for such thoughts not to have occurred to him and Tristan le Beau was many things, but saint he was not.

'How long was Esmerée your lover?'

'A year? Two? Lord, Francesca, I didn't count the days.'

Francesca nodded as though she understood, except she didn't understand, not at all. Tristan might say his arrangement with Esmerée had ended, but he must be fond of her. Why else would he keep her at des Iles? Had he married her off to his friend in order to keep her close? Was she truly happy with Roparz? It was all a little too convenient. Slowly, she slid her hand from under his. 'It sounds extremely awkward.'

'What does?'

'Esmerée living at des Iles.'

He shrugged. 'Does it?' His face was blank. Puzzled. As though he had no idea why she would say such a thing.

'It is most peculiar. Tristan, surely you see that?'

He looked away, flushing. 'I'm not the only man who's taken a mistress.'

'Aye, but to have her living in des Iles—in your most important castle—can't you see how odd it is? When you're in residence, you must run into her all the time.'

'You will recall I have not spent much time there of late.' He shrugged. 'In any case, as I said, my relationship with Esmerée was purely a business transaction. I like Esmerée very much, but I never loved her. Our union was purely physical.'

'You paid for her services.'

'She wasn't reluctant, if that is what you are thinking.'

She raked him with her eyes, taking in his dark hair, those blue eyes that had once, or so she had thought, looked at her with such warmth. *What am I to you? A failed business transaction? Another woman who gives you physical release? Or is there more to us than that?* She sighed, unable to tear her gaze from that firm jaw, that sculpted mouth. Tristan le Beau. Even with all his arrogance, his coldness, he was a handsome devil. 'I don't suppose she was.'

That puzzled look was back in his eyes. 'Francesca, I apologise for not telling you about Esmerée years ago. On my honour, she stopped being my mistress the moment I decided to marry.'

'Why didn't you mention she was living at des Iles before now?'

'It makes a difference?'

'Of course it does! Tristan, I've said I'll go back with you to des Iles, but I've no wish to be living under the same roof as your former mistress.' She gripped the bedcovers. 'You must see it will be impossible.'

'She's married to my steward, she is Lady Esmerée de Fougères. I can't send her away.'

'Château des Iles is not your only castle.'

His eyes narrowed. 'You expect me to dispense with Roparz? He's my friend, not to mention that he's also a most efficient steward. I want my best steward in charge of my main holding.'

'I'm asking you to have the decency to house your friend and his wife elsewhere. God knows you've plenty of castles to choose from.'

'I can't do that.'

'Why not?'

Tristan shoved his hand through his hair and glowered—that was the only word for it—at the torn tapestry lying at the foot of the bed. Despite the warmth of the bedcovers, Francesca shivered. She had never really crossed swords with Tristan before and she didn't like it. Was this merely the arrogance of a great lord used to commanding others? There was something odd in his manner, some reluctance she couldn't pin down. What was it? Did it concern Roparz?

Roparz had shown Tristan great loyalty and clearly Tristan thought of him almost as a brother. Indeed, Roparz was perhaps the only stable element in Tristan's life. No wonder he was so valued. Tristan's parents had never given him much warmth, it was possible that the bond between him and Roparz made up for that. Roparz was his rock.

Was that why Tristan refused to give Roparz an appointment elsewhere? If so, much as she hated the idea of coming face-to-face with Lady Esmerée de Fougères, she might have to accept it.

At heart, Francesca was sure Tristan wasn't as cold as he pretended. He had made love to her so sweetly last night. It had surely been more than mere physical release on his part. He'd been tender and loving. A man who could make love like that was far from cold. Whatever it was that sparked between them was more than any business transaction, it had to be. Their marriage had been contracted for dynastic reasons, but the instant she had laid eyes on him she had known there was only one man for her. Tristan le Beau. That had not changed.

Tristan, I love you. The words echoed through her mind. She had loved him from the start, she had even told him as much. However, she would be the first to admit that her love had been immature. It had been based mainly on his looks and the carnal attraction—unexpected and overpowering—that had flared between them. Her feelings were stronger now, the girlish infatuation had blossomed into deep love.

If I want to keep him, I shall have to fight for him.

She drew in a breath. 'Tristan, why did you come to fetch me from Provins?'

He gave her the oddest look. 'You know the answer to that—to tell you Count Myrrdin was ill.'

'You didn't have to come in person, you could have sent someone else.'

'I wanted you to hear it from me.'

'Why?'

A muscle twitched in his cheek. 'I've no idea.' His voice was dry. 'Let us say it was an impulse I am beginning to regret.'

You, my lord, are a liar. Francesca bit her lip and pushed her disappointment aside. She longed for him to admit that he had been worried for her, that he wanted to tell her about Count Myrrdin's illness personally because he knew how upset she'd be. She wanted him to say something—anything—that revealed that he cared for her. Her heart squeezed. Even though she'd known their relationship had begun as a useful dynastic transaction, she'd hoped it would turn into something more meaningful. And then Lady Clare had arrived and all she could think was that the county Tristan had married her for would never be his.

With a start, she realised she had changed in the months they had been apart. She was older and, she hoped, a little wiser. Although the original nature of their relationship—a dynastic alliance—might be no more, she had cause for hope. Tristan must value her, he had come to Provins in person, when he could have sent someone else.

Tristan wasn't one to wear his heart on his sleeve. Despite that, he was loyal to those he cared for. He valued Roparz more than most—witness the way he refused to send him to a remote holding on the edge of his county.

If Francesca wanted to keep Tristan, she must prove that there was more to them than a dusty agreement forged because Count Tristan des Iles and Count Myrrdin de Fontaine held adjoining counties.

When Tristan had dragged her away from the revel in the palace, she'd given him the benefit of the doubt. She'd told herself that his knightly upbringing—being fostered away from his parents, not to mention his father's harsh treatment of him after his mother's death—was responsible for his apparent coolness.

At their wedding, she'd been innocently confident in her role as the Fontaine heiress. She'd been certain she could change him. She gritted her teeth. No, that was wrong, she'd imagined he had it within him to be a loving, caring husband.

Deep down, she still felt the same. The fire between them still burned as last night had proved. Francesca couldn't imagine joining with another man in the way she did with Tristan. She lost herself completely, and she was confident it was the same for him. Were all men so giving when it came to making love with their wives? Her experience was limited, but she felt sure they were not.

During her stay at Paimpont, Francesca had had leisure to think. She had observed that many married men were careless of their wives' affection and she had seen them sow their seed where they might. Not all men were cast in that mould, of course—some could be faithful…they honoured their marriage vows. Such men surely felt affection for their wives. Tristan swore he had kept his marriage vows, as she had kept hers.

Tristan did care about her. He might not be able to express his affection in words, but she believed his tenderness in bed spoke for him. She would hang on to that and pray that he would learn to acknowledge his feelings.

Likely he saw love as a weakness. If she wanted him, she would have to teach him that far from being a weakness, love was a great strength. However, there was something Tristan must be made to understand, she wasn't going to let him trample all over her.

'Tristan, I really don't want to meet your former mistress.'

Silence. Then, in a troubled tone, 'I am sorry, but Lady Esmerée and Sir Roparz will not be leaving des Iles.'

Francesca clutched at the bedcovers. Saints, she hoped she was right about loyalty and affection being behind Tristan's insistence that Sir Roparz remain with him at des Iles, because if she was wrong, if Tristan was incapable of such feelings, there would be no hope for them.

A loveless marriage wasn't for her. If that was all he had to offer, she would have to be strong. She would quietly withdraw from his life, leaving him free to make a dazzling dynastic alliance elsewhere.

Eyes prickling, Francesca rolled over and presented him with her back. She heard him sigh. The bed rocked as he pushed to his feet and she listened to him undressing—the faint click of a belt buckle being unclasped; the *thud, thud* of boots being tossed into the corner.

The St Méen wall-hanging lay across the foot of the bed, heavy as a millstone. Irritably, she kicked it away and it landed on the floor with a soft thump.

Tristan padded over. Out of the corner of her eye—not that she was watching him—she saw him bend to pick it up.

'What's this doing here?' He placed it on a coffer.

'I thought I might mend it, but I fear it is beyond repair.'

Tristan just looked at her, a muscle twitching in his cheek. Then he got silently into bed.

The next morning the bailey was filled with sunlight as Francesca and Tristan took their leave of Lady Clare and Sir Arthur. Overhearing Tristan's last hurried conversation with Sir Arthur, Francesca gathered Tristan had persuaded Sir Arthur to send a small deputation of men to look over Sir Joakim's manor. Sir Arthur's men were, apparently, to report back on anything unusual. That, more than anything, proved how concerned Tristan was about the threat posed by Sir Joakim.

There was no sign of the Benedictine novices, who had set out early on their return journey to St Michael's, and their farewells finally made, Francesca and Tristan clattered across the Fontaine drawbridge in the midst of a large troop of Sir Arthur's knights.

Tears not far away, Francesca sat stiffly in the saddle and didn't look back. It was hard to believe she was missing Count Myrrdin's funeral.

Despite the sun, the forest of the Brocéliande echoed her sombre mood. The trees marched alongside them, dark sentinels whose trunks were stained with grey lichen. The trackways beneath the unfurling leaves were heavily shadowed. Even the screech of a hawk sounded like a soul in torment. Shutting her mind to her surroundings, Francesca rode in a daze.

Then, somewhere near the eastern fringe of Brittany, the trees thinned and Francesca emerged from her abstraction to overhear two of the knights talking.

'Journey's end is in sight,' one knight said. 'The sea's just ahead.'

'And not above time,' his companion replied. 'I'm starved.'

The track became narrow. Through a thicket of hawthorn, Francesca caught her first glimpse of the ocean, a breathtaking expanse of heaving grey water. Filled with awe, her jaw slackened. She had never seen the sea before. She'd heard it was vast, and in her mind she'd imagined a large lake. This was—heavens—a world of water.

They slowed the horses and wound along the rim of a tall granite cliff in single file.

On the landward side, the path was edged with prickly clumps of gorse—the flowers flashed like gold in the evening light. The clifftop path looked safe, none the less the sea was so far below them that Francesca's stomach dropped to her toes whenever she looked down. The wind was keen, white-tipped waves were rolling onshore, she could hear them crashing in some rocky cove hundreds of feet below. A scattering of small islands sat out in the bay—dark and wooded. The air was heavy with salt.

Up here on the cliff, the wind flicked the horses' manes this way and that; it tugged strands of Francesca's hair free of her veil. Seagulls screeched and wailed as they sliced briskly through the air. The sound—mournful and edgy—tugged at her heart.

Esmerée.

Francesca wasn't looking forward to the next few hours.

'There it is.' Tristan drew rein and pointed at the next promontory. 'I brought you this way so you could see it at its best.'

Château des Iles.

Francesca stared. A curtain wall ran the length of the cliff—the easternmost end caught the last of the sinking sun and glowed in the fading light. Jutting up behind the merlons and crenels were the towers and turrets of a sprawling castle that would have been at home in any ballad. Château des Iles was huge—a complicated mass of masonry that dominated the skyline. Saints, Tristan's castle dominated the landscape. It looked completely impregnable. There were turrets and walkways and fortified towers. There were sloping roofs and conical roofs. It was hard to know where to look first.

'It's magnificent.'

They rode on with Francesca trying not to gape. Tristan's castle was double the size of Fontaine, why, it was larger even than Count Henry's palace in Provins. It should have looked out of place here at the edge of Brittany, yet it did not. Francesca lifted her gaze to the white clouds pushing in from the sea, and for an instant it seemed that Château des Iles was a ship, setting sail through a foaming sea towards the islands in the bay.

'Tristan?' Licking salt from her lips, she pointed at the islands. 'Are those islands inhabited?'

Tristan's saddle creaked as he turned to look at her. 'A hermit lived on one of them in my father's day, I am not sure if he is still there. There are a couple of fishermen's cottages. Otherwise, there are only birds.'

Francesca turned her attention back to the castle. Even though she'd heard of its grandeur, she'd had no idea it was so large.

The clifftop track widened out as they approached the castle on its rocky promontory, and as they neared the gatehouse, Tristan drew rein so that she might ride up beside him. He gave her a crooked smile and reached across to lightly touch her brow. 'You are worrying about Esmerée. Don't.'

Francesca held her head high as they rode into the bailey.

Tristan took Francesca's hand. 'I'll show you to our bedchamber and then I must beg your leave, I need to speak to Roparz.'

'Of course. I am sure you have much to catch up on.'

Tristan was aware of Francesca taking everything in as he led her swiftly through the hall and past the curious gazes of his retainers. There would be time for introductions later. Hurrying along the corridor, he stopped at the foot of the stairwell.

'I should warn you, there are a lot of steps. Our bedchamber is at the top.'

'Very well.'

He hoped she had forgiven him for insisting that

she missed Count Myrrdin's funeral. Her voice was quiet, far too polite, and her cheeks pale. Was she fretting about meeting Esmerée? He didn't want that, though in light of her reaction when she'd learned that Esmerée was living at des Iles, it seemed highly likely.

Yet what could he do? Tristan held in a sigh. His meeting with Roparz couldn't wait, they had an agreement, and he wasn't about to make changes without first consulting Roparz.

Francesca was out of breath by the time they reached the bedchamber. The sun was setting, and a shaft of fiery light blazed through the window. Dropping his hand, she made straight for the window embrasure.

'A triple lancet facing the sea,' she murmured. 'Heavens, you can see for miles.'

'You like it?'

'How could I not? Tristan, it's breathtaking.'

Tristan's chest tightened. Francesca was in his bedchamber at last. Her body—feminine and so beguiling—looked impossibly tempting with every curve limned by sunlight. Had he done the right thing bringing her here without first alerting Roparz? Lord, he hoped so.

He cleared his throat. 'My father had the windows enlarged. This chamber is so high that there is no need for defensible window slits.'

She rested her hand on the window embrasure. 'What's that booming noise?'

'The waves.'

'It sounds like thunder.'

Tristan went to stand at her side and covered her hand with his. 'Aye.'

She was seeing the bay at its best. The sky was fiery, clouds were splashed with crimson and gold. Even as they looked, the rim of the sun nudged the horizon and the islands looked as though they were floating in a gilded sea. Waves rippled the surface as they rolled to shore.

'Beautiful,' she murmured.

The sunset gleamed in her grey eyes, lighting up the silver and gold flecks he loved so much. It shone on her ebony braid and put colour in her cheeks.

'Beautiful,' Tristan echoed.

Inhaling deeply, she turned and took stock of the bedchamber.

The ancient coverlet on the great bed was emblazoned with the des Iles colours, three large cinquefoils, sewn on to silver silk. The coverlet was worn in places, Tristan half-expected a comment on its age, but Francesca said nothing. She seemed transfixed as she stared at it, and he thought he knew why. The silver silk reflected the colours of the setting sun—gold, apricot, crimson.

Her keen gaze moved swiftly on. It lingered briefly on a side-table, on the door to the small chamber Tristan sometimes used as an office. She glanced at the pegs on the wall, at the travelling chests lined up by one wall. And she froze.

'Those are my travelling chests.' Her eyes were puzzled. 'You've had them carted from Provins.'

When she set her hands on her hips, Tristan knew he was in trouble.

She cocked an eyebrow at him. 'You decided that I was coming to des Iles all that time ago? Even before I agreed?'

He stepped closer. Smiled. 'I hoped to change your mind, yes.'

'You presumed a great deal. Before the revel, I'd planned to leave Paimpont and go to Monfort.'

'To stay with friends.'

Her face darkened. 'Sir Ernis has been talking, I see.'

Tristan lifted his shoulders. 'He mentioned you had friends there.'

'I have one particular friend and she needs me. She asked for my advice.'

'Oh?'

'On running a manor. You wouldn't understand.' A wave of her hand took in the lancet window and the great bed with its silken bedcover. 'Tristan, you were born to all this, my friend was not. She's expected to act as housekeeper at Monfort, but her origins are humble. She is anxious to please and has asked for my help. Sir Guy—'

'Sir Guy? I thought Sir Eric held Monfort, the knight who married Lady Rowena de Sainte-Colombe?'

'So he does. Sir Guy is Sir Eric's steward.' The anger faded from Francesca's expression as she looked earnestly up at him. 'Sir Guy has been kind to Helvise. Tristan, Helvise is my friend and she has had a difficult time of it. She is happy at Monfort and doesn't want to lose her place there.' She touched Tristan's chest. 'I offered to help—to teach her how to run a manor so Sir Guy will allow her to stay.'

Tristan nodded as though he understood, though in truth he was puzzled. 'Why would Sir Guy cast her out?'

'She's not been trained to run a manor. And she has a child.'

Tristan thought he understood. 'She has no husband.' Unmarried women with babies were often shunned. Tristan didn't know Sir Guy, so he couldn't comment on whether the man might take exception to having Helvise in charge of the household.

'Exactly. You know how judgemental people can be. I feel a certain kinship with Helvise, like her I don't have noble blood, although thanks to Count Myrrdin—' her face clouded and she swallowed hard '—thanks to Count Myrrdin I have been trained. I understand the workings of a manor. I can help her. I may not have aristocratic blood running through my veins, but managing a household is the one part of my training that has stood me in good stead.'

'I don't doubt it. At Paimpont Sir Ernis mentioned you were a godsend when it came to the estate accounts. And that the storerooms have never been better stocked.'

Further, Tristan had seen for himself how the cobwebs had been banished from Paimpont. He'd seen the polished tables and the flowers, and the fresh rushes strewn on the hall floor.

'Thank you, I did try to help.' Her expression brightened. 'At least some of my training took.'

Tristan couldn't deny that she had wrought wonders at Paimpont. However, something in her tone felt wrong. He homed in on it. '*Some* of your training?'

Her eyes were frank. 'I am not a noblewoman.'

'Nobility is not defined by birth, it is defined by actions.' He lifted her hand and brought it close. 'You, my heart, are every inch a lady. Always have been. Always will be.'

Her face softened. 'You are just being chivalrous.'

'Chivalry be damned, I mean it.' He looked her up and down and grinned. 'You are every inch the lady.'

She gave him a shy smile, worryingly it was tinged with sadness. 'Tristan, I see what you are about. You want to get me into bed again.'

Tristan didn't reply. Naturally, he wanted to get her into bed, but her smile—the sadness—was particularly concerning because he could see it had nothing to do with Count Myrrdin's death and everything to do with their marriage and her place in the world.

'My lord, I am neither fish nor fowl, and your eagerness to bed me betrays it.'

He looked blankly at her. 'I beg your pardon?'

'Don't you see? I can't resist you and well you know it.'

If it hadn't been for the shadows in her eyes, Tristan would have smiled. 'You seem to think that's a bad thing.'

She gave an emphatic nod. 'It is, it proves my point.'

He waited.

'I can't resist you. I've never been able to resist you. Tristan, you make me behave in the most unseemly fashion, you turn me into a wanton. When I'm with you, I hardly recognise myself.'

'I'm your husband. That is as it should be.'

'Is it?'

'Of course it is! Think of Count Myrrdin. Everyone in Fontaine knows how he and his countess adored one another.'

She frowned at the front of his tunic. 'It's true he never stopped mourning her.'

'Exactly.' Tristan took in a deep breath. 'It was the same with my parents. They only had eyes for each other, and when Mama died, my father was so full of grief he had little care for anyone else.'

Francesca's grey eyes filled with sympathy. Her fingers curled into his tunic. 'Tristan, I am sure your father loved you.'

He drew back sharply. Lord, he was trying to comfort her, the last thing he wanted was her sympathy. 'All I am saying is that our mutual satisfaction in the bedchamber does not name you wanton. You are a passionate, giving woman and

I am blessed to have you as my wife. Francesca, I do not wish to hear such nonsense ever again.'

Holding down a rush of anger, he turned to the door. This was his fault. If he hadn't removed himself so completely from her life— No, he wasn't completely to blame, those letters had gone astray. None the less, he had failed in his duties as a husband.

Francesca had a warm heart. It was plain from what she had told him about her friend at Monfort that she needed to be needed. What she didn't need was a husband who married her and then dashed off in the service of the duchy. He'd been proud. Arrogant. He'd assumed too much and he'd not taken her youthfulness into account. She'd been sixteen when their marriage had begun. So young.

Those blasted lost letters had a lot to answer for.

Well, he would make up for it. He had to, he needed her too. His need for Francesca was a fire in his blood whenever he looked at her, it was an ache in his heart at the thought of losing her. He couldn't lose her. He had to convince her of her worth. He had to prove she could trust him and in order to do that he was going to have to tell her about Kristina.

Except he couldn't tell her about Kristina until he had warned Roparz that someone else was about to be let in on their secret. He must speak to Roparz without delay.

'Francesca, we shall speak more of this later. By now Sir Roparz will have heard of our arrival. He will be waiting to give me his report.'

I need to ask Roparz about what might have happened to those lost letters. And then we shall have to discuss Kristina.

Mon Dieu, would Francesca ever forgive him for keeping so large a secret? His stomach tightened. He must tell her. And as soon as he had spoken to Roparz, he would.

She was frowning in the direction of her travelling chests. Well, that was something he could help with.

'I apologise for removing your belongings from Paimpont without your leave.'

Her eyes met his. 'You'll let me return to Champagne?'

'I'd prefer that you chose to stay. Lord, I'd offer your friend Helvise a place here, if it would encourage you to remain.'

She went very still. 'You'd offer Helvise a place at des Iles? That is most generous.'

'Francesca, I am not entirely heartless. Life can be hard for women who have children out of wedlock.' He shrugged. 'In any case, it seems a small price to pay if it would encourage you to stay. However, if you must return, I won't hold you.' Tristan forced a smile which felt all wrong. He suspected it wouldn't feel right until he had bared his soul to her. He had to tell her about Kristina, he couldn't think of a better way of proving how much he trusted her.

He could only pray that in telling her about Kristina, he wouldn't alienate her for ever. Learning about his daughter would surely test their marriage more than anything that had happened so far. 'I'm hoping to persuade you to stay. Francesca, I have to leave you for a space, I must speak with Sir Roparz. I'll come for you at suppertime. If you've a mind to join us in the great hall, you can meet everyone then.'

'Thank you, Tristan,' she said softly.

Francesca stared at her travelling chests and listened to Tristan's footsteps retreating down the stairs. It had been high-handed of him to remove them from Paimpont without her leave, but she couldn't bring herself to be angry with him, particularly since he had offered to find space for Helvise at des Iles. It was the last thing she had expected.

He really wants me. Of course, wanting alone

wasn't enough, wanting—*desire*—was too close to lust. To forge a lasting marriage, they would need love. On both sides.

Well, they were finally together at des Iles. Perhaps here they could come to understand—to *love*—each other. She would give it until summer's end. By then she would surely know if Esmerée had a place in his heart.

She would give it until Michaelmas. And if she and Tristan were no closer, she would return to Champagne. She would lend Helvise a hand, and when she was confident Helvise could cope, she would retire to her own manor at St Méen.

Chapter Eleven

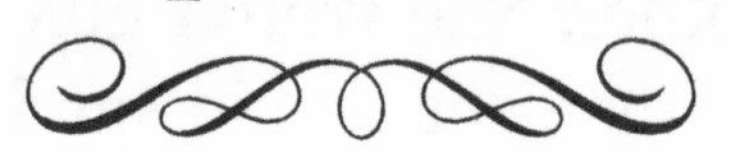

Tristan strode into the steward's office just after sunset. The narrow window was lit by the faintest of glows and Roparz was at his desk, reading a scroll in the light of a flickering lantern.

Dropping the scroll on to the desk, Roparz rose and gripped Tristan's shoulder. 'Welcome home, my lord. Sergeant Olier told me you were back. You made good time, I must confess I didn't expect to see you for another couple of weeks at the earliest.' He lifted an eyebrow. 'Count Myrrdin?'

Tristan grimaced. 'The count is with God, he died the day we arrived in Fontaine. To my mind he'd been waiting to see Francesca.'

'It seems likely, I know that he and Lady Francesca were close. God rest him.' Roparz gave Tristan a penetrating look. 'Were the funeral rites concluded so swiftly? No, don't tell me, you can't have stayed for the funeral, there wouldn't have been time.'

'No.' Tristan nudged the door shut with his boot, he didn't want their conversation to be overheard. 'We decided to miss it.'

Roparz went still. 'We?'

'Francesca came with me, didn't the sergeant say?'

'Countess Francesca is here in des Iles? *Mon Dieu*, does she know about Esmerée?'

'Yes, I have told her.'

'And?'

Tristan rubbed the bridge of his nose. 'As you may imagine, it has created difficulties.'

Roparz clenched his jaw. 'And what about Kristina? Have you told her about Kristina?'

'Not yet, I wanted to hear your views first.'

Roparz relaxed. 'Thank you.'

'How is she?'

'Kristina? In rude health, as usual.'

Tristan walked to the desk, picked up the scroll Roparz had been working on and dropped it back on the table. 'Roparz, we need to talk about Kristina, but first—has anything unusual happened since I left?'

Roparz shook his head. 'On the contrary, it's been unusually quiet. Why?'

'We have much to discuss. I fear the rebel alliance is not entirely spent.'

Roparz watched him intently. 'Oh?'

'When I found Francesca in Provins, she was being accosted by Sir Joakim Kerjean.'

'*Mon Dieu*, he must have gone straight to Champagne as soon as he learned her whereabouts. What happened?'

'Francesca was attending a masked revel at the palace. Kerjean was trying to seduce her. It was pure chance that I arrived at the right moment.' Tristan scowled at the scroll on the desk. 'He's bold to the point of recklessness. When Francesca and I set out for Fontaine, he followed us. And he wasn't alone.'

Roparz lifted his eyebrows. 'He has men?'

'Outlaws only. Disreputable-looking crew, I doubt there's anyone of note among them, although that may change. I had to promise a donation to St Michael's to pay for the escort of a group of Benedictine novices to get us safely to Fontaine.'

'An escort of novices?'

Tristan made a dismissive gesture. 'Knights who've had their fill of the world, it's common enough.'

'Aye, but novices don't usually bear arms.'

Roparz's eyes glittered. 'Your donation must have been generous.'

Tristan gave him a wry smile. 'It was. Roparz, even with our makeshift escort we weren't secure. Kerjean broke into Francesca's manor in Fontaine and left a very clear message—Francesca was at risk there.'

'*Bon Sang*, so that's why you brought her to des Iles. What the devil is he up to?'

'I imagine Kerjean's current aim is to stir up trouble and weaken us here in Brittany. The duchy means nothing to him. The man's a vulture, he feeds on disorder. Doubtless he's hoping the duchy will fall apart again so he can pick over the carcass. My hunch is that he is planning to rebuild the wretched so-called alliance.'

Roparz let out a slow whistle. 'How many men do you suppose he can muster?'

Tristan scrubbed wearily at his face. 'Lord, I have no idea. He will need money if he's going to attract anyone of standing. We shall have to be on our mettle. Sir Arthur's men are keeping an eye on Kerjean's manor, and I have sent word to Baron Rolland in Rennes advising him of my suspicions.'

'I'll double the watch,' Roparz said.

'Thank you. And we shall need more eyes and ears in the alehouses and the markets.'

'Consider it done.' Roparz tapped his finger thoughtfully on the table. 'Tristan, I must tell you that until I'm certain these outlaws have been run to ground, I won't be happy for you to claim publicly that Kristina is your daughter.'

'You're as fond of that child as I am.'

'I can't deny it, she's a sweetheart. I hope you are not thinking of telling Francesca about her.'

'And if I am?'

'I must counsel against it. Kerjean will want to attack you where you're weakest. Suppose he discovers Kristina is your child and not mine? I wouldn't put it past him to use her against you. Kristina's very life might be at risk.'

'Hell burn it, Roparz, I'm not planning on a public announcement. Not if there's a whisper of suspicion that these vermin are gathering strength again. It's Francesca I'm concerned about, she needs to know.'

Roparz gripped Tristan's arm. 'Tristan, you cannot tell Francesca about Kristina! God knows what might happen if word gets out. We've kept this secret for so long, why not wait until we are certain it is safe?'

Tristan's eyebrows snapped together. 'Francesca won't breathe a word to a soul if I ask her not to.'

'It's too soon, we can't risk it. Jésu, Tristan, this is Kristina we are talking about.'

Tristan rubbed his brow. 'But Francesca needs to know. I have to tell her.'

'Why?'

'I want her to understand that I trust her.'

'And do you?'

'With my life.'

Roparz gazed at him, mouth slightly agape. Then he gave a harsh laugh. 'Lord, I never thought I'd see the day.'

'What day?'

'It's finally happened.' Roparz swore under his breath. 'I must say your timing is perfect.'

Tristan looked blankly at him. 'What in blazes are you talking about?'

'You love her. The impossible has happened, Tristan le Beau has fallen in love.'

Tristan blinked and felt himself go still. *I love her.* The words felt right, they sank deep into his mind, where they felt perfectly at home. *I love her.*

So that was what this was all about. That was why he could not stand the thought of further separation. That was why he wanted her safe. Why he constantly wanted her at his side. He didn't simply need her, he loved her.

Tristan lifted the quill from its stand and found

himself twirling it in his fingers. 'She wrote to me, you know.'

Roparz shook his head, his eyes shadowed and full of doubt. 'That's not possible, I never saw her letter.'

'Francesca didn't write just once, apparently she wrote several times.'

Roparz made an impatient movement. 'Do you have proof? I didn't see a solitary letter.'

'Roparz, I believe her.'

'Forgive, me, Tristan, it's clear you're not thinking straight.'

'I'm not?'

'You're besotted.'

Tristan's father's voice echoed in his mind. *Love? Just another word for weakness. A warrior is better off without it.* He pushed the memory aside, this was not the moment to dwell on what grief had driven his father to do after his mother's death. 'You're forgetting something. Roparz, I wrote to Francesca. My letters didn't reach her either.'

Roparz spread his hands and raised his eyebrows.

Tristan gave Roparz a straight look. 'Oh, of course I believe you had no hand in this. I trust you. Just as I trust Francesca.'

Roparz stood there, fists opening and closing, whilst the shadows drew in around them. He cleared his throat. 'So I see. My lord—Tristan—I understand that Lady Francesca must be told, but I implore you to wait until we have the outlaws in irons.' He paused, mouth grim. 'If anything happened to that little imp, you'd never forgive yourself.'

Tristan's jaw tightened. Maybe Roparz was speaking sense. 'I shall think about it. Francesca will have to know sometime and I would prefer it to be sooner rather than later.'

'Naturally.' A crease formed on Roparz's brow. 'Tristan, someone must have intercepted those letters. Kerjean? But how?'

'It could have been Kerjean. If he wanted to send messages to allies further afield, he would have been using the same Champagne trade routes that we do.' He sighed. 'We shall talk more later. In the meantime, I need a bath and a shave. How is Esmerée?'

'Apart from complaining of feeling as large as a whale, very well.'

'I am glad to hear it.' Tristan looked his steward in the eyes. 'Thank you, Roparz, for everything. You're a friend in a million.'

Francesca stood by the bedchamber window as the sun slipped below the horizon and the sea turned slowly from gold to grey. Violet shadows were gathering in the troughs between waves, the Baie des Iles was beyond beautiful and the sight should have soothed her.

Unfortunately, it did nothing of the kind. Francesca's stomach was churning and her hands shaking. It would be suppertime soon, and the thought filled her with dread. It was bad enough to be meeting Tristan's retainers for the first time, never mind that she would be meeting his former mistress as well.

She must find a way to shift the balance of power in her favour. Twisting a strand of hair round her finger, she found herself staring at the coffers that Tristan had brought from Paimpont. As she moved towards them, she heard grumbling and muttering as someone came up the stairs.

Mari came in, chest heaving. 'Saints, what a climb. Here, my lady, I brought your saddlebag.'

'Thank you.'

Mari set her hands on her hips as she caught her breath. Her face creased in puzzlement when she saw Francesca's travelling chests. 'What are those doing here?'

'My lord had them sent on from Champagne.'

Whoever had transported her coffers must have locked them for travelling and they had, Francesca was pleased to note, returned the keys to the locks. Moving to the largest, she turned the key.

Mari stood at her elbow, her eyes full of curiosity. 'Did you know these would be here, my lady?'

'No, although as it happens I am more than happy to see them.' Francesca heaved back the lid. 'We shall be going down to the great hall for supper shortly. I would like water to bathe in and you shall help me find my best gown.'

'The lavender silk you were married in?'

'Yes, that will do very well.'

Francesca couldn't tell Mari how much she was dreading meeting Lady Esmerée de Fougères. As far as she was aware, Mari had no idea that Lady Esmerée had in the past been linked with Tristan. Fortunately, she didn't need to know.

Mari's eyes brightened. 'You want to make an impression. Quite right, my lady.' She bent over the coffer. 'We can't have Lord Tristan's household thinking he has brought a bunch of ragged pedlars home with him. We shall have to find the amethyst circlet he gave you, it's perfect with that gown.'

Tristan paused at the entrance to his great hall to link Francesca's arm with his. 'You look charming tonight, my lady,' he murmured.

'Thank you.'

'I shall introduce you generally before we are seated. You can meet people individually tomorrow.'

'Very well.'

Francesca kept her chin up and tried to smile. Her stomach was full of butterflies and her heart was pounding. It was most strange, she felt involved in what was happening, yet at the same time she felt as though she was looking on from a great distance.

The great hall was lined with long tables spread with snowy-white cloths. An army of retainers sat at the benches and the air was filled with noise—the roar of the fire behind the high table on the dais; the hum of conversation and guffawing of laughter; the shuffling of rushes underfoot.

The great hall at des Iles was larger than the hall at Fontaine, and the air shimmered with candle haze. The scent of beeswax was strong. Chunky iron candle stands lined the walls; more candles marched down the centre of each of the tables.

Tristan waved at a servant and conversation ceased as though cut off with a knife. A heartbeat later dozens of benches scraped the floor as everyone scrambled to their feet. Faces turned to stare. Save for the crackle of the fire, all was quiet.

Gently, Tristan gripped her hand. 'My friends,

it is my great pleasure to present my lady wife to you. This is the Countess Francesca des Iles. I trust you will serve her as faithfully as you have served me.'

In the pause that followed, Francesca felt the sting of tears, Tristan's standard on the wall opposite was a blur of black and silver, she could see nothing else. She hung on to her smile and tried not to mind that every eye in the hall was focused on her.

Someone on the dais gave a cheer. It seemed to be the signal for general chaos as the hall erupted into cheers and shouts.

'Welcome, Lady Francesca!'

'Countess Francesca, welcome!'

Tristan turned to her, face lit with a smile. 'You see? Everyone is anxious to meet you.' As the cheering subsided, Tristan ushered her towards a couple of high-backed cushioned chairs at the head of the high table. 'Please, my lady, take your place at my board.'

Francesca stepped on to the dais and took her seat. She stared blindly at her trencher and the moment she'd been dreading was upon her.

Tristan leaned forward to indicate the man seated on her other side. 'Francesca, the reprobate next to you is my steward Sir Roparz de Fougères.'

Sir Roparz had light brown hair, grey eyes and an open, honest countenance.

'Good evening, my lady, I am glad to see you here at last.'

'Good evening, Sir Roparz.' Francesca was pleased to hear her voice was steady. 'It is a pleasure to meet you, Tristan has spoken of you often.'

Sir Roparz bowed his head, and then he in turn was leaning back to introduce the woman on his right—a pretty and very pregnant woman with brown hair and eyes.

'Countess Francesca, this is my wife, Lady Esmerée,' Sir Roparz said quietly.

Francesca's smile felt stiff. 'Lady Esmerée, good evening.'

'Good evening, countess.'

Lady Esmerée's brown eyes studied her and she gave a slight nod. Francesca had no idea what it meant. It could be her imagination, but it seemed that Lady Esmerée's smile was as forced as hers. It wouldn't be surprising, she must feel awkward too. Next to Lady Esmerée stood a small girl. With a sense of relief Francesca turned her attention to her. About three years of age, the girl had the prettiest blue eyes Francesca had ever seen. Her eyelashes were extraordinary, thick and dark.

'Mama, me next?' the child said, clutching at Lady Esmerée's skirts.

Francesca felt her smile soften. 'And who is this?'

'My daughter, my lady.' Lady Esmerée looked sideways at Tristan, who was watching the proceedings, his face oddly blank. 'Her name is Kristina, she wanted most particularly to meet you.'

Francesca held out her hand. 'Good evening, Kristina.'

The girl skipped forward, lightly touched Francesca's hand and danced out of sight behind her mother once more.

'What a pretty child,' Francesca said. 'You and Sir Roparz must be very proud.'

Lady Esmerée lifted an eyebrow at Tristan and her lips curved into the oddest of smiles. 'Oh, I am, my lady, very much so. Everyone loves her.' She paused. 'Especially her father.'

Sir Roparz cleared his throat.

'Enough of this,' Tristan cut in testily. 'Lady Esmerée, it's late. Shouldn't Kristina be abed?'

'As you wish, my lord. She so wanted to meet your countess.'

Tristan gestured a maidservant over. Kristina obligingly held up her arms and was carried out of the hall, thumb in mouth.

The rest of the meal passed as though in a dream.

They had arrived at the castle without warning or fanfare, yet Tristan's servants had conjured a feast. Platter after platter was laid before them, Francesca's head whirled with the scale of it.

Fish from the bay had been baked in a pie, she forced down a morsel. It was hard to eat, she was exhausted and very much on edge. Grief; the journey from Fontaine; meeting Lady Esmerée—all had taken their toll.

Game from the nearby forest had been simmered in wine, she managed a nibble. She tried some stuffed goose. She found herself gazing in disbelief at great platters of cheese, nodding as each one was identified for her. A tart goat's cheese made locally. A light creamy ewe's cheese. A smoked variety that had been carted in from Rennes and was new to her. She sipped at her wine.

The candles burned down, wax dripped into pools on the candle stands. Francesca sat on the high-backed chair that looked like a throne and looked over the company with her heart in her throat. Saints, it was hard to keep smiling, she felt like death. Should she be mentally preparing herself to take control of this huge household? Or to face a future alone?

At length, when the hall had become little more

than a dazzle of candlelight and a buzz of sound, Tristan touched her hand.

'Time to retire, I think.'

Shooting him a grateful look, Francesca allowed him to pull back her chair and they swept from the hall.

Francesca woke alone. She sensed immediately that the day was well advanced and was astonished at how soundly she had slept. Perhaps the incessant beat of the waves had lulled her. Pushing back the bedcovers, she padded over to the great lancet and drew back the curtain. White horses were dancing on the crests of the waves, ragged clouds raced across a blue sky. Judging by the length of the shadows, the morning was far gone.

How odd, it wasn't like Mari to let her oversleep. Of course, Mari herself might be lying in, she certainly deserved a rest. Mari was no longer young and they'd had a trying journey with a lot of grief at the end of it.

A door slammed and quick footsteps sounded on the stairs below. Somewhere nearby a woman was crying. Hurrying to the door, Francesca lifted the latch and caught the sound again. Dear Lord, something dreadful must have happened, a woman was sobbing as though her heart would break.

Snatching a gown at random, Francesca pulled it on and grabbed a shawl. She didn't stop to lace her gown, that crying was simply too distressing. She hurried to the stairs.

After two turns, she met Mari coming up, eyes troubled. Mari grabbed her by the hand and glanced over her shoulder, towards the solar door. 'Oh, no, my lady, don't go down there. You must come away.'

Francesca dug in her heels, the sobbing was coming from inside the solar. 'What's happened? Mari, please let go of me.'

Mari tightened her grip, even going so far as to give another tug as though to draw her back upstairs. Her face looked pinched and her mouth tight. 'Come away, my lady, the solar is no place for you this morning.'

Francesca stood her ground. Mari had never been the most biddable of maids, but she wasn't usually quite so stubborn. 'What's happening? Mari?'

The solar door burst open and Sir Roparz stalked out, his face dark with some heavy emotion. Francesca must have made a movement, for he glanced briefly in her direction, gave her a curt nod and clattered on down the stairs.

From inside the solar came a low wail and more unrestrained sobbing. The woman wasn't alone.

Francesca heard a murmur, someone was offering her comfort.

'Mari, stand aside, if you please.'

Mari choked out a protest, Francesca shook herself free and stepped over the threshold. Tristan stood by the fireplace, Lady Esmerée in his arms. Francesca halted, her feet felt as though they'd been nailed to the floor.

Tristan was too busy soothing Lady Esmerée to see her. 'We'll find her,' he said, easing back to look into Lady Esmerée's face. 'Esmerée, if we have to tear this duchy apart stone by stone, we'll find her.'

Lady Esmerée let out a low keening sound. 'You swore she'd be safe.' She curled her fingers into Tristan's tunic.

Tristan's mouth was grim. 'Esmerée, in all likelihood she's playing hide-and-seek somewhere in the castle. Have you checked the kitchens? The chapel? The garden?'

'Aye. Aye. Everywhere. Tristan, we've looked in all those places. I tell you, she's been kidnapped!'

'We don't know that.' Tristan tipped up Lady Esmerée's chin. 'You told no one of her connection to me?'

As the words left Tristan's mouth, Francesca's stomach dropped. They were talking about Kristina. The child's dark-lashed blue eyes—beautiful and strangely familiar—flashed before her. The truth hit her. Kristina must be Tristan's daughter. His *daughter.* A wave of nausea rolled over her.

'I told no one.' Lady Esmerée's fingers clenched and unclenched on Tristan's tunic and her wedding ring flashed in the light. 'Tristan, you must find her, you must.' Her voice broke on another sob and she stumbled to a nearby chair and buried her face in her hands.

'We will find her, Esmerée, never fear.'

Francesca took a deep breath and stepped fully into the solar. Her mind was a maelstrom of whirling thoughts.

Tristan had misled her, he had a daughter. Francesca should have made the connection last night, indeed she would surely have done if she had not been so exhausted. Though he hadn't admitted it, the child's kinship to Tristan was clear in her eyes, in those compelling blue eyes she had inherited from her sire. From Tristan.

Francesca had thought she was getting to know him, she had imagined they understood each other. Bile rose in her throat. How wrong she had been. Afraid she might actually be ill, she put her hand to her mouth.

Lady Esmerée—Tristan's former mistress and

the mother of his child—was weeping loudly on the chair, wiping her tears with her veil. 'Find her, Tristan. For the love of God, find her.'

Francesca felt as though the sky had fallen in, he'd lied to her. Tristan the honourable, Tristan the chivalrous. He had lied.

'Tristan?' Francesca said, in a choked voice.

There was movement behind her, Sir Roparz was back. He went to his wife's side, helped her to her feet and slid his arm about her thickened waist. 'Come, my love. You must rest.' With a last glance in Francesca's direction, he led her from the solar.

Tristan's eyes were bright as sapphires, his face was drawn. He looked utterly drained.

Francesca swallowed. 'Kristina's your daughter.'

'Yes.'

'You lied to me.' A hand reached towards her, she batted it away. 'Tristan, you lied.'

He shook his head. 'No, I—'

'If you didn't lie, you misled me. You allowed me to think Roparz was her father, that's just as bad.' Francesca's chest ached. She felt hurt. Used. As she stared at him, it came to her that she'd never seen him look so worried before. The shock of seeing him so vulnerable jolted her out of her anger and she made herself take a few steadying breaths. 'Saints, Tristan, you look like death.'

He shoved his hand through his hair and grunted.

Francesca felt hurt and used, but suddenly she saw that her feelings must be put aside. Her anger could wait. A child had gone missing and that child must surely come first. She stiffened her spine. 'What's happened to Kristina?'

Blue eyes looked steadily into hers. 'She's vanished. Not in the castle, apparently.'

'How can that be?'

'Her bed was empty this morning.' Tristan's voice cracked and his throat worked. When he reached for her hand a second time, she allowed him to take it. He loved Kristina and it was obvious he was frantic with worry. 'For Kristina's safety, we have told absolutely no one of her relationship to me.'

Francesca stared at their linked hands. 'Your work for the duchy made enemies, you feared she wouldn't be safe.'

He let out a great sigh. 'You understand, *Dieu merci*. Francesca, you have to believe me, I had no mind to deceive you. I intended to tell you as soon as possible, yet I feared for her.'

'Do you think someone has discovered she is your child?'

'I can't see how, less than a handful of people know the truth.' The desperation in his eyes told another story—he was afraid she'd been kidnapped.

'Has there been a ransom demand?'

'No, nothing.' He pulled her towards him. 'Francesca, I am truly sorry you had to learn about Kristina in this way. It was never my intention to hurt you.' Leaning in, he kissed her cheek. 'We shall talk more later, for now, I must leave you.'

'You're going to look for her.'

He released her and stood back. 'Kristina can be a handful. She loves going into the village, one possibility is that she's found a way to get there on her own. She might have sneaked into the back of a supply cart when no one was looking.'

Francesca felt his anxiety, the harbour would be a dangerous place for a child her age. If Kristina was there, Tristan needed to find her quickly.

At the door, he looked back. 'Until later, my heart.'

Chapter Twelve

Mari was waiting for Francesca in the bedchamber. 'This gown today, my lady?' she asked, gesturing at the bed, where she had laid out a blue linen gown. 'The one you have on is rather shabby.'

'Thank you, Mari, that will be fine.' Unwinding her shawl, Francesca draped it over a coffer. Pretending a calm she did not feel, she went to the ewer to wash. Her mind was a confused jumble. Fury—Tristan had misled her; hurt—he hadn't taken her into his confidence about Kristina; regret—she'd not won his trust after all.

Oddly, she wasn't surprised. Tristan's harsh upbringing had taught him not to rely on others, and whilst they had known each other for four years, they'd been apart for much of that time. It was only recently that they were truly beginning to get to know and understand each other. Trust must surely follow. Saints, if they were to have a future together, it must follow.

Yet how could it, when one moment he was introducing her to his retainers as his countess, and now this!

Questions swirled through her head. How old was Kristina? When had she been born?

Francesca found herself thinking back to a frosty December morning in Fontaine when a messenger had ridden in from des Iles. Her innards tightened. It had been during the first year of their marriage, and Tristan had told her he must return to his castle on a matter of some urgency. In those early days it hadn't been his habit to discuss matters of estate business with her, he'd simply informed her that Sir Roparz had sent for him. Back then, she had been too in awe of him to insist on details.

Tristan had been gone a week, and on his return he had simply said that Roparz had married and he'd wanted to attend the ceremony.

Well, that might well have been the truth, or part of it. Francesca splashed water on her face and reached for the drying cloth. Kristina must have been born that December. Had Tristan gone back to des Iles to secure his daughter's future? He'd told her that Roparz had wanted to marry Esmerée, and Francesca had seen with her own eyes that Roparz treated his wife with the utmost consideration. None the less, Tristan must have been worrying about Kristina ever since her birth.

Lady Esmerée has given him a child, whereas I have not.

Francesca's heart clenched. *Am I barren?*

She'd yearned to give Tristan a child, and all these months she'd assumed that they had simply been unlucky. But what if it was more than that? Clearly, Tristan had had no difficulty fathering a child. What if the problem lay with her? Tristan wouldn't want a barren wife.

Saints, this wasn't promising—the more she thought about her future with Tristan, the more difficulties she found. Was their marriage doomed?

She had tried so hard to win his trust, yet he continued to keep her in the dark. She stared blindly into the washbowl. Here she was, happily thinking she had won him over because he had finally told her about his father, and here she was—his countess—when the plain truth was that Tristan didn't really trust her, not with matters close to his heart.

Would he ever trust her? Her mouth twisted. When their marriage had begun, she'd believed her greatest rival was the duchy. More recently, she had learned about Esmerée. And now there was

Kristina. It was a lot to swallow, but she thought she could do it because these recent revelations all proved how wrong her initial judgement of his character had been.

She'd thought Tristan callous—a ruthless lord with little in his head save power and politics. But the latest evidence showed that he had dealt with Esmerée responsibly. He hadn't discarded her, he had stood aside so that Sir Roparz might win her. And she'd never forget the bleakness in his eyes in the solar just now. Tristan cared about his daughter. In short, Tristan had a heart, which meant there was hope.

Francesca became aware of Mari muttering quietly to herself as she hunched over a coffer. 'Mari, did you say something?'

'I warned you not to go into the solar, my lady. I knew no good would come of it.'

Goosebumps rose on Francesca's skin. Tristan had made it clear that he didn't want anyone to know that Kristina was his daughter.

'Mari, how long were you listening outside the door? What did you hear?'

Mari sat back on her heels. 'Enough to know that your husband deceived you. My lady, I can't believe Lord Tristan had the nerve to marry his mistress to his steward. And that poor child. What kind of a life will Kristina have? My lady, you've married a monster.'

Briefly, Francesca closed her eyes. 'It is not your place to judge him. Mari, when you were walking past the solar, was anyone else in earshot?'

Mari gave a firm headshake. 'No.'

Not entirely convinced, Francesca reached for Mari's hand and tugged her to her feet. 'I beg you not to rush to judgement. You don't know everything.'

Mari gave her a sour look. 'I do know when a man is spinning yarns, and that man is a deceiver.'

Francesca hung the drying cloth on a hook. 'For the sake of little Kristina, I would ask you to set your antipathy aside.'

Mari's eyes widened. 'You feel sympathy for his bastard?'

'Kristina is an innocent. Mari, listen. Everyone in the castle believes Sir Roparz is her father, and with good reason. My lord has enemies who wouldn't hesitate to use that child to bend him to their will.'

'And if people think she's Sir Roparz's daughter, she'd be safe?'

'Exactly. So I need to ask you again, do you think anyone else overheard what was said in the solar?'

'No, my lady, it's not possible. Until you came on to the landing, I was the only one about.'

Francesca let out a breath. 'Thank heaven. Mari, I want you to swear—on your mother's soul—that you will tell no one else what you heard. As far as you are concerned, Sir Roparz is Kristina's father.'

Mari gave a brusque nod. 'Very well, my lips are sealed. I wasn't anywhere near the solar. I heard nothing.'

'And one thing further...'

'My lady?'

'There is to be no more listening at doors.'

Mari's cheeks went crimson and she hung her head. 'I am sorry, my lady, it won't happen again.'

Francesca smiled and held out her comb. 'Thank you. Please help me with my hair, and then we had better go downstairs. A little girl is lost and our help will be needed.'

Mari took the comb and gave a slight nod. 'Of course, my lady.'

Francesca asked for directions to the steward's office, and when they got there, they found it empty. She stood in the corridor, biting her lip, wondering where Sir Roparz might be when a passing maidservant saw them.

The maidservant bobbed her a curtsy. 'May I help you, my lady?'

'Thank you, yes.' Tristan had mentioned going to the village in search of his daughter and in his absence Francesca thought to offer Sir Roparz her help. He knew the castle, he would know where she might look. 'I was hoping to speak to Sir Roparz.'

'He's in the guardhouse, my lady, directing the search for Kristina. Shall I show you the way?'

'Thank you, we should like to help. What is your name?'

'Adèle, my lady.'

Francesca and Mari followed Adèle through the hall. Servants were rushing this way and that, calling the child's name.

'Kristina? Kristina!'

Clearly, every able-bodied person in the castle was looking for Kristina. Page boys were flinging back coffer lids, doubtless fearing that the little girl had climbed inside and become trapped. Cupboards were being turned out, pots and linens were strewn every which way.

'Kristina? *Kristina!*' The castle walls echoed. 'Kristina? *Kristina!*'

Outside, the bailey was a whirl of activity. Horses were being led out of the stables and grooms were combing through the empty stalls, calling the child's name. On the castle walls, pairs of men-at-arms paraded up and down the wall walk—one with his eyes trained on the bailey whilst his fellow studied the cliffs and paths outside the castle.

The wind was brisk. Tristan's standard streamed from the topmost tower and Francesca could taste salt on her tongue. Beneath the cacophony of men shouting orders and of stable boys calling for Kristina came a subtler sound—the eternal beat of the waves on the rocks beneath the castle.

When they reached the gatehouse, Adèle pointed to a door at the top of a short run of steps. 'You'll find Sir Roparz up there, my lady.'

The door was ajar. Smiling her thanks, Francesca started up the steps. At the top, she looked back. 'Mari, please wait in the courtyard.'

'Yes, my lady.'

In the guardhouse, a harassed-looking Sir Roparz was scowling at a mail-clad soldier.

'Kristina wasn't in the chapel, captain?' Sir Roparz asked.

'No, sir.'

'You asked Father Paol if he'd seen her?'

'I did, and I'm sorry, sir, Father Paol hasn't seen your daughter since supper last eve. No one has.' The captain hesitated, a pleat in his brow. 'Sir Roparz, we have searched her usual hiding places.

The kitchens, the stables, everywhere. I'd swear on my mother's life Kristina isn't in the castle. Perhaps Lord Tristan will find her in the village.'

Sir Roparz rubbed his brow. 'We'll search again, captain, everywhere.'

The captain blinked. 'Even where we have just looked?'

'Every nook and every cranny. Everywhere.'

'Very good, sir.' The captain saluted.

Francesca stood aside as the captain tramped out.

Sir Roparz lifted a helmet from a hook on the wall and tucked it under his arm. His smile was strained. 'My lady, if you are looking for Count Tristan, he's down in the village. I am about to join him. If you like, I can relay him a message.'

The tension in Sir Roparz's face told Francesca more than words ever could. Tristan's steward loved Kristina as though she were his. She shook her head. 'I'm not looking for Tristan, Sir Roparz. I'd like to help. I know I am new to des Iles, but there must be something I can do.'

Sir Roparz scrubbed his face. 'That is kind of you, my lady. However, you're unfamiliar with the lie of the land, you won't know where to begin.'

Francesca touched his sleeve. 'There must be something.'

He drummed his fingers on the top of his helmet and regarded her thoughtfully. 'Aye, there is, but it might be awkward. I am not sure I can ask it of you.'

'Please go on, sir. I am anxious to help.'

'It's my wife. She's in the chapel making her confession to Father Paol.'

Francesca struggled to keep her face clear of emotion. 'Aye?'

'I shall be taking a small troop of horse soldiers into the village to aid Tristan in the search, and I may be some while. I don't want Esmerée to be on her own when she's finished her confession. She's close to her time and—'

'You would like me to keep Lady Esmerée company whilst you are in the village?' It was the last thing Francesca wanted to do. Hearing that Lady Esmerée had borne Tristan a child had knocked her back, she wasn't really ready to face the woman. However, Sir Roparz stood before her, fingers drumming on his helmet and a tight pleat in his brow. Francesca's chest ached. She hardly knew the man, but it was obvious he was deeply concerned about his wife, it would be churlish to refuse him.

'If you could, my lady.'

Francesca thrust her misgivings to one side and managed a smile. 'Of course.'

Face clearing, Sir Roparz jammed on his helmet. 'Thank you. Esmerée will be out of her mind with worry and I don't want anything to happen to the new baby.'

'You may rely on me,' Francesca said. It wouldn't be easy, she would have to keep a tight rein on her hurt if she wasn't to add to Lady Esmerée's distress. She would do it though, Lady Esmerée surely had enough to worry about without her adding to her woes.

Sir Roparz held her gaze for a long moment. 'Thank you again, my lady, you are grace itself.' With a bow, he gestured for Francesca to precede him back into the bailey.

Mari was standing in a patch of sunlight, watching as the last cask of wine was offloaded from a merchant's waggon.

'That cart's from Champagne,' Mari said, as the carter, a brawny, unkempt man with messy hair and beard, shouldered the cask and bore it into the hall.

'Oh?' Francesca hardly heard her, she glanced abstractedly at the cart before her gaze settled on the chapel, a neat stone building with Romanesque arches. A gold-painted cross glinted in the sun.

Saints, what was she to say to Lady Esmerée? She wrapped her arms about her waist. She wanted answers to a thousand questions and not one could be posed to a woman whose daughter had gone missing.

Lady Esmerée, when did you tell Sir Roparz you were carrying Tristan's child?

Do you love Sir Roparz?

How long have you known my husband? Did you love him? Do you love him still?

Did you know you were carrying Tristan's child when he and I were married?

With an effort, Francesca shoved the questions to the back of her mind. Lady Esmerée needed comfort, not an interrogation, which meant that Francesca ought to ensure that others were present when she spoke to her. That way, she would be less likely to blurt out something untoward.

'Mari, would you recognise Lady Esmerée's maid?'

'I think so.'

'Lady Esmerée has need of her. Please be so good as to fetch her. Bring her to the chapel porch.'

'We shall be joining Lady Esmerée in the chapel, my lady?'

Francesca nodded. 'She is near her time and Kristina's disappearance has her desperately worried. Sir Roparz doesn't want her left alone.'

'Very good, my lady.'

Mari headed back to the castle entrance. Francesca leaned against a wall, closed her eyes and turned her face to the sun. Had Kristina been found? If she had gone to the village, surely the villagers would look out for a little girl—especially if they believed her to be the daughter of the castle steward? Lord, she hoped so.

Heavy footsteps approached the waggon. A horse stamped his hoof and a sudden shifting of air made her open her eyes. The carter stood before her. His expression was so cold it seemed to steal the heat from the sun. And he was standing too close for comfort, so close Francesca could tell what he had been eating last eve. Onions. Garlic. Stiffening, she pushed away from the wall.

'You are Lady Francesca?' His voice was uninterested, but there was a calculating gleam in his eyes.

Francesca's heart skipped several beats and she found herself glancing up at the wall to check that the guards remained close at hand. She told herself not to be so jumpy, she was surely safe in Tristan's bailey.

'I am.'

The carter gave an ugly smile and leaned in. 'My, my, what a stroke of luck. We hoped to find you quickly, but we didn't expect to do so when delivering the first consignment.'

Goosebumps rose on Francesca's arms. Overhead, a gull mewed and the guards went on pounding the wall walk. Drawing a deep breath, she was about to summon help when a large hand clamped over her mouth.

With a jerk, the carter pulled her into the shadows between the waggon and the wall. 'Be calm. If you want the knight's brat to live, be calm. We wouldn't want you to do anything that might make us hurt her, would we?'

Francesca didn't move a muscle. Saints, Kristina *had* been kidnapped. Her mind raced. It hadn't escaped her that the carter had referred to Kristina as the knight's brat. *Dieu merci*, the kidnappers must believe Roparz to be her father. That had to be a good thing. On the other hand, what had they done to her? The poor child must be terrified.

Francesca held the carter's gaze and tried to peel his hand from her mouth. This man was in league with Tristan's enemies, she was sure. Was he taking orders from Sir Joakim?

The carter glanced briefly over his shoulder, he was probably checking that they remained unobserved. 'You won't cry out?'

Francesca shook her head and the carter's hand

lifted, though he kept a vice-like hold of her wrist. She kept her voice low. 'You have Kristina?'

The carter gave a slight nod.

'Where is she? What have you done with her?'

'She's safe.' The carter's eyes were cold as stones. 'She does a lot of screeching, we've taken her where no one can hear her. Still, we shouldn't expect a spoilt knight's brat to be brave.'

An image of Kristina, huddled and frightened, flashed into Francesca's mind. 'You devil, she's little more than a baby.' The man shifted closer, bringing with him the smell of onions. She noticed that he was missing several of his teeth.

'You want to help her, my lady?'

'Of course!'

Keeping her fast by her wrist, the carter plucked a filthy strip of leather from his belt.

Backing up against the wall, Francesca eyed it suspiciously. 'What's that for?'

His grin chilled her to her core. 'There'll be no screeching from you.'

He was going to gag her! Francesca looked him firmly in the eye. 'I want to help Kristina, I give you my word I will not cry out.'

'Your word has no currency with me, *ma dame*.' An oilcloth served as a door at the back of the waggon, the man's lip curled as he shoved it aside. 'Shut up and get in.'

Heart in her mouth, Francesca climbed into the cart. The carter followed.

Empty of its cargo, the bed of the waggon was littered with straw and dirty sacking. It was very gloomy. Francesca peered through the murk at the cold gleam of the man's eyes. The idea of being gagged made the hairs rise on the back of her neck.

He gave her a nasty grin. 'My lady, you will be silenced. Behave, and we'll send the girl back safe and sound. Otherwise, that knight won't be seeing his whelp again.' He made a slicing gesture across his throat and shrugged. 'Makes no difference to me either way.'

Francesca soon discovered the carter wasn't working alone. As the waggon rattled through the castle gates, another man lifted the oilcloth and vaulted into the back. With lank hair and a rank, unwashed stink about him, he was no more prepossessing than his accomplice. Francesca sat on some straw and sacking and hung her head, trying to look defeated. With luck, the man would dismiss her as harmless.

That these men were outlaws, she had no doubt. It was chilling to discover they had been looking for her, specifically for her. What were they planning? The only ray of light in this was that they had no idea that Kristina was Tristan's daughter.

Despite the straw, every rut in the road rattled her teeth. She tried to recall the lie of the land, resolving to at least try to imagine where on the road they might be. That swaying must mean they had reached the turn in the road just before the gatehouse. She could hear the shriek of gulls and the hushing of the waves.

Abruptly the waggon stopped. She frowned. They couldn't have got far, no more than a few dozen yards.

The carter's accomplice shifted and it was then that she noticed he was holding a small flask. Francesca's skin crawled. Too small to contain wine or ale, it looked like the sort of medicine bottle one might buy from an apothecary. A filthy hand reached for her. She jerked back, but the side of the waggon bit into her spine, there was nowhere to go.

The gag was wrenched from her and before she knew it the carter's accomplice had firm hold of her nose. He was a large man and he overpowered her shamefully easily. He shoved her on to her back and, using his knees, he pinned her in place.

'Let go of me! What are you—'

The mouth of the flask was pushed against her lips. 'Open up, my lovely.'

Francesca tried to resist. She clenched her jaw and kept her lips firmly together, except she couldn't do that for long, the grip on her nose was merciless. *I can't breathe!* The man's smile was cruel. Her lungs began to ache; her heart pounded; her head swam.

'Come on, my lovely.' His smile widened, the brute was enjoying this. 'Admit defeat or suffocate.'

Francesca held on until her lungs were at bursting point. Black spots danced in front of her eyes. She gulped in a breath and snapped her mouth shut. She was too slow. A sickly bittersweet fluid coated her tongue and trickled down her throat. What was it, poppy juice? Whatever it was, it must have been expensive. Such potions weren't available to everyone. She coughed again and immediately felt the cold press of the flask against her lips.

A callous laugh filled the shadowy interior. 'That's it, my pretty.'

Francesca sucked in another mouthful of air and more bittersweet liquid slipped down her throat. Her head swam. The straw rustled. Something was drumming against the bed of the waggon. Vaguely, she realised it was her heels.

A few more minutes of this treatment and her

vision blurred. The drumming slowed, the black spots melted into one other and her limbs turned to lead. Darkness engulfed her.

Chapter Thirteen

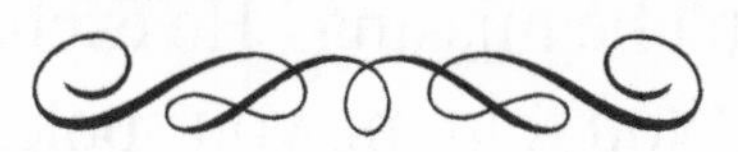

Back in the bailey, Tristan reined in and dismounted smartly. At his side, Roparz did the same. Their hearts were heavy, neither the villagers nor the fishermen had seen Kristina.

Tristan's boots had barely hit the ground before the captain of his guard hurtled down the guardhouse steps, his face creased with worry.

'Captain, you've news? You've found Kristina?'

'I'm sorry, *mon seigneur*, we haven't. We've combed through the entire castle several times. Kristina is not in des Iles.' The captain squared his shoulders. He seemed to be having difficulty looking Tristan in the eye. 'My lord, I'm afraid there's more bad news. I have to tell you that Countess Francesca is missing.'

Tristan's veins turned to ice. 'Francesca, missing?' Vaguely, he was aware of handing Flint over to Bastian. He dragged off his helmet. 'What do you mean she's missing?'

The captain gulped. '*Mon seigneur*, her maid alerted us when she couldn't find her.'

Tristan stared, he couldn't seem to take it in. 'Francesca can't be missing.' He exchanged glances with Roparz. 'You told me you spoke to her before you met me in the village.'

'So I did. I was concerned for Esmerée and asked the countess to speak to her.'

'Where was Esmerée?'

'She was in the chapel when I left to join you.'

Tristan looked at his captain. 'I take it you've searched the chapel?'

'Of course, my lord. After the countess's maid told us Lady Francesca had also vanished, it was the first place we looked. Father Paol hadn't seen her and Lady Esmerée said the last time she saw your wife was earlier this morning, in the solar. My lord, as far as we can see, Lady Francesca has left the castle.'

Roparz gave Tristan a bleak look. 'Hell burn it, Tristan. What is going on?'

Cold sweat trickled down Tristan's back. *Fear.* First Kristina and now Francesca. He strode towards the guardhouse, Roparz and the captain at his heels. 'The two disappearances have to be linked.'

Francesca would never have gone on her own. She'd been shocked and hurt that he hadn't told her about Kristina, and she might yet decide to push for an annulment, but he knew her and she wouldn't dream of leaving without first bidding him farewell.

'I agree,' Roparz said. '*Mon Dieu*, what do we do?'

'We wait, my friend. If I am not mistaken, we will shortly be receiving a ransom demand.'

Tossing his helmet on to the guardhouse table, Roparz met his gaze. 'Kerjean is behind this?'

'I'd stake my life he is involved.' Tristan strode up and down and wished he had more to go on. Where had Francesca and Kristina been taken? Were they together? Were they safe? Conscious of the captain hovering anxiously at his elbow, he picked his words with care. 'Roparz, what I can't fathom is how Kerjean found out about Kristina. We were so careful.'

With a sidelong glance at the captain, Roparz's reply was equally guarded. 'It certainly is a mystery.'

'Captain, find the countess's maid, would you? I'd like to speak to her.'

'Yes, my lord. The maid did mention that when

she left the countess in the bailey, a consignment of wine was being delivered.'

'Wine?' Roparz frowned. 'I didn't order any wine, the cellars are full.'

The captain cleared his throat. 'The carter told the guards it was a gift, Sir Roparz.'

'A gift?'

'Aye, from Count Henry of Champagne.'

Tristan swore. 'That wine is not from Count Henry, Joakim must have arranged this. Captain, find Mari, would you? She might have noticed something else.'

'At once, my lord.'

'Bring her to the steward's office, Sir Roparz and I will be in there. Come, Roparz, we have letters to write.'

'You're alerting Baron Rolland?'

'Not only Baron Rolland. Roparz, I suspect there is more to this than the kidnapping of two people dear to my heart. The peace of the Duchy is again at risk. We must rally the troops, Kerjean cannot be allowed to start bonfires all over Brittany.'

Francesca woke shivering. All was dark. And cold, deep cold, her skin was nothing but goose-bumps.

Where am I?

Her first thought was that she must be outside, then she realised that, overhead, an awning of some kind was flapping in a brisk wind. And the dark wasn't total, beyond the awning she could see stars. She was in a crude shelter, under a coarse blanket.

Her head was pounding and her mind was muzzy. When she moved her hand to rub her brow, the ache intensified. Stifling a groan, she closed her eyes and lay still, trying to orient herself. The ground was hard. Lumpy. Tentative exploration revealed that the walls of the shelter were made out of rough stone blocks and, save for the awning, the roof was open to the elements. She seemed to be alone.

What had happened?

Events flooded back in a painful, gut-twisting rush. Kristina—Tristan's daughter, for heaven's sake—had disappeared. The face of the carter from Champagne swam into her mind's eye. Oddly, she caught a faint whiff of onions, garlic and stale sweat. Was he close by? She shuddered. It was surprising her hands were free, her kidnappers must have been confident the drug—whatever it was—would do its work. Her lips worked. The taste of the bittersweet liquid lingered on her tongue. Her mouth tasted sour and her throat was parched.

A salty scent was sharp in her nostrils. Nearby, waves were smashing against rocks and she could hear the suck and drag of the sea shifting shingle. Wherever she was, she was by the shore. Her heart lifted. Perhaps she wasn't far from des Iles.

She stared at the stars beyond the awning and a shadow in the shape of a man moved across them. She lifted her head. The man's features were lost in the dark, but she knew who it must be.

Pushing upright, she tried to swallow. 'Sir Joakim?' Her voice sounded rusty.

'Lady Francesca, how lovely, you are awake.' He laughed. 'I've been looking forward to renewing our acquaintance.'

'Where is Kristina? What have you done with her?'

The shadow that was Joakim Kerjean moved closer. 'The brat's behind you in the corner.'

Thrusting the blanket aside, Francesca scrambled through the dark, so anxious to reach Kristina, she didn't care that she was crawling. When a jagged rock cut into her knee, she barely noticed it. Her fingers encountered another blanket and a slight huddle of warmth. Kristina was curled up on her side.

Francesca gave her a gentle shake. 'Kristina?' The child didn't move, she didn't as much as murmur. Sitting back, Francesca pulled her on to her lap and smoothed her hair out of her face. 'Kristina?'

Nothing.

Francesca curled her arms about Tristan's daughter and scowled through the dark at Sir Joakim. 'Have you hurt her?'

'She's fine.' The knight's voice was bored, careless. 'She was yelling her head off. Thought I'd use her to test a little of the potion I'd bought for you.'

Francesca felt a flare of anger. 'You drugged a child? What is that stuff?'

'I have no idea.'

'I would have thought you'd want to know what you were buying. Whatever it was, you must know the doses are different for children.'

'Are they?'

'You might have killed her!' Francesca laid the back of her hand against Kristina's face and felt the slow, steady huff of her breath. *Dieu merci*, she was alive. 'You'll send her back to des Iles?' Francesca's thoughts were still clouded, the after-effects of the potion, she supposed. She must remember to guard her tongue, it wouldn't do to betray Kristina's true parentage. 'Your man said you would return her to

Sir Roparz and Lady Esmerée if I came with him. Here I am. You are honour-bound to release her.'

Kerjean let out an amused snort. 'She can go back to her parents as soon as you sign a letter for me. It's only a formality, you understand, since I already have your seal.'

My ring! Francesca's heart shifted as she felt for Tristan's ring. It wasn't on her finger, Kerjean had stolen her ring! 'You, sir, are a thief.'

He let out a bark of laughter. 'I've been called far worse, I can assure you.' His tone went hard. 'My dear lady, you will sign that letter.'

'If you have my husband's seal, you don't need my signature.'

'I want your lord husband to be in no doubt that we have you in person, and that you are alive. I have a proposition for him and I suspect he will respond more favourably if he is aware that I have you entirely at my mercy.'

Sir Joakim's statement made hideous sense. Francesca swallowed hard, her throat felt as though it was full of thistles. 'I must have something to drink.'

She heard a grunt and the shadow moved away. 'We have ale. One moment.' Sir Joakim left the shelter.

Whilst he was gone, Francesca adjusted Kristina's blanket and laid her gently on the ground. With a sigh, she leaned back against the wall, absently rubbing her empty ring finger. She felt hollow inside, she'd worn Tristan's ring every day since her marriage and she felt naked without it. Lost.

Kerjean's footsteps crunched away. Francesca stared at the stars beyond the awning and willed her mind to clear.

'Biel!' The wind threw Sir Joakim's words into the shelter. 'Fetch ale. And food. We must look after our hostage, she is valuable.'

I am a hostage.

The footsteps returned, the stars vanished and that dark shape—it was like looking at a demon—was crouching before her. Then came a metallic creak and a pale glow illuminated Sir Joakim's face, he had brought a lantern with him and had opened the shutter. His yellow hair looked as though it had been gilded. The lantern light also revealed the awning above them to be a sail. Yes, it had definitely been a sail. Staring at the sail, something shifted in Francesca's mind. She knew exactly where they were.

'We're on an island in the bay.' She placed her palm on the crude stone wall. 'This is Hermit's Rock. You brought us over by boat?'

'Clever girl.'

'You're a fool if you think you can get away with this. How many men can you call on? Half a dozen? A dozen? Tristan has a whole garrison. Most of the villagers are fishermen—this island will be surrounded in no time.'

The fair head shook. 'No, it won't. When Count Tristan understands we have you as our honoured guest, dear lady, I can assure you that he will fall in with our plans. In this letter, I ask him to come alone. If he wants to see you alive, he will do as I ask.' Sir Joakim yawned. 'I tire of this conversation. Here.' An ale skin was thrust into her hand. 'Drink.'

Removing the stopper, Francesca took a suspicious sniff. 'I've had enough poison for one day, how do I know you haven't doctored it?'

With a sound of exasperation, Sir Joakim snatched the ale skin back. 'It's safe.' He took a long swallow. 'See?'

With a nod, Francesca took the ale from him and drank deep. It was surprisingly refreshing and she drank as much as she could. It might be some time before she was offered more.

A scroll was waved in front of her. She stoppered the ale skin and set it aside.

'Sign this,' Sir Joakim said.

Parchment crackled as it was unrolled. Seeing a dark, round blob at the bottom, Francesca touched it. Sealing wax. She let out a sigh. 'You've already been free with my ring. This is Tristan's seal.'

'Sign, damn you.'

'You swear on your knightly oath, you will send the child home?'

White teeth grinned though the dark. 'My dear lady, I swear. We simply await your co-operation.'

'She will not be harmed?'

'The brat will not be harmed. Sign.'

An inkpot and quill were set before her. Francesca spread the parchment on her knees and scrawled her name at the bottom, next to Tristan's seal.

'Thank you, dear lady,' Sir Joakim said. The document rustled as he took it from her. 'Next, I must ask you to unbind your hair.'

Francesca stiffened. 'What?'

'Be calm, I have no designs on your virtue. A lock of your hair will be one final proof that you are *entirely* within my power.' A silver blade glinted in the lamplight. 'Hurry up.'

Francesca reached for her plait.

As dawn pushed back the night, Francesca stood in the entrance of the ruined hermitage, wrapped in a blanket to keep out the worst of the wind. During the night, thick clouds had rolled in and the sun was lost behind them. Scant feet away, waves hissed and frothed as they rushed past the tiny island on their way to the shore. The smell of woodsmoke mingled with the briny tang of the sea. Her captors had lit a small fire in the shelter and a trail of smoke rose into the air before being whisked away by the wind. Presumably, with Francesca known to be their hostage, the outlaws could afford to be bold.

She gazed at the cliffs. The tide was in and white spume rose and fell at the foot. Higher up, the castle walls seemed to melt into the grey of the sky. It wasn't yet light enough for her to see Tristan's standard.

By now, Kristina would be safely back with her mother. Tristan would be relieved.

How would he react to Sir Joakim's summons? Sir Joakim seemed certain Tristan would arrive soon, Francesca wasn't so sure. It wouldn't be sensible for Tristan to put himself at risk in such a way.

What will he do?

She fingered her empty ring finger as she stared at the entrance to the harbour. She didn't like to think about what might happen to her if Tristan didn't come, but she didn't want him to do anything rash. Surely he would be sensible. Surely he would stay away.

The wind tugged at her blanket as she stood there, staring.

Shortly after dawn, a small fishing boat nosed out of the harbour and sailed out into the bay.

Tristan sat in the stern and pinned his gaze on Hermit's Rock.

What were they doing to her? Was she safe? Absently, he touched his pouch, the pouch in which he'd put that dark twist of hair. One moment he'd been thanking God that Kristina was safe and the next…

Mon Dieu, Tristan had faced some bleak reversals in his life, but when he'd cracked the seal on the letter and that lock of Francesca's hair had fallen out, he'd gone weak at the knees.

Sir Joakim had Francesca.

Had those bastards hurt her? Sweet Lord, let her be safe.

Tristan had galloped straight to the village. He'd hauled two fishermen—Ivon and Alan—from their beds. He'd been deaf to every objection.

'Think, Tristan, it's clearly a trap,' Roparz had

said. 'We need a plan. Racing alone into the mouth of hell will achieve nothing.'

Tristan's mind had room for only one thought. 'I can't abandon Francesca.'

'*Mon Dieu*, man, no one is asking you to abandon her. Hermit's Rock is a small island, we can surely surround it. There are plenty of boats in the village and you have an entire troop at your command. Capturing a handful of outlaws should be child's play.'

An image of Francesca lying bloodied and still on the shingle had flashed into Tristan's mind. He had stared at that dark lock of hair before shoving it into his pouch. 'Kerjean wants to negotiate. He will kill her if we try anything else. I won't put her at risk, I have to see what he wants.'

The trouble was, Tristan knew only too well what Kerjean was after. The man was using Francesca to drum up support for the disbanded rebel alliance. Doubtless he needed money to tide him over until more men could be persuaded to rally under his banner.

'There's no need to rush into things,' Roparz had said. 'I urge caution. You've sent word to Rennes, surely it makes sense to wait until reinforcements arrive? We can negotiate then.'

'To hell with sense.' Tristan hadn't listened, he

couldn't. He was haunted by that image of Francesca lying motionless on the shingle. Had Kerjean hurt her?

And now, even though he was grimly aware that his actions were dictated by passion rather than reason, Tristan was sitting in Ivon's boat with the smell of fish filling his nostrils as the fishermen set the sail.

'Going to be a storm,' Ivon muttered, jerking his head in the direction of a mass of dark clouds.

Tristan grunted, his gaze never shifting from the rock in the bay. He hoped to hell he wasn't too late. The sail bellied out with the wind and the little vessel surged into the grey, heaving waters.

After what seemed like an eternity, Tristan leapt out of the boat and on to Hermit's Rock.

'Thanks, friends, wait here.' He drew his sword.

Kerjean was waiting in front of the ruined hermitage, hand clamped round Francesca's arm. She didn't appear to be hurt, although her skin was pale and her eyes looked enormous. Relief flooded through him. Tristan strode towards them, his boots crunching through a patch of shingle. He couldn't take his gaze off Francesca. Her veil had gone and her hair streamed like a dark pennon in the wind.

Her lips pursed, her eyes were as stormy as the sky. 'You shouldn't have come.'

He made his voice light. 'Thought you might need to know that I reply to letters when I get them.'

The faintest of smiles lifted the corner of her mouth. 'None the less, you shouldn't have come.'

Sir Joakim jerked his head at the fishing boat rocking up and down on the shoreline. 'Those men are unarmed?'

'They are fishermen, Kerjean. They have knives. They gut things.' He sighed. 'Look, you have a proposition to put to me, get on with it. What do you want?'

'It's quite simple, my lord, I want you to join us.'

Tristan hoped the surprise didn't show, he was under the impression that he was here to pay a ransom for Francesca's freedom. 'You don't want money?'

'Gold is always welcome, my lord. If you want to support us in that way, I won't stop you. However, I was hoping to persuade you to join our cause. With your backing, others will soon join us.'

Tristan snorted. 'You're insane, Kerjean, the alliance is dead.'

'Is it?'

Pointedly, Tristan glanced about. 'Face it, you've

been chased from the mainland and all that is left to you is a barren rock on the edge of the ocean. I doubt you can muster a dozen men. This is your last, desperate stand. It will fail.'

'It won't fail if you join us.'

Kerjean's fingers were white on Francesca's arm, he had to be hurting her. Tristan reined in his anger and prayed he looked calmer than he felt. In truth, he was watching Kerjean like a hawk, waiting for the slightest sign of weakness.

'Why in hell should I join you?'

Kerjean's fair hair lifted in the wind. 'With you as our ally, our fortunes would turn. More men would rally to our cause.'

'What cause?'

'The cause of freedom, le Beau.'

'Freedom?' Tristan gripped his sword. He was finding it increasingly hard to hang on to his temper. 'Anarchy, more like. Your so-called alliance has never been more than a gang of robber barons. Duchess Constance is a minor and you and your friends have been taking advantage of that for years.'

'We have no quarrel with the duchess, le Beau, we question the rule of that foreign king and his puppet. In my opinion, you made a grave error supporting Baron Rolland.'

'I don't give a damn for your opinion. I support the rule of law. Always have, always will. Kerjean, however you dress it, you and your cronies don't fight for anyone's good but your own. You're a bunch of outlaws.' Tristan felt a muscle tick in his cheek. 'I work for Brittany. You work to feather your nest and to hell with everyone else. You and your accomplices are nothing more than a pack of wolves. You want to tear the duchy limb from limb. You will fail.'

A seagull shot past them, heading for the cliffs. With a sly smile, Kerjean shifted his grip on Francesca and captured a trailing length of hair. With slow deliberation, he wound it around his wrist. 'I am surprised you defend yourself in so passionate a fashion, Lord Tristan. I really did hope that you would join us.'

Tristan's gaze flickered briefly to Francesca. Her eyes had never seemed so large, nor her face so pale. It came to him that even with a tattered blanket wrapped around her, she was the most beautiful woman in the world. He would do anything to save her.

'This is lunacy, Kerjean. For God's sake, release my wife. Put her back in the hermitage. We can talk just as easily with Francesca in the shelter.'

'I think not.' Pulling Francesca by her hair, Kerjean reeled her in until her body touched his. 'She is my security, and in any case I enjoy having her close. It's a pity you won't join us though. There I was, thinking you'd be certain to follow in your father's footsteps.'

Tristan felt himself frown. 'What are you talking about?'

'Didn't you know?' Kerjean sneered. 'Count Bedwyr was one of us. He supported the cause.'

For a moment it seemed that the wind stopped blowing, everything went still. Then another gull flew shrieking past them and the steady beat of the waves resumed. A gust of wind lifted the edge of Francesca's blanket.

Tristan took in a deep breath of salty air. 'Don't be ridiculous.'

'Your father was one of our most valued allies.'

'You, sir, are a liar.' Tristan almost went for Kerjean's throat, it took all his willpower to resist. 'Hell burn it, release my wife.'

Kerjean looped his arm about Francesca's waist, pinning her tight against him. 'In good time, my lord. First, I would have your answer. Will you join us? I am anxious to put this unpleasantness behind us.'

'My father would never side with thieves and traitors.'

A blond eyebrow lifted. 'You are mistaken, my lord. Count Bedwyr joined the alliance shortly after your mother died.'

Kerjean's statement gave Tristan pause. His father had, by all accounts, been beside himself after his mother's death. Who knew what a man might do when out of his mind with grief? Doubt balled in Tristan's gut—when all was said and done, how well had he known his father?

Kerjean twisted the knife. 'How far would your precious English prince trust you if he knew you were the son of a traitor? Would you still have a county to call your own?'

Ugly words. Words that couldn't be true. As they washed over him, Tristan felt a niggle of doubt. Never in a thousand years would he have imagined that his father would kill himself. Yet he had done so. Could his father have joined the alliance?

Never, that never would have happened.

Tristan put iron in his voice. 'You're bluffing. How would you know? Firstly, you're too young to remember. I myself was only a lad and you're younger than I. Secondly, I doubt there's anyone else in your ragbag so-called alliance who can remember that far back.'

'I have it from a reputable source, my lord.'

The wind blew Tristan's hair into his eyes. Impatiently, he shoved it back, it was sticky with salt. 'Kerjean, this is ridiculous. Join you? The answer's no. Release my wife.'

'I don't think so.' Sir Joakim shrugged. 'Very well, my lord, I accept you won't join us. It was a long shot, I admit. However, there is another way you can help.'

Tristan laughed. 'You've nerve, I'll give you that. Kerjean, I am not going to help you in any way whatsoever.'

Kerjean gave a thin smile and shifted his hold on Francesca. His hand moved and suddenly there was a knife pressed against her throat. 'We'll see. I want a ship. The vessel that brought us to this benighted isle is fine for hugging the shore, but it is hardly seaworthy. We need a proper seagoing vessel.'

Tristan felt his eyebrows snap together. 'You marooned yourself on this island, you can rot here for all I care.'

'A ship, Lord Tristan, is surely not too much to ask.' Sir Joakim gave an oily smile. 'Since I have your lady at my mercy. *Olivier! Biel!*'

Two thugs appeared from nowhere. The blood beat in Tristan's ears. Francesca was still as a statue, her face was strained, yet she remained calm. Thank God she was a level-headed woman. 'Release. My. Wife.'

'Give me a ship and you need never see me again.'

Tristan didn't reply. *Stay calm, my heart. A few moments more and we shall be out of this.*

'If you are not going to see sense, le Beau, I shall have to change your mind.' Kerjean dropped the knife and his sword scraped clear of its scabbard.

His own sword in hand, Tristan lunged forward. He must take care. Francesca was struggling to twist away from Kerjean, but the man hadn't let go of her hair. She couldn't get away, she was too close to Kerjean's sword.

Tristan's heart thumped. He was about to make the most delicate manoeuvre of his life, nothing less than precision would serve. Utter precision. 'Forgive me, my heart,' he said. Quick as lightning, he sliced at her hair.

Francesca gasped, tumbled to the rocks and scrambled out of harm's way. For a moment Tristan couldn't breathe. There she was, lying on the rocks exactly as he had imagined earlier. Except—*Dieu merci*, there was no blood, just the appalling desecration of her head shorn of that beautiful mass of hair.

Kerjean, gaping with shock, stood stock-still,

an untidy hank of black hair in one hand and his sword in the other.

Tristan pushed the sight of Francesca running her fingers through her shorn locks out of his mind and stepped within fighting distance of Sir Joakim. 'You have a choice, Kerjean. A fair fight, or surrender. Which is it to be?'

Kerjean's mouth curled into a sneer. 'My lord, you must have forgotten, you are outnumbered here.'

Tristan beckoned him forward. 'Very well, if it's a fight you're after, I'm your man.'

Francesca rose shakily to her feet, staggered to a large rock and leaned against it. Tristan's blue eyes gleamed, bright and determined. Francesca was no expert on hand-to-hand combat, but even she could see that Tristan's stance was firm, and the grip on his sword unwavering. He and Sir Joakim were slowly circling each other.

At a guess, she would say that Sir Joakim was reluctant to engage. Each time Tristan pressed closer, Kerjean skipped sideways. If he continued, it wouldn't be long before he ended up with wet feet, he was very close to the water.

'Biel?' Sir Joakim's voice was tight with anxiety, his men had slunk away. '*À moi!* To me! Olivier?

Pierrick!' Eyes hunted, he glanced frantically at the hermitage.

No one appeared. Sir Joakim's cronies, if they hadn't already put to sea, were apparently content to remain out of sight. Kerjean swore under his breath, and Tristan and he continued their unnerving, circuitous dance for the advantage.

Tristan was the taller of the two and that should surely give him the advantage in terms of reach. His shoulders were broader and he exuded confidence. He made a testing pass.

Sir Joakim sidestepped.

Tristan made another pass. Sweat gleamed on Sir Joakim's brow. His heel splashed in the shallows. More swearing. Waves buffeted his calves.

The fishing boat Tristan had arrived in lay slightly offshore. Francesca caught her breath as Tristan made a gesture with his left hand and the fishermen reached for their oars. They were beaching the boat a few yards away, Tristan wasn't alone.

And there was more, Francesca had clear sight of the village and harbour. A flotilla of fishing boats was spread out across the bay, headed towards Hermit's Rock. Even better, Tristan's colours were flying from one of the masts. Francesca felt a smile form. With his back to the sea, Kerjean hadn't noticed the boats.

Tristan, on the other hand, had. 'Sir Roparz,' he murmured. His sword sliced through the air and Kerjean danced backwards. Tristan levelled his sword at Kerjean's throat. 'You don't watch your back,' he said, in a conversational tone that bordered on insulting. 'It's quite a weakness.'

Kerjean barked out a laugh and struck out wildly. Steel clashed against steel. Francesca could hardly breathe. Sword weaving this way and that, Tristan pressed harder, edging Sir Joakim inexorably into the shallows. The flotilla drew closer.

Tristan smiled. 'If I were you, Kerjean, I'd yield. I played on these islands as a boy and those rocks can be damned slippery.'

'God rot you.' Sir Joakim's sword swung wide. A wave splashed against him, he lost his footing and tumbled into the seething foam.

Chapter Fourteen

Thunder rolled overhead as Francesca hurried out of the rain and into the castle, the storm had finally broken.

Tristan kept close, his face was tight, she couldn't read him. Since leaving Hermit's Rock he hadn't let her out of his sight, even going so far as to ride back from the village with Francesca sitting before him on his saddle. Back in the bailey with rain falling all about them, he'd ordered Sir Roparz to escort Sir Joakim to the dungeon. Then he'd taken her firmly by the hand and had marched her out of the rain and into the hall.

A number of servants were working in the great hall—carrying logs, folding linen—and a small silence fell as everyone looked their way. Francesca had never felt less like a lady and she took care not to meet anyone's eyes. Her clothes were damp and stiff with salt; she was chilled to the bone and her skin itched. With her free hand, she clutched the coarse blanket tightly about her, she was using it as a veil to hide her shorn hair. Her ruined hair and bedraggled state would inevitably raise questions and she wasn't ready to deal with them. For the time being she was simply relieved to be free of Sir Joakim.

Tristan gestured at a maidservant. 'Where's Lady Francesca's maid?' he demanded.

'I believe she's in the solar, my lord.'

'Take my lady straight to our bedchamber. Then you may tell Mari that her mistress has need of her. My wife will want a fire and hot water to bathe in.'

The maidservant curtsied. 'Very good, *mon seigneur*.'

Tristan cupped Francesca's cheek with his hand. 'I shall join you once I have seen Kerjean under lock and key. Until later, my lady.'

Upstairs, Francesca huddled on a stool by the fire until she stopped shivering. She watched the flames and listened to the thunder as it moved slowly to the north.

Mari burst in. 'Oh, my lady, thank heavens you are all right. I didn't sleep a wink for worrying about you. What happened? Where have you been? Bastian said something about you passing the night on Hermit's Rock.' Pausing for breath, Mari grimaced at the blanket. 'And why have you got that filthy thing on your head?'

Mari plucked the blanket from her and her face fell. 'Oh, my lady, your hair, your poor hair.'

With a grimace, Francesca ran her hand through what was left of her hair. 'It's that bad?'

Mari's lips worked. 'What happened?'

The moment Tristan had lifted his sword was sharp in Francesca's mind. 'I was trapped by my hair, Lord Tristan cut me free.' A reminiscent shiver ran through her. It had been so close, she had actually felt a brush of air as the tip of his sword had flicked past her neck. The accuracy of that stroke was too unnerving to contemplate. If Tristan had misjudged it…

Mari stepped behind her and Francesca felt a gentle tug on her hair.

'It's not very ladylike,' Mari muttered. 'Far too short. And very messy. Would you like me to tidy it up?'

'Thank you, I am sure it looks hideous.'

'Honestly, that man.' Mari tutted. 'Was there no other way to free you? Did he have to chop off your hair?'

Francesca felt a smile form. 'He did his best. I am lucky Lord Tristan is a master swordsman, Sir Joakim didn't care whether I lived or died.'

Mari covered her mouth with her hand, her eyes were shiny with tears. 'Oh, my lady.'

Francesca rose from the stool and gave her a swift hug. 'Come, Mari, there is nothing to cry about. Lord Tristan and I are both safe, and my hair will soon grow. They will be bringing up the water soon, please help me disrobe. I am sticky with salt.'

There was much Francesca needed to resolve with Tristan. He must be made to understand that if their marriage had a future, he would have to abandon his penchant for secrets. Most importantly, there was Kristina and Esmerée.

Tristan had a child. Francesca had prayed to give him an heir, but in all their time together she had never quickened. Until learning about Kristina, it hadn't been something Francesca had really worried about. Yes, it had crossed her mind, but she'd kept faith that she would some day have his baby.

Learning about Kristina threw her relationship with Tristan into a different light. Clearly, Tristan had no problem fathering children. Again her thoughts plagued her. *What about me? Am I barren? Am I? If Tristan wants a legitimate heir, he might have to find a new wife.* The very idea of Tristan remarrying made her curl up inside.

Stiffening her spine, Francesca turned her back

to Mari so her gown could be unlaced. She and Tristan had much to sort out and she had no mind doing it looking like a drowned rat. When she next saw him, she needed to look presentable. At least as presentable as was possible, given what he had done to her hair.

Francesca was reluctant to leave the bedchamber after she had bathed. It wasn't that she was ashamed about her altered appearance, her reluctance stemmed from the fact that she was unsure of her ground as Tristan's countess. Until she knew where she stood, she would feel awkward among his retainers. And they would surely feel awkward with her. So, until she and Tristan had resolved matters, it was surely best she kept to the bedchamber.

She sat on her stool by the fire, talking to Mari. At length, brisk footsteps sounded on the stairs and the door opened. Tristan had a wine flask dangling from one hand and two silver goblets in the other. He set them on the side-table.

Francesca smiled at Mari. 'Thank you, Mari. That will be all.'

Gesturing for Mari to wait, Tristan locked eyes with Francesca. 'Adèle tells me you ate nothing at noon. Would you like Mari to send up a tray?'

'I had an apple and some bread earlier.'

He studied her, a slight frown between his eye-brows. 'That's not very sustaining.'

'I am not hungry, thank you.'

He nodded at Mari, who went out. 'What about wine? Would you like some?'

'Thank you.' Francesca's stomach was churning, wine might make this conversation easier. She drew in a breath and plunged straight in. 'How is Kristina coping after her ordeal?'

'Kristina seems fully recovered, she was eating the kitchens out of spiced buns when I last saw her.'

'I am glad to hear it. Tristan, when were you going to tell me that she is your daughter?'

He paused in the act of pouring the wine. 'I am sorry, my heart. I wanted to tell you. I thought you had enough to contend with after Count Myrrdin's death. It seemed wrong to burden you further. Here.' He handed her a goblet.

'Thank you.' Francesca sipped the wine as he drew up Mari's stool and sat down. She lowered her goblet and met his gaze straight on. 'Tristan, hearing about Kristina has disturbed me greatly. How could you keep her existence from me for so long? She's not an infant, she was born in the first year of our marriage—over three years ago. You could have told me about Kristina a number of times in the past three years and yet you did not.'

'I had my reasons.'

Francesca tapped the side of the goblet. 'You feared that if these alliance people learned Kristina was your daughter, they might use her against you.'

'That's it, exactly. *Bon sang*, Francesca, I had to keep her existence dark. You've seen for yourself what ruthless men can do. Kerjean's outlaws kidnapped Kristina not knowing she was my daughter—imagine what they might have done to her if they had known the truth.'

'None the less, you should have told me about her.'

He drew back. 'How could I? You said it yourself, if word got out that she was mine, she would have been a target for every outlaw in the duchy.'

'You didn't trust me.'

A pleat formed in his brow. 'That's not true, of course I trust you.'

'You didn't trust me three years ago.' Francesca swallowed hard. Despite the wine, her throat was dry. She gulped down another mouthful. 'I can understand that, I was young and untried and incredibly naive. We were practically strangers.' Leaning forward, she touched his hand. 'I'll have you know that Count Myrrdin had taught me about honour and discretion and loyalty, your secret would have been safe with me.'

Strong fingers gripped hers. 'My heart, I am sorry. A new husband and wife have a lot to learn about each other—and from each other. It takes time.'

She squared her shoulders and freed her hand. 'You didn't trust me after Kristina was born, just as you didn't trust me when you decided to bring me here after Papa's death. Tristan, we travelled together all the way from Champagne and I thought—hoped—that we were finally coming to understand each other. I thought our marriage had a chance. How wrong I was. Nothing has changed.'

Dark eyebrows came together in a deep frown. 'Everything's changed. What about those letters?'

Francesca took heart from the fact that Tristan looked more confused than angry. Firmly, she shook her head. 'Forget the letters, nothing has changed, deep down. If it had, you would have told me about Kristina. You still don't trust me.'

Blue eyes holding hers, Tristan set his goblet down on the matting and leaned his elbows on his knees. 'Francesca, I do trust you. I wanted to tell you about Kristina, indeed I knew it would be wrong for you to arrive here in ignorance. As I told you, in the wake of Count Myrrdin's death, it seemed cruel to burden you with yet more.' His mouth twisted. 'It was hard enough telling you about Esmerée, I was certain that telling you I had a daughter too would be a step too far. And then there was Kerjean—my fears that he would attempt to revive the alliance meant that Kristina was no longer as safe as I had hoped.

'Francesca, I swear I wanted to tell you. In truth, I was on the point of confessing all when we arrived at des Iles. Roparz counselled against it.'

Firelight played over the planes of Tristan's face, accentuating his sharp cheekbones and strong jaw. With a sigh, he leaned back and dug into his pouch. A signet ring—the ring he had given her on their wedding day, the one Sir Joakim had stolen—glittered in his palm. Finely sculpted lips twisted as he stared at it.

'Francesca, I am sorry if you think I misled you. I have made many mistakes in my life and doubtless I will make many more, but I have no regrets as far as our marriage is concerned.' Swallowing, he held out the ring. 'I need you to put this back where it belongs.'

Francesca searched his face. Her fingers itched to pick up the ring—her hand felt naked without it. However, he hadn't said a word about love. Perhaps he couldn't. 'Why?'

A line formed in his brow. 'I need you, Francesca.'

'You need heirs and you have decided I will suit you? Is that it? Tristan, have you considered this—what if I am barren? What if I cannot give you an heir? Would you still want me as your wife?'

'You're not barren.'

'You can't know that.' She looked sadly at him. 'You have fathered a child with Esmerée, but you and I— Tristan, we had all that time together, and nothing. What if I am barren?'

'We are young, Francesca, there is no rush.'

'Tristan, you cannot simply dismiss this. I could be barren and you need an heir.'

He sat very straight, the ring glittered in his palm. 'Francesca, you are overwrought. I do not for a moment believe you are barren and I refuse to discuss this further. You are my wife and you suit me, you suit me very well.' A dark eyebrow lifted and his voice changed, became tinged with laughter. 'Besides, you must realise by now that the idea of trying to get you with child has always held appeal.'

Taken with the urge to touch his cheek, she glanced swiftly away. He was simply too handsome. Never mind that he hadn't declared that he loved her, all she could think was that she wanted to be in his arms again. How could that be? 'Tristan, please don't.'

'What?'

'You're trying to seduce me and I shan't let you.'

He smiled. '*Dommage.* Pity.'

'It is true that we have never had problems with the carnal side of our marriage.' She tore her gaze from him and stared into the fire. 'Tristan, we won't be young for ever, what happens when our blood cools and the fever abates?'

'Francesca, you're my wife, wedding vows should last for life.'

'Even though the grand alliance that you hoped to forge with Fontaine has come to nothing? I bring you no lands. I am no one, Tristan.'

He shrugged. 'You suit me.'

'I suit you.' Francesca stared at the ring in his palm and swallowed. Her mind was in turmoil, save for one thing—she would like nothing better than to reach for the ring. Tristan seemed earnest about wanting to keep her as his wife and yet there had been no mention of love. 'I bring you no lands. I bring you nothing.'

She held her breath and waited. If he loved her, her lack of breeding and fortune might not matter.

Smiling, he shook his head. 'You bring yourself and that is all I want. Here.' He twitched the goblet out of her hand and set it on the matting. Firmly, he pushed the ring back on to her finger. 'You are my wife, Francesca. I will have no other.'

Francesca's throat closed and her vision blurred. It wasn't quite the declaration of love she had been longing for. Was it enough to sustain a marriage? She blinked and his dark features swam into focus. His forehead was creased, he looked almost anxious.

Surely more than mere pride was at stake here? *Tristan cares about me, I believe he really cares. He does not know how to express it.*

'You'll wear my ring?' His voice was husky. 'You'll stay?'

'I will stay.'

Tristan's forehead cleared as though by magic. Francesca prayed she had made the right decision. He must love her, he just didn't know how to tell her. She curled her fingers round the ring. 'There is one condition.'

'Name it.'

'No more big secrets.'

Tristan lifted her hand and kissed it. 'Very well, no secrets.' Tugging on her arm, he manoeuvred her on to his lap and nuzzled her neck. 'I expect that means I must tell you about the army of mistresses I have waiting for me in Rennes.'

She shot him a startled look, caught a glint in his blue eyes and knew he was teasing. Tristan had already told her that he had been faithful to her during their separation and she believed him. She also believed him when he said that he had considered telling her about Kristina when they'd arrived as des Iles. Tristan had a powerful sense of right and wrong, he didn't lie. His sin, as far as she was concerned, was that he hadn't been open with her. He'd kept things hidden. She understood it though, he'd been trained in tight-lipped self-reliance.

In one sense, she should be flattered he'd wanted to tell her about Kristina. It was a start.

Was it enough for her to risk the pain of losing him again?

It had to be. She loved him, and if there was the slightest chance of finding happiness with him, she must take that risk.

She gave him a warm smile. 'Saints, an army of mistresses? You must have learned a lot about the arts of love, I expect a full confession.' Sliding her fingers along his cheek, she aligned his mouth for a kiss and prayed she wasn't deluding herself about the true nature of his feelings for her.

Tristan needed to love her. At some point she was going to have to tell him that she hated the idea of Tristan's former mistress remaining at des Iles.

And what did he intend to do about Kristina? Now he had these outlaws locked up, was he going to make a public acknowledgement that Kristina was his daughter? There were many challenges ahead of them and the only certainty was that they were not going to be overcome in a day.

Francesca pressed her lips to his.

Relieved beyond measure that Francesca had taken back his ring, Tristan tried to ignore the disquiet that had sat like a lump of lead in his gut. Kerjean's accusation echoed in his head: *Count Bedwyr was one of us. He supported the cause.*

Kerjean had to be lying, Tristan's father was no traitor. Tristan could hardly bear to think about it, yet he had done little else since leaving Hermit's Rock. Could he be wrong about his father? Had he joined the alliance?

His father had killed himself, there was no argument there. Tristan had thought about it for years, it had seemed so out of character. Was it possible that his father had done something on impulse he later regretted? Could he have joined the alliance? And had remorse then driven him to despair?

Francesca leaned against him and murmured against his mouth, 'Kiss me, Tristan.' Her teeth nipped his upper lip, her breasts pressed against his chest. It was the most welcome of distractions. 'I need to be held.'

Drawing back, Tristan looked deep into her grey eyes and his worries faded. He would think about his father's involvement with the alliance later. He had Francesca in his arms, his ring was back on her finger and all was going to be well between them. She had agreed to stay. And she wanted him to hold her. Well, that he could do.

The crackle of the fire faded as their lips met. She must be exhausted, after her ordeal she would need proper rest. When he pulled the hairpins out of her veil, the pounding of the waves below the castle seemed to fade. The fire was less bright. There was only Francesca. Her veil slid to the floor. Sight of that dark hair, falling in short, glossy waves about her face, gave him a jolt. Thank God, he hadn't wounded her.

Self-consciously, she touched her hair. 'Mari says it is most unladylike. I must look like a page boy.'

'Not at all, you are far too pretty and feminine to be mistaken for a page.' Catching her chin, he gently turned her head this way and that. 'I am truly sorry, my heart.' His mouth curved. 'Still, at least we can be sure that no one will be able to constrain you by your hair for some time.'

'That's true. Mari tidied it up for me.'

'So I see, she did a good job.' He felt a smile form and combed through it with his fingers, testing the texture. Her hair had the sheen of black silk. He leaned in and felt the tension ease away. It smelt of her—Francesca and that faint fragrance of jasmine, two scents that would be linked in his mind for ever. 'It's got more curl than it had when it was long, I rather like it.'

Her eyes went wide. 'You like it?'

'Aye. Perhaps it will catch on.'

She laughed. 'Flatterer.' She kissed his nose. 'I am simply thankful that you are such a skilful swordsman, my lord.'

'Part instinct, part training. I had to get you away from him.' He gripped her fiercely, saw her flinch and immediately slackened his hold. 'What's the matter?'

'My arm.' Extricating herself from his hold, she rubbed her upper arm. 'It's a little tender.'

'He bruised you?' Tristan swore softly. 'Let me see.'

Pushing her from his lap, Tristan rose and reached for the clasp on her belt. She didn't argue as he carefully, methodically stripped her of her clothes—belt, gown, undershift. When he got down to bare skin, he swallowed hard. She was so lovely. Her skin was creamy and faintly perfumed. More jasmine. More Francesca. The dark shadow on her upper arm held his gaze.

'The cur, his fingers left marks.' He kissed the bruise, looping his arm about her waist as she slid her arms about his neck. 'One moment, little one.' He stood back and twirled her about, examining every breathtaking inch of her—the gentle curve of her buttock, that slight indentation at the base of her spine, the slender legs. 'No more bruises.'

'No.'

'Dieu merci.' Noticing her downcast eyes and her pink cheeks—*I am making her shy*—he led her to the bed. 'I don't suppose you had much sleep last night.'

'He drugged me, it took a while to wear off.'

Tristan set his jaw. Bruised. Drugged. He flung back the bedcovers. 'In you get, you need proper rest.'

She arched an eyebrow at him. 'Tristan, it's the middle of the day!'

'You need rest.' Tristan spoke firmly, to hide his need. Truly, Francesca was his weakness. Despite the hour, he had to have her in his arms again. She needed rest and he needed to feel her body resting safely against his.

Much as he might want her, for today, he would simply hold her. He would watch over her until she fell asleep. It was strange how the need to keep her safe overrode other more basic needs.

She scrambled under the covers and he was struck with another thought. 'Francesca?'

'Aye?'

'Kerjean has yet to explain how you fell into his hands. Roparz mentioned a consignment of wine.' Walking to the window, Tristan closed the shutters and the light dimmed. She would rest better in the half-light.

She yawned. 'I was in the bailey waiting for Mari and the carter spoke to me. I got the impression he had been hoping to find me.'

He looked sharply across, all he could see was the top of her head peeping out from the nest of blankets. 'The carter was looking for you personally?'

'I think so.' Another yawn. The sheets rustled. 'He told me they had Kristina. I couldn't bear the thought of her being frightened, so I went with him.'

'You weren't forced?' Tristan stared at the bump under the blankets. So that was why the guards on the walkway hadn't noticed anything amiss, there hadn't been any struggle because she had gone willingly.

'You would have done the same, I am sure.'

Shaking his head at her, Tristan came to lie on top of the bed. Shifting the bedcovers, he folded her in his arms. 'That was very brave. And very foolish.' And very like Francesca. She'd not found it easy learning that Kristina was his child and yet she had voluntarily put herself in the hands of outlaws to save her. He frowned. No, that didn't do her justice. Francesca hadn't simply climbed into that cart because Kristina was his, she would have done the same for any child.

She gave a little sigh and Tristan kissed her forehead. It wasn't long before her body went lax in his arms. The wind rattled the shutters and the curtains shifted in a slight breeze. The fire was painting flickering patterns on the walls, Tristan watched them shift and sway. He wouldn't stay long, just long enough to ensure that she was deeply asleep.

He listened to the wind and the drumming of the waves. Francesca had been drugged and threatened for Kristina's sake. That didn't mean she was going to be happy living under the same roof as Kristina and Esmerée.

Yet what could he do? Roparz was his most trusted knight, his right-hand man. He was best qualified to be steward of des Iles and Tristan had had it drilled into him by both Lord Morgan and his father that the steward of your main holding was your right-hand man—your rock.

I can't lose Roparz.

Tristan pressed another kiss to Francesca's forehead.

It made no sense to dismiss Roparz. Militarily, it made no sense at all.

He sighed. Perhaps dismissing Roparz from des Iles might be avoided if he spoke to Esmerée. Yes, if Esmerée realised the full extent of Francesca's involvement in Kristina's rescue; if she understood that Francesca had deliberately put herself at risk for Kristina's sake, she would surely be grateful. Perhaps the two women might even become friends.

He would speak to Esmerée as soon as he could. And then he would interrogate Joakim Kerjean. Once Tristan had got Kerjean to admit that he had been lying about his father's involvement with the alliance, he would pack the man off to Baron Rolland in Rennes.

Count Bedwyr was no traitor.

Alone on the tower watch point above their bedchamber, Francesca leaned against the parapet wall and looked out to sea. The tide was at the ebb and the rocks in the bay looked larger than usual. Spiky and sharp. Dark seaweed drifted in the shallows like dirty washing. It had stopped raining hours before, though the sky remained overcast and a gloomy mass of clouds was piled in the western sky. The breeze was bracing, it tugged at her veil and sent shivers down her neck.

Behind her, the door creaked and Lady Esmerée stepped on to the parapet.

'Excuse me, Lady Francesca, is it convenient for me to speak to you?'

'Of course.'

Veil flying in the wind, Lady Esmerée came to her side. She glanced briefly at Hermit's Rock and touched Francesca's hand. 'My lady, I have come to thank you. Lord Tristan tells me you put yourself in harm's way to ensure Kristina's safe return.'

Francesca smiled. 'You are welcome, anyone would have done the same.'

Slowly, Lady Esmerée shook her head. 'No, my lady, I don't think they would, particularly given the circumstances of Kristina's birth. You are Lord Tristan's wife—discovering we had a daughter must have been a shock.'

Francesca's face felt stiff. 'I won't deny it, it did knock me back.'

'None the less, you went with those outlaws for Kristina's sake.' Lady Esmerée's voice trembled with emotion and she dropped to her knees and bowed her head. 'I am thankful beyond measure, my lady, Kristina means the world to me.'

'Please, Lady Esmerée, there's no need to kneel.' Cheeks hot, Francesca urged Lady Esmerée back to her feet. 'Lord Tristan tells me your daughter is recovering well. He mentioned something about spiced buns.'

Lady Esmerée's lips softened. 'Kristina loves them, they make her very greedy.'

Francesca squeezed Lady Esmerée's hand and made her voice bright. 'I am happy your daughter came to no harm and that is thanks enough. Please say no more about it.'

Lady Esmerée nodded and turned away. 'Bless you, my lady, you are all grace.' At the door she hesitated and looked back. Her eyes were glassy with tears, she looked deeply uncomfortable.

Francesca felt a sinking feeling. 'There's more, isn't there?'

Lady Esmerée stood in the doorway, wringing her hands, the very image of misery.

'Lady Esmerée?'

'I feel terrible, my lady. Your bravery puts me in the shade. You saved my child.' Her voice broke. 'Whilst I have done you a great wrong.'

Francesca felt a chill that had nothing to do with the wind. 'What? What have you done?'

Lady Esmerée hung her head. 'I made full confession to Father Paol and he suggested that I tell you too. I am so ashamed.'

A flurry of rain dampened Francesca's veil. Calmly, she gestured at the door. 'Come, my lady, it's raining again. We can continue this conversation in the solar.'

Chapter Fifteen

Francesca was bursting with questions and she felt oddly nervous. None the less, she held her tongue until she and Lady Esmerée were seated before the solar fire. What was Lady Esmerée talking about? What could she have done? And did Tristan know about it?

She leaned back against a cushion. 'Your mention of making a confession is intriguing, Lady Esmerée. Please, continue.'

'As you wish.' Lady Esmerée wiped away a tear and folded her hands in her lap. 'My family lived in the village. My lady, I have known Count Tristan all my life.'

'You became his *belle-amie*—his mistress.'

Cheeks bright, Lady Esmerée stared at the floor. 'Yes, my lady. It was shortly after my father's death.' Her chin came up. 'Sinful though it was, I wasn't ashamed, I was proud to be Lord Tristan's, as you say, *belle-amie*. He looked after me and he didn't shame me, he never took other lovers.'

'You loved him?'

'So I thought, though I never dared tell him, you know how aloof he can be.'

Francesca nodded and waited.

Lady Esmerée lifted her gaze, her eyes bleak. 'All went well until Lord Tristan told me he was planning his wedding. A dynastic alliance, he said. My liaison with him was ended. I was devastated. Only after you had married him did I discover I was carrying his child.'

'And then Sir Roparz married you.'

'Aye.' Lady Esmerée's expression softened. 'Roparz asked for my hand. My lady, please understand, it wasn't until long after Kristina was born that I came to appreciate my husband's qualities.' She grimaced. 'Before that happened, I was bitterly jealous. I harboured much resentment against both you and Lord Tristan.'

'You felt wronged.'

'Aye.'

Francesca braced herself as it dawned on her that an unconventional woman like Lady Esmerée, a merchant's daughter who had openly taken a noble lover despite the difficulties that must have caused in a small village where everyone knew her, wasn't likely to sit idly by if she believed herself wronged.

'What did you do?'

Lady Esmerée looked away. 'When Lord Tristan was called to serve the duchy, he wrote to you. His letters came via des Iles.'

The realisation came in a flash. 'You intercepted our letters! You destroyed them.'

White about the mouth, Lady Esmerée glanced covertly at the fire. 'Yes, my lady, I am ashamed to say that I did.'

Francesca felt a wave of nausea sweep through her. She stumbled to her feet. All that pain, all those months of waiting in vain for Tristan to reply. All that time during which she had been made to question her place in the world. And she hadn't been the only one to suffer—Tristan had been made to think she had turned her back on him. He'd come to believe she didn't trust him enough to appeal to him for help.

'How did you get them? What did you do with them?'

'I persuaded Sergeant Jagu—he mans the gatehouse—to give them to me. My lady, you mustn't blame the sergeant, I told him I would pass them on to Roparz.'

'And then?'

Swallowing, Lady Esmerée gave a guilt-laden nod towards the leaping flames in the hearth. 'I burnt them.'

'What, all of them?'

'Aye, every one.' Lady Esmerée was chewing her lip, a tear tracked slowly down her cheek. 'Can you forgive me, my lady?'

Francesca rubbed her brow. 'I…I am not sure.' Her nails were digging into her palms, she actually wanted to hit the woman. She wouldn't, of course, but she wanted to. Badly. 'Lady Esmerée, do you understand how much trouble you caused?'

'I am truly sorry, my lady.'

'This is very hard to accept.' Francesca set her hands on her hips as she thought it through. Something about Lady Esmerée's confession didn't fit and she was determined to puzzle it out. 'You love Sir Roparz?'

'Very much, my lady.'

'You didn't love him at first,' Francesca said, thinking aloud. 'How long have you loved him?'

'It did take a while. Roparz was kind to Kristina. I kept thinking he would be bound to reject her, and he never did. He idolised her from the day she was born and she, in turn, idolises him. I was slower to love him back.' Lady Esmerée smiled sadly. 'Roparz was very patient. It took a couple of years for me to learn to love him.'

Francesca did a swift calculation. She had last written to Tristan in the autumn of the previous year, he should have received that letter and he hadn't. 'You could have stopped destroying our letters once you had found love. Yet you didn't, you continued to destroy them. Why?'

Worried eyes met hers. 'Once I'd started burning them, I had to continue. My lady, many of the later letters referred to earlier ones. If the later letters had been delivered, either you or Count Tristan would have been sure to realise that something was amiss.'

'So you not only destroyed them, but you read our private correspondence first! And, having done so, you couldn't stop because you were afraid of being found out.'

'Exactly. My lady, I am truly sorry. Can you forgive me?'

Francesca gave a heavy sigh. 'I shall try.'

'Thank you. My lady, please do not chastise Sergeant Jagu, it was entirely my fault.'

'Sergeant Jagu will not be blamed.'

'Thank you.' Lady Esmerée rose. 'I realise I am in no position to ask for favours, but I would beg you not to mention this to Lord Tristan. It might poison his relationship with Kristina.'

Francesca stiffened. 'I can't think Lord Tristan would be so petty as to allow your sins to reflect badly on your daughter.'

'Nevertheless, I would rather Lord Tristan did not know what I have done. He might mention it to my husband and that I could not bear. Against all expectation, I have found happiness with Sir Roparz. He may never forgive a wife who behaved in so dishonourable a fashion.'

'You ask a great deal. Lady Esmerée, I am reluctant to tell tales, but the loss of those letters caused much misery, it almost destroyed my marriage. Lord Tristan must be told.'

Lady Esmerée groaned. 'My lady, please—if Roparz learns what I have done, he will despise me.'

'I doubt that.' Francesca held herself very straight. 'Lady Esmerée, it is my firm belief that husbands and wives should not keep secrets from one another. I shall tell Count Tristan about the letters. However, you may be assured that I will ask my lord not to discuss the letters with Sir Roparz.'

Lady Esmerée clasped her hands together. 'God bless you, my lady.'

'Thank you for your confession, it can't have

been easy.' Francesca held her gaze. 'I feel confident Count Tristan will respect your wish for discretion. Lady Esmerée, I appreciate that what you tell your husband is your affair, however, I would strongly recommend that you confess all to him too.' She smiled. 'I am sure it is a course Father Paol would endorse.'

Tristan was so involved with military matters that Francesca saw little of him that day. Private conversation had to wait until he joined her in their bedchamber that night and Francesca was already in bed when he came quietly in.

'Tristan?'

He gave her a preoccupied smile and began to disrobe. 'I am sorry if I woke you.'

'I wasn't asleep.' Absently, Francesca twisted a lock of hair round her finger. It felt odd to have such short hair, it would take a while to get used to it. 'Is your interrogation of Sir Joakim progressing? Will you be sending him to Baron Rolland in Rennes?'

Tristan drew off his tunic and shook his head. 'Not yet, the man's as closed as a clam. On the island he claimed my father was supporting the rebel alliance. I'm reluctant to hand him over until he's told me all he knows.'

'He could have been bluffing about your father.'

There were dark circles under Tristan's eyes. Clearly, Sir Joakim's remarks about Count Bedwyr had cut deep.

He sighed. 'I pray so. I've had enough of Kerjean for one day.' Tristan pinched out the candles, leaving only the glow of the fire to light the chamber. The mattress dipped as he got into bed and warm arms reached for her. He gave a heavy yawn. 'Was there something you wanted to tell me?'

She kissed his chest. 'You're tired, it can wait.'

A large hand ruffled her hair, his lips curved into a weary smile. 'I can tell by your tone it's important. Tell me.'

'First, I should like you to promise that you will not breathe a word of what I am about to tell you to Sir Roparz.'

Catching her by the chin, he looked deep into her eyes. 'What's happened? Francesca?'

'Promise me.'

'I promise. Whatever it is, I shall not mention it to Sir Roparz.'

'It concerns our lost letters.'

His fingers stilled in her hair. 'You've discovered what happened to them?'

'Aye.' Resting her head against Tristan's chest,

Francesca told him everything that Lady Esmerée had told her concerning the burning of their letters.

His eyes widened. 'Esmerée? Esmerée destroyed our correspondence?'

'Yes.'

Tristan rolled on to his back and stared at the curtains on the opposite wall. 'The letters all came via des Iles, yet I find it hard to credit she would do such a thing.' His chest heaved. '*Mon Dieu*, Francesca, I admit you have surprised me. I never would have thought her capable of such deceit, but now you have told me I can see how she might have been angry.'

'She loved you.' Francesca hugged him to her. 'I think she hoped for marriage.'

A dark eyebrow lifted. 'I couldn't have married Esmerée.'

Francesca's stomach tightened. 'She wasn't noble. She brought no dowry.'

Turning towards her, Tristan framed her face with his hands. 'Francesca, don't. Esmerée, charming though she is, is not you. There is no comparison.'

She looked at him and ached to be loved. Even exhausted, Tristan was impossibly handsome—the only man on earth to possess such long-lashed blue eyes, such jet-black hair. Sadly, she ran her fingertips across his chest. 'Tristan, you married me because of my dowry, you would never have considered me otherwise.'

His fingers tightened on her scalp. 'That might be true, but having wed you, I am loath to let you go. You are my wife and I need you and you alone. You have taught me that I do not need a noble wife with a fat dowry.'

Shifting her in his arms, Tristan rolled her on to her back. Warm lips met hers. 'My heart, you must never doubt me,' he murmured. 'Never.'

He kissed her mouth, lingering there for a while, touching his tongue to hers before moving on to kiss her cheeks and eyelids. He even kissed her cropped hair before angling her head to kiss her neck. Then he slowly began working his way down—neck, collarbone, breasts…

He lifted his head. 'Don't doubt me, Francesca.'

'I don't.' Francesca sighed as Tristan's lips moved inexorably over her skin. She was lying, she did doubt him. Even as her blood heated and her limbs moved restlessly against his, a cold hand had hold of her heart. *Don't doubt me.* If by that he meant that he loved her, why did he not tell her? If he loved her, he would surely tell her.

Strong legs nudged against hers, and she ran the sole of her foot up his muscled calves, relishing in the feel of his masculine strength. The contact, the rhythmic pushing of body against body, all this she loved. Saints, but her handsome husband was the best of lovers, he could push all thought from her head. All thought save one.

Tristan might tell her he wanted and needed her, but nothing had changed. He was keeping her as his wife because he was fiercely honourable and he didn't want to break his wedding vows. Not once had he said that he loved her. His feelings were not truly engaged.

Francesca passed the next few days in a state of limbo. Tristan seemed to go out of his way to avoid her and she couldn't understand it. It was extremely disheartening. He seemed to have reverted to his old ways—namely, no sooner had he allowed her close, than he retreated behind his duties. Somehow, she must find a way to break the pattern.

She set out to explore the castle with Mari while she tried to work out what sort of marriage Tristan expected. There was much that was unusual about Château des Iles and she and Mari got lost many times as they learned their way about the labyrinthine corridors.

They came across a small terrace set between the castle walls. It had been transformed into a garden and, apart from a solitary stone bench, was crammed with plants in pots. Arrow slits in the western wall looked out over the ocean. Francesca asked a maidservant about the garden and was told Tristan's mother had made it. Judging by the orderly lines of pots and the lack of weeds, it was still carefully tended. Cracks in the paving were filled with wild thyme, tiny pink flowers nodded in the breeze. There were pots of herbs—chives, rosemary and bay.

People's faces became familiar and the names soon followed. There was Paskella, who worked in the bakehouse—she was who was responsible for the currant buns so beloved of Kristina. Antoine and Guirec worked in the stables. Father Paol was usually in the chapel. There was Nazaire, the blacksmith—over the days, the list grew and grew.

Francesca and Mari discovered that the wine cellar beneath the great hall had been hollowed out of the rock. Francesca told herself it was important she learned the lie of the land, but in truth she would far rather be getting to know her husband. After he had rushed to her rescue at Hermit's Rock, everything had seemed so promising. She'd been certain that she and Tristan were about to develop that deep intimacy that went far beyond mere physical connection.

Sadly not. After pushing his ring back on to her finger; after promising there would be no secrets between them, Tristan had become his old self. He was cool and distant. Ever the efficient warrior; ever the loyal servant of the duchy. Was there really no room in his heart for him to become the loving husband she longed for?

At night Francesca was able to cling grimly on to hope, for he held her in bed, kissed her forehead and told her to sleep. Unfortunately, he didn't confide in her. And, apart from a chaste goodnight kiss, he didn't touch her again. Even the passion they had once shared seemed to have vanished, like smoke in the wind.

Each night, Francesca would tell herself that as soon as Tristan had finished his interrogation of Sir Joakim, he would find time for her. She knew he wanted heirs. And whilst passion alone was no longer enough, she was getting to the point where if passion was all Tristan had to offer, she would try to make the best of it.

What had he said? *Wedding vows should last for life.*

It seemed he intended to be faithful. Was she wrong to want more from him than mere passion?

She'd hoped for a soulmate. Despite her hopes, it was becoming clear that Tristan's idea of a good marriage didn't chime with hers. Perhaps it never would.

Each dawn she woke to find he had left their bedchamber, and wherever she made enquiries as to his whereabouts, she received the same answer:

'Sir Roparz, where is Lord Tristan?'

'Interrogating Sir Joakim, my lady.'

She would try not to frown. 'Surely he can't *still* be interrogating Sir Joakim?'

'I'm afraid that he is.'

After several days when Francesca received a similar response, she came to a decision. Tristan had to be made to see that his insistence on scouring Brittany for every last outlaw was a form of escape. If he didn't want more from life than that, their marriage was at an end.

Just because I am far below him in rank, he thinks I will accept everything he does. Well, he is about to find otherwise.

She marched into the steward's office. 'Sir Roparz, I would like to speak to my husband.'

'He's dealing with the outlaws, my lady.'

She made her voice firm. 'I need to speak to him without delay. Where is he?'

'In the dungeon.'

'I should like you to take me.'

His eyebrows shot up. 'To the dungeon? My lady, I can't do that.'

'I am sure that you can.'

'The dungeon is no place for a lady.'

'Nevertheless, I am asking you to take me.' Her foot tapped. 'At once, if you please.'

Sir Roparz searched her face and nodded. 'Very well. It's cold down there, you will need a cloak.'

The entrance to the dungeon was beneath the guardhouse. The door was oak, dark with age and banded with iron, it looked strong enough to withstand attack from a horde of Vikings. Sir Roparz spoke to guards stationed at either side of the door and a large key was produced.

Francesca shivered. 'Lord Tristan is locked in the dungeon?'

'He's not prepared to run the risk of Kerjean escaping.'

The door grated open. Francesca braced herself, she'd never been inside a prison and she wasn't sure what to expect. She wasn't sure what to expect from Tristan either, he was a loyal warrior of the duchy and Sir Joakim and his cronies had been causing havoc for years.

A flight of roughly hewn steps ran sharply downward. Peering in, Francesca could see the faint glimmer of a torch at the bottom.

'Follow me, my lady. Please take care, the steps are slippery.'

At the foot of the steps, a tunnel sloped downward—the dungeon had been hewn from the rock upon which the castle was built. Dark walls glistened. As they descended, they passed studded door after studded door, the place was literally honeycombed with cells. Torches hissed and spat. As Sir Roparz had warned, the air was chill.

At the end of the corridor, the final door was ajar, Sir Roparz came to a halt outside it. Tristan was talking inside, his voice echoed round the rocky walls.

'Kerjean, if you refuse to give me proof, you will rot here until Doomsday.'

'Damn you, le Beau,' Sir Joakim said. 'I've told you a thousand times, I have no proof. I was simply told your father served the alliance.'

'That is your final word?'

'I can't help you. Hell burn it, le Beau, what is the point of this? The alliance is finished. You, of all people, should know that.'

'Very well, you will remain here. You will be fed and watered, but you will never see the light of day. All that could change, however, once you tell me what I want to know.'

'It matters not to me,' Sir Joakim said, in a dull voice. 'I am a dead man either way.'

Francesca moved to the doorway. Sir Joakim was slouched on a stone ledge, chains about his wrists and ankles. His beard had grown, he looked dirty and dishevelled, but he didn't appear to have been beaten, in truth he looked surprisingly hale.

Tristan turned her way and his face went blank. 'This is no place for you, my lady.' He took her wrist in a fierce grip, walked her back into the tunnel and scowled at Roparz. 'What possessed you to bring her here?'

Francesca tugged her wrist free. 'Don't blame Sir Roparz, I insisted he brought me.'

'You shouldn't be here.'

Francesca looked pointedly towards the cell. 'Nor should Sir Joakim. Tristan, your part in this is ended. Send Sir Joakim to Baron Rolland, let him deal with him.'

Tristan gave her a look so cold, she shivered. 'Kerjean and his men remain here until I am done with them.'

Dread filled her. Francesca had heard about the lengths some men were prepared to go in order to extract information from their enemies. Prisoners would be flogged, they'd be put on the rack. Surely Tristan wouldn't resort to torture? Not Tristan. 'Tristan, I should like to speak to you, and preferably not down here.'

'Very well.' His voice was curt. Efficient. 'Roparz, lock up behind us, will you?'

Francesca hurried along the corridor and up the steps.

'Where are we going?' Tristan asked.

She didn't hesitate, the sun was shining and they needed to be somewhere they could talk without being interrupted. 'Your mother's garden.'

She swept on, through the bailey and on to the sloping path between the castle walls that led up to the garden terrace. Tristan followed in silence, she didn't need to look back to know that her discovery of his mother's garden had surprised him.

Reaching the door in the wall, Francesca shot back the bolts, turned the key and stepped out into the wind. Above her, the gulls cried and wheeled.

Tristan followed. His expression was stony, though the eagerness with which he drew in a lungful of fresh air told her that he was secretly relieved to be out of the dungeon.

He nudged a pot of mint with his boot. 'I'd forgotten about this place.'

'I was told your mother loved it.'

'So she did.'

Stepping up to him, Francesca laid her hand on his sleeve. 'Tristan, what are you doing in that dungeon?'

He frowned down at her, jet-black hair ruffled by the wind. 'You know what I am doing. Kerjean accused my father of being a rebel, I intend to prove him a liar.'

'I thought their cause was dead and that Kerjean and his men are merely outlaws.'

Tristan shrugged. 'That is true, up to a point. Kerjean would need a great deal of money to revive the rebel alliance.'

'He would also need a great deal of support from powerful men. That's why he wanted you to join them.'

Tristan nodded.

'Tristan, Sir Joakim made that accusation to get under your guard. He succeeded.' A muscle twitched in Tristan's cheek, Francesca ignored it. 'I can see what he said has cut deep, but you might need to accept that you will never know the truth of it.'

'My father was a cold man, not a traitorous one. I won't have him slandered.'

She looked up into his eyes, they were full of shadows. 'Even at risk of your soul, Tristan?'

He stiffened. 'What do you mean?'

She focused on the wall behind his head. 'You've been interrogating that man for days and you're getting nowhere.'

'He'll break in time, everyone does.'

She drew back, frowning. 'And how will you ensure that he breaks? You heard him—he has nothing to lose. Sir Joakim knows he will be accused of treason and there is only one penalty for that.'

'Death.'

'Exactly. Even if Sir Joakim knows more that he has told you, it's obvious he has no intention of helping you. Are you planning to put him on the rack?'

His eyes went wide. 'I beg your pardon?'

Thank goodness, her question had shocked him. Which must mean that he hadn't been planning on using torture. 'Well, it seems to me that you have set out on that path.'

'Lord, Francesca, I wouldn't torture the man.'

'Wouldn't you? Are you sure? You're refusing to send him to Baron Rolland, and he is refusing to speak.' She spread her hands. 'It seems like an impasse to me.'

'Francesca, I must know about my father. Surely you understand?'

She leaned towards him. 'Why? Why must you know?'

He looked at her as though she had grown two heads. 'I would have thought it was obvious, this touches on my honour.'

'You are saying that if your father sided with the alliance, then *your* honour is in question?'

'Yes.'

'I don't see why you must shoulder responsibility for your father's deeds.'

'You're a woman, you wouldn't understand.'

Anger flared, a scorching burn in her belly. 'No, likely I wouldn't. Tristan, I know you for a man of honour.' She drew in a calming breath. 'I love you, Tristan.'

His hand caught hers, his eyes held some deep emotion. Yearning? Longing?

'Francesca—'

'Let me finish, I beg you. Tristan, I loved you from the beginning. I think I told you.'

'You did.' His voice was husky, his gaze wistful. It gave her strength. And hope.

'Tristan, back then my love was untried, we didn't know each other very well. I love you more truly today, I know you for an honourable man. You are honest and hard-working.' She gave a self-deprecating smile. 'Indeed, sometimes you are a little too hard-working for my liking, but I accept that as your nature. I will always love you. And I have to tell you that my love will not change, whatever we discover your father did.' Reaching up, she lightly touched his mouth. 'Tristan, you say you want to keep me as your wife. Yet you know nothing about my family. What if one day you were to discover that my mother was a thief, and my father a murderer? Would you want me then?'

Tristan slid his arms about her waist and pulled her tightly against him. 'It makes no difference to me what your parents were. You are not a thief and you are not a murderer. You are Francesca. You are my heart.'

Triumph filled her. Tristan did love her! He wasn't ready to see it, his obsession with his father's honour was blinding him to all else, but she was certain he loved her. If only she could set his mind at rest concerning his father, they could finally get on with their marriage.

'Tristan, would you hold a man guilty for his father's sins?'

'Of course not.'

'Then you should give yourself the same courtesy. Tristan, whatever your father did, you are not your father.'

A small smile played about his mouth. 'I see I

married a clever woman.' His smile faded and he rested his forehead against hers. 'My heart, I accept what you say, but I cannot rest until I know the nature of my father's involvement with the rebel alliance.'

Chapter Sixteen

Tristan couldn't tear his gaze from Francesca. He could see the silver and gold flecks in her eyes and her smile held a warmth he knew was reserved solely for him. As he looked at her, his uncertainties about his father were in some way diminished. His wife was a sorceress, a beguiling, clever sorceress and he blessed the day that she became his bride. He could so easily have chosen another woman. Yet this one, the woman who brought him nothing save her beautiful self, held the key to his heart.

It had been mere chance that he had chosen her. Lord, he'd been lucky, the idea of life, of a future without her was unbearable. Torture. How she did it he had no clue, but sometimes simply being in Francesca's company set the world to rights. Was it a weakness to desire her company as much as her body? He'd always thought so.

'Tristan?' Her voice cut into his thoughts. 'What

happened to Sir Joakim's accomplices, are they in the dungeon too?'

'Naturally.'

'Have you questioned them?'

'I've been concentrating on Kerjean.'

'I take it he isn't inclined to talk?'

'No.'

Her expression became pensive. 'As we were leaving the island, I noticed that one of the outlaws looked quite a bit older than the others. He might know the extent—or not—of your father's involvement. Why not interrogate him?'

Tristan straightened. 'That is a good idea.'

She tipped her head to one side. 'I'm surprised you didn't think of it yourself.'

'I should have done, if I hadn't been blinded by fury.' He touched her cheek and gave her a crooked smile. 'I was obsessed with the idea of proving Kerjean's guilt. I wanted him punished for having the temerity to plan your abduction. You, my heart, are my weakness.'

'I am your weakness?' She laughed. 'You make it sound as though I am some kind of affliction.'

He caught her hand. 'Perhaps you are. When I think about what might have happened to you had I not gone to that blasted revel, my thoughts scramble. That should not happen. I need to be master in my own mind.' He shrugged. 'You are my Achilles' heel.'

She put her hand to her breast and her eyes danced. 'Tristan, you really know how to woo a woman.'

Bemused, Tristan simply looked at her. Contrary to his expectation, Francesca seemed pleased by what he had said. Surely no lady would be happy to learn that her husband could not command his thoughts for thinking of her? Women. What a mystery they were.

Determined to focus on the matter in hand, he took a deep breath. Except—blast it, when Francesca smiled at him in that manner, his mind filled with thoughts that had little to do with interrogating outlaws and everything to do with taking her in his arms and kissing her until the world was lost to them. He cleared his throat. 'I shall interview the other rebels shortly.'

She squeezed his hand. 'I shall come with you.'

He felt a frown form. 'Francesca, I am not going to resort to torture.'

'I know that, you dolt.' Looking down at their hands, she interlaced her fingers with his. 'This is important to you, I'd like to be present.'

Firmly, he shook his head. 'You're not going back into that dungeon.'

'Thank heaven for that, it makes my skin crawl.'

He smothered a laugh. 'The dungeon's not meant to be pleasant, it's a deterrent.'

Grey eyes studied him. 'What will you do, have the outlaws brought up to the solar? I suppose you have enough guards to interview them there.'

His lips twitched at her assumption that he would agree to her being present. 'Francesca, I never said you might witness the interrogation.'

A line formed in her brow. 'I need to be there.'

'Why?'

Lifting his hand, she kissed it. 'Because I love you.'

He had no answer to that. And before he knew it he found himself agreeing to her request. 'I don't think the solar is the right place, the steward's office would be better.'

When Francesca tipped her head back and gave him a smile that took his breath away, Tristan realised that if his wife wanted something and it was within his power to give it to her, he would do so. Lord, it would seem he could deny her nothing. She who gave him his strength was truly also his weakness.

Dust motes flickered in a shaft of light pouring through the windows. Tristan sat behind the steward's desk with Francesca at his right hand and Roparz on his left, quill in hand.

In front of them, heavily chained and hedged in by guards, stood the older of the outlaws. He was about fifty years of age, and his face and shaven head bore many scars. Yet it wasn't the scars so much as the lack of expression in the man's eyes that bore witness to a life filled with violence and shattered dreams. His name was, apparently, Albin.

'And you were witness to this meeting with my father?' Tristan was asking. He was more pleased than he could say that he'd taken Francesca's advice and had Albin brought up from the dungeons. They'd been questioning him for half an hour and what Albin had told him had relieved his mind. He wanted confirmation, before witnesses, that he had it right. 'It must have happened years ago, my father died when I was a squire.'

Roparz's quill scratched its way swiftly across the parchment, everything that was said was being carefully recorded.

'Aye, my lord, it was years ago, all right. Sir Joakim's sire, Sir Gregor, thought Count Bedwyr might be persuaded to join us. He was wrong, your father would have none of it.'

Thank God. Tristan exchanged a swift smile with Francesca before turning back to the outlaw. 'And were there other witnesses to my father's refusal of Sir Gregor's terms?'

'None that are alive, *mon seigneur*.'

'Albin, as you see, my steward is recording what you say. Are you prepared to repeat this before Baron Rolland?'

Albin's eyes flickered. 'What's in it for me?'

Sir Roparz looked up. 'What's in it for me, *my lord*?'

Tristan lifted an eyebrow. 'You have family, Albin?'

'A wife. No children, my lord.'

'I can't promise you your freedom, that will be Baron Rolland's decision, but I can promise that your wife will be cared for.'

'Thank you, my lord.' Albin hesitated, chewing his lip.

'There's more?'

'Aye.'

'Go on.'

Albin shifted and his chains clanked. 'If you've a mind to sue for mercy on my behalf, I'll tell you. Otherwise…' He shrugged and folded his lips together.

Tristan kept his gaze steady. 'I have already said

I will speak up for you. I will ensure your wife is provided for. More than that I cannot do.' He leaned back in his chair. 'Albin, you might like to consider that the more helpful you are at this stage, the more persuasive I am likely to be on your behalf. And the more generous with my aid to your wife.'

Albin's mouth worked. Eyes fixed on Tristan, he took a wary step backwards. His chains rattled. 'It…it concerns Countess Suzanna, my lord.'

Tristan's brow furrowed. 'My mother?'

'It wasn't sickness that killed her.'

Tristan leapt up and was round the table in an instant. Dimly, he heard Francesca's gasp of dismay, and the scrape of Roparz's chair as he too pushed to his feet. Tristan glared at Albin. 'Of course it was sickness, my mother caught a chill.'

The grizzled head shook. 'No, my lord, she did not.'

'What are you saying?'

'Countess Suzanna was murdered.' Albin's voice sounded rusty, he licked his lips. 'There were those in the alliance who believed that your father needed a little persuasion before he would come round to their way of thinking.'

Tristan struggled to find words. 'My mother was murdered?' Albin had to be lying—his mother had caught a chill and had died soon after, everyone knew that. The man had to be lying.

'My lord, Countess Suzanna was murdered.'

Hollow inside, Tristan glared at Albin, but he wasn't really seeing him. He was thinking back, racking his brains to try to remember the little he'd been told of his mother's death. 'Lord Morgan said she died of a chill.'

'My lord, she was poisoned.'

Tristan's mind reeled. 'Someone got into des Iles—is that what you are saying?' He grabbed the front of Albin's tunic. '*Jésu*, how was it done?'

'It…I don't know exactly. I was Sir Gregor's sergeant back then, and a comrade and I overheard him talking. Your mother was killed to try to force Count Bedwyr into siding with the rebels. That's all I know.' Albin's throat worked. 'Benedig—my comrade—had a very loose tongue, he died shortly afterwards and I always wondered why. I wouldn't have put it past him to attempt to use what we'd heard to feather his nest.'

'Benedig was silenced?'

A shrug. 'I imagine so. Leastways, his death gave me pause. Until now, I've not breathed a word to anyone.'

Tristan felt stunned. The idea that his mother had been killed as an attempt to force his father into joining the rebels would never have occurred to him. 'Does Kerjean know his father is implicated in my mother's death?'

'No, my lord, Sir Gregor took the secret to his grave.'

Wheeling about, Tristan let out a huge sigh. Francesca looked as stunned as he was, and her grey eyes were full of fellow feeling. A lump formed in his throat.

'Roparz?'

'My lord?'

'I need to think. Get this man back into the dungeon, will you?'

'Yes, my lord.'

'And see that he has a decent meal.'

'Of course.'

Tristan stalked out of the office, his thoughts in complete disarray.

Francesca waited as long as she could before going in search of him.

Tristan wasn't hard to find, she knew exactly where he'd be and there he was, sitting on the stone bench in his mother's garden. Francesca didn't know what she was going to say, but if he needed comfort, she wanted to be there for him.

He looked up, eyes bleak.

She gripped the door. 'If you don't want company, I can come back later?'

Slowly, he shook his head. 'Stay. Please.'

Crossing the terrace, she settled beside him on the bench. She could smell rosemary, he had picked a sprig and was twirling it in his fingers. Setting the sprig aside, he took her hand and their fingers laced.

'I am so sorry, Tristan.'

His smile was tight, his blue gaze seemed to look into her soul. 'I must confess, Albin's statement about my mother—*Jésu*, I never saw that coming.'

'How do you feel?'

'I am not sure.' His chest heaved. 'Mother—murdered. I can't seem to accept it and yet in a dreadful way it makes complete sense.'

Francesca leaned her head on his shoulder. A bee, buffeted by the wind, was buzzing around the pot of chives. As she watched the bee moving from purple flower to purple flower, an extraordinary thought came to her—one that would explain much about Tristan and his warped relationship with his father.

'Tristan, has it occurred to you that your mother's death might explain why your father kept you at arm's length?'

His muscles tightened. 'How so?'

'Albin implied that Lady Suzanna's death was part of Sir Gregor's plan to draw Count Bedwyr into his net.'

'Aye.' He gave a puzzled frown. 'Go on.'

'What if that wasn't the whole truth? What if your mother was killed to show your father what he stood to lose if he didn't join Sir Gregor?'

He gave a harsh laugh. 'What more was there? My mother's death destroyed my father, she was his world.'

Francesca gripped his hand. 'Yes, I am sure that is true. I had heard how your father adored her.' She drew in a breath. 'However, I think there was more for your father to lose, much more.'

He made a sound of exasperation. 'For pity's sake, speak plainly.'

'There was you, Tristan. Your father had you.'

Tristan sat there, eyes holding hers. He didn't move a muscle. The bee buzzed among the chives, a gull shrieked over the cliffs and Tristan simply stared at her.

Francesca tore her gaze from his and leaned on his shoulder. 'You were the real target, I feel sure. By killing Lady Suzanna, Sir Gregor was warning Count Bedwyr what might happen if he didn't fall in with their plans. You, Count Bedwyr's heir, would be killed.'

She waited, watching the bee and listening to the gulls.

At length, he sighed. 'That version of events could be true, although with only Albin as our witness, I don't suppose we shall ever verify it.'

'Your father must have been at his wits' end after your mother died, no wonder he wouldn't allow you to attend her funeral.'

Tristan gave her a sharp look. 'He thought I'd be safer in Vannes?'

'Exactly, by keeping you at arm's length, he hoped to protect you.'

Tristan shook his head and swore softly. 'The devil of it is we shall never know for sure what my father thought.'

Francesca gave a sad smile. 'That is true, but it must help to know that Count Bedwyr's apparent coldness could have been born out of love rather than indifference.'

'Love,' he murmured, staring at the pot of rosemary with troubled eyes. He drew in a lungful of air. 'Francesca, we have learned that my mother was murdered and my father threatened by outlaws and rebels. This could cast my father's death—his mortal sin—in a new light.'

She gave him a gentle smile. 'I was wondering when you would come to that, it could indeed.

It's entirely possible that your father, threatened at every turn, decided that the best way to protect you was to remove himself from play.'

Tristan's face drained of colour. 'My father died to save me? He sacrificed himself?' He rubbed his brow. 'Lord, what a turnaround. I wouldn't have thought it possible, and yet—it is plausible.'

'Your father loved you, Tristan, I am sure of it.' Lifting his hand, Francesca kissed the back of it. 'The pity is that we shall never truly know your father's motives. We can't know everything.'

'No.' He rubbed his brow. 'All these years I thought him indifferent.'

'You will need to come to terms with what we have learned. However, I believe your father loved you as much as he loved your mother.' Reaching up, she slid her hand about his neck, tugged him close and kissed his cheek. 'You are easy to love.'

The response she hoped for, the response she ached for—an answering declaration of love—never came. Instead, he looked enquiringly at her. 'Francesca?'

She held in a sigh and her hand fell away. 'Aye?'

'Do you ever wonder about *your* parents—your real parents?'

'After Lady Clare came to Fontaine I thought about them endlessly. I never stopped wondering who they were, what sort of lives they lived and whether they were still alive. Lately, I've hardly thought of them at all.' She pressed another kiss to his cheek, and a wave of sadness swept over her. 'Since you came to Provins I've had other things on my mind.'

He gave her a sombre look. 'Saying farewell to Count Myrrdin. I know it was a wrench.'

'It does hurt, in part because I feel guilty for staying away so long. However, since coming to des Iles, I am learning to think of him as my father again. When I fled to Paimpont, I seemed to forget it.'

The wind tossed a lock of raven-dark hair into his eyes. Impatiently, he pushed it back. 'Count Myrrdin died more easily for seeing you. Francesca, he loved you and I am sure he always thought of you as his daughter.'

Francesca blinked, Tristan was talking about love, how extraordinary. Her heart thumped, she couldn't breathe for hoping he was leading into admitting that he loved her.

'Count Myrrdin might not be your sire, Francesca, but he was your true father. He taught you everything of importance.'

She gave him a quizzical look. 'You're talking about my training? About learning to run a household and putting visitors at their ease? Keeping servants happy?'

'Nothing so mundane, I assure you.' A strong arm went round her waist, drawing her against the warmth of his body. 'He taught you how to do what he did best, namely to inspire love and devotion in other people.'

'In other people?'

'Mari adores Brittany, yet she trailed all the way to Champagne simply to stay at your side. Mari loves you. Your new sister, Lady Clare, loves you. Everyone who meets you learns to love you.'

Francesca looked deep into Tristan's eyes. 'Everyone?'

His mouth went up at a corner. 'Everyone,' he said firmly. 'And I include myself in that number. Francesca, I love you with all my heart.'

Francesca's vision misted and her throat tightened. Blindly, she reached for him and smiling lips met hers.

Time stopped. As the kiss drew out, she could no longer feel the salty breeze toying with her veil. The gulls stopped crying; the bees stopped buzzing. Tristan was warm and strong and his arms were wrapped tightly round her. There was nowhere else she would rather be.

Tristan loves me.

When she came up for air, she was breathing hard and couldn't stop smiling. 'It's good to hear that you consider me more than just a weakness. Say it again, if you please.'

His mouth curled into a warm smile. A loving smile. 'Francesca, I love you.'

With a sigh, she slid her fingers into his dark, wind-ruffled hair. 'I've waited a long time to hear that.'

He gave her a confused look. 'I've been telling you for years.'

'No, you haven't.'

His gaze was unwavering. 'My heart, I have.'

My heart. She blinked. *My heart.* Her throat tightened. 'Saints, I never realised.' She curled her fingers into his hair. 'You should have made it plainer.' Even as she spoke, she realised that Tristan's harsh upbringing had made that impossible. His father's apparent rejection had led him to believe that love was a weakness. She had been his weakness. 'We almost lost each other. I was convinced you needed a dynastic alliance.' She tipped her head to one side. 'Admit it, you married me because you thought I brought you Count Myrrdin's lands.'

'I can't deny it, back then I thought I needed them.' He shook his head, a rueful smile playing round his mouth. 'If I'd held the entire duchy, it wouldn't have been enough. My father's death, you see. I felt such shame. Such guilt.'

She studied him. 'You thought more responsibility would help you atone for your father's sin.'

'Just so.' Leaning closer, he nuzzled her neck. 'My guardian angel must have been watching over me because my desire for atonement led me straight to you. Francesca, you are infinitely more important than any estate. I thank God we have found each other again.'

'Amen to that. I pray that nothing comes between us. Ever.'

A warm kiss landed on her chin. 'So, you'll not be returning to your friend in Provins?'

She gave a swift headshake. 'I think not. If you are still in agreement, I shall invite Helvise to des Iles.'

'She would be most welcome.'

'Thank you.' Even as she spoke, Lady Esmerée's face swam into focus at the back of Francesca's mind. She frowned pensively at the pot of rosemary.

A large finger angled her face back to his. 'Why the sigh?'

She shrugged. 'I was thinking about Lady Esmerée. Her child will be born soon, I think.'

Tristan stiffened. 'You don't want her to stay at des Iles.'

'No, that isn't what I'm saying. I admit I wanted her to leave at first.' She smiled and touched his cheek. 'That was when I believed you to be a hopeless case.'

Dark eyebrows came together and she held in a laugh. 'There's no need to scowl, but for a long while I thought you so far beyond love that all you ever thought about was your duty to the duchy. Ironically, it was Lady Esmerée and your treatment of her that gave me hope. This was a woman, not a duty. You didn't simply discard her, when many men in your position would have done. Besides, how could I ask you to send Sir Roparz away?'

'Thank you, my heart, you are all that is generous.' Tristan took a deep breath. 'There is something you need to know, it concerns Kristina.'

'Aye?'

'As you know, it is my earnest wish that you and I should have children. That is in God's hands. However, Kristina will always be my daughter, even if she would never take precedence over our children.'

'You wish to acknowledge her?'

'Yes. The rebellion is over, there is no longer any reason to hide her away.' He shoved his fingers through his hair. 'I shall give her a grant of land, a manor that will be ring-fenced from my other properties. What I am saying is that Kristina's land won't be available for any children we might have. Francesca, I don't have to have your agreement to do this, but I should be pleased if you would give it.'

Her lips curved. 'Of course I give it. How could I not? Papa allowed me to keep St Méen, after all.'

'So he did.'

Heart full, Francesca sifted his hair through her fingers, gently measuring its length. She drew back with a frown. 'Tristan, your hair really needs cutting, you do realise it is longer than mine?'

Tristan laughed and pulled her fully on to his lap. 'Francesca des Iles, I do love you.'

* * * * *

If you enjoyed this story, you won't want to miss the other great reads in Carol Townend's KNIGHTS OF CHAMPAGNE *miniseries*

LADY ISOBEL'S CHAMPION
UNVEILING LADY CLARE
LORD GAWAIN'S FORBIDDEN MISTRESS
LADY ROWENA'S RUIN

MILLS & BOON®

Hardback – March 2017

ROMANCE

Secrets of a Billionaire's Mistress	Sharon Kendrick
Claimed for the De Carrillo Twins	Abby Green
The Innocent's Secret Baby	Carol Marinelli
The Temporary Mrs Marchetti	Melanie Milburne
A Debt Paid in the Marriage Bed	Jennifer Hayward
The Sicilian's Defiant Virgin	Susan Stephens
Pursued by the Desert Prince	Dani Collins
The Forgotten Gallo Bride	Natalie Anderson
Return of Her Italian Duke	Rebecca Winters
The Millionaire's Royal Rescue	Jennifer Faye
Proposal for the Wedding Planner	Sophie Pembroke
A Bride for the Brooding Boss	Bella Bucannon
Their Secret Royal Baby	Carol Marinelli
Her Hot Highland Doc	Annie O'Neil
His Pregnant Royal Bride	Amy Ruttan
Baby Surprise for the Doctor Prince	Robin Gianna
Resisting Her Army Doc Rival	Susan MacKay
A Month to Marry the Midwife	Fiona McArthur
Billionaire's Baby Promise	Sarah M. Anderson
Seduce Me, Cowboy	Maisey Yates

0217 GEN STD HB